THE

LOST GIRL KING

'Doyle is one of my favourite writers, and The Lost Girl King is another breakneck adventure full of folklore and family love. Prepare to be transported!' **Ross Montgomery**

'Few do page-turning, high-stakes, and warm and witty adventure as well as Catherine Doyle, and The Lost Girl King is a writer at the height of her powers' **Kiran Millwood Hargrave**

'Nobody writes peril, wit and wonder as well as Catherine Doyle. The Lost Girl King is real magic' **Dave Rudden**

'A thrilling adventure – loveable characters, magical folklore and a seriously scary villain. Truly one of the best fantasy stories I've ever read' **A.F. Steadman**

'Beautifully written, breathlessly exciting, and full of heart and humour, this is an epic adventure like no other' **Louise O'Neill**

D0543071

'A glorious gulp of a summer adventure' **Piers Torday**

'What a fantastic story! I was utterly gripped'
Abi Elphinstone

'Packed full of heart and humour, The Lost Girl King is the perfect mix of nail-biting action and spellbinding magic'
Anna James

'A book I look forward to reading again and again'
Katie Tsang

'Echoes The Lord of the Rings and Narnia, whilst being original and fresh. It's sure to become a classic'
Aisha Bushby

'I fell headlong in love with this absolutely enchanting adventure' **Tamzin Merchant**

'If the world needs saving, I want Amy and Liam Bell and the Fianna on my team! The Lost Girl King is an extraordinary adventure' **Clare Povey**

'I was totally transported by this book. Fizzling with folklore and fun' **Francesca Gibbons**

THE LOST GIRL KING

Books by Catherine Doyle

The Storm Keeper trilogy:

The Storm Keeper's Island

The Lost Tide Warriors

The Storm Keepers' Battle

The Lost Girl King

THE
LOST GIRL KING

CATHERINE DOYLE

BLOOMSBURY
CHILDREN'S BOOKS
LONDON OXFORD NEW YORK NEW DELHI SYDNEY

BLOOMSBURY CHILDREN'S BOOKS
Bloomsbury Publishing Plc
50 Bedford Square, London WC1B 3DP, UK
29 Earlsfort Terrace, Dublin 2, Ireland

BLOOMSBURY, BLOOMSBURY CHILDREN'S BOOKS and the Diana logo
are trademarks of Bloomsbury Publishing Plc

First published in Great Britain in 2022 by Bloomsbury Publishing Plc

A catalogue record for this book is available from the British Library

ISBN: PB: 978-1-5266-0800-0; Waterstones: 978-1-5266-6080-0;
eBook: 978-1-5266-0798-0

2 4 6 8 10 9 7 5 3 1

Typeset by RefineCatch Limited, Bungay, Suffolk
Printed and bound in Great Britain by CPI Group (UK) Ltd, Croydon CR0 4YY

MIX
Paper from
responsible sources
FSC® C171272

To find out more about our authors and books visit www.bloomsbury.com
and sign up for our newsletters

For Ellen

Chapter One

THE HOUSE BETWEEN WORLDS

Way out west, where the roads run out and the craggy hills of Connemara slope down to meet the Atlantic Ocean, a yellow house sat on the edge of two worlds. It was a home lined with books and filled with knick-knacks, surrounded by stony mountains that groaned in the winter and blossomed in the spring.

The house belonged to Amy Bell's grandmother, Dorothy, and by the time her mum's car was trundling up the driveway towards it, Amy was fast asleep in the back seat. Her full-mouthed snores fogged up the window, which made little difference to the view of the grey mist outside.

'Here we are then. All in one piece,' announced Mum, as the engine sputtered to a stop. 'I expect you two to be on your best behaviour. Don't go making any trouble for Gran.'

In the front seat, Amy's older brother, Liam, looked up from his book. 'Mum,' he huffed. 'You know how responsible I am.'

'Yes, love.' Mum glanced pointedly at Amy in the rear-view mirror. When she received no answer, she launched into her loud operatic voice, usually reserved for school mornings. 'Wakey-wakey, sunshine!'

Amy stirred. 'Sunshine? Where?'

'Not here,' said Liam. 'I wouldn't get your hopes up.'

The rain had followed them all the way from the city, and was tip-tapping against the car windows.

Mum folded her hands in her lap. 'Let's just give it a minute.'

Liam pushed his glasses up his nose and squinted through the windscreen. 'I don't think a minute will do it, Mum. I can barely see the mountains through this fog.'

Amy scowled. It was bad enough that she had to spend her first week of school freedom so far away from her friends, Lily and Gita, whose families were off camping on the Aran Islands together, but now she was trapped inside this stubborn rain cloud. It was hardly a recipe for adventure.

'What kind of summer is this?' she mumbled.

'An unpredictable one,' said Mum brightly. 'Which are the best kind, if you ask me.'

Amy's scowl deepened. It was easy for Mum to be chirpy. Her new boyfriend Paul was whisking her away to Santorini in the morning. A paradise, by the looks of the photos, where the sea was so clear it sparkled and all the restaurants served rainbow-coloured drinks with tiny umbrellas. 'There's nothing unpredictable about the rain in Connemara. I'm going to be so *bored* here.'

'I did tell you to bring a book,' said Liam, who wasn't at all bothered by the rain. In his opinion, the outdoors was fraught with danger anyway. He hated insects and sports, and was the only person he knew who could get sunburnt on a cloudy day. To Liam, a rainy week at Gran's house was *better* than a week in sunny Santorini. 'I've got a really interesting one about sharks, if you want to borrow it. But don't dog-ear the pages.'

'I'd rather eat a bowl of my own hair,' said Amy, her heart sinking at the distant roll of thunder. She pressed her forehead against the window and yelped at the sudden appearance of a face on the other side. 'Gran!'

Gran's smile was bubblegum-pink and her eyes were the bright blue of a behaving sky. She rapped her knuckles against the glass. 'Are you coming out, or do I have to climb in and fetch you?'

Amy swung the door open and launched herself into her grandmother's arms. She couldn't help being pleased to see her, even if there was no adventure in sight.

Liam shoved his book into his hoody and clambered out after her. Gran had to stand on tiptoes to gather him into a hug.

'Goodness, you're as tall as a beanstalk!' She craned her neck, shouting into the car. 'What have you been feeding him, Darcy? Miracle-gro?'

Mum waggled her fingers in greeting. 'Well, one of us needs to be able to reach the lightbulbs!'

'Too right.' Gran patted Amy primly on the head. 'Don't worry, love. You'll catch up.'

Liam patted her on the head too. 'Maybe someday.'

Amy stuck her tongue out. 'Actually, I like being small. It's much better for sneaking around.'

'I'll try not to read too much into that,' said Gran, as she shooed them towards the house. 'Let's get out of this deluge before it makes a puddle of us. I've made rhubarb crumble so I suggest we do the sensible thing and start dinner with dessert.'

Mum said goodbye, planting a wet kiss on each of their cheeks before hopping back into the car and speeding away. Liam and Amy waved her off from the doorway, both of them feeling a bit disgruntled at how delighted she was to be leaving.

4

In the hallway, Gran shed her raincoat like a butterfly emerging from a chrysalis. She was wearing her personality underneath – a gold blouse, blue trousers, and bright yellow wellies. She took the children to warm up in the living room, where a fire was crackling. Liam beat Amy to the shaggy beanbag in the corner, flinging himself into it with gusto.

'You're too big for it now,' said Amy, nudging him with her shoe. 'You're going to burst it.'

'Nice try,' said Liam, as he stretched his hands behind his head. 'You're never too big for a beanbag.'

'Whatever.' Amy kicked her trainers off and sank into the over-stuffed armchair by the fireplace. The bookshelves on either side of the mantelpiece looked even more lopsided than usual, and for a heartbeat, she wondered if this would be the trip where they finally toppled over and flattened her.

She looked up at the books, their gilded spines winking at her as she tried to guess how many it would take to *really* squish her. The well-thumbed copy of *Old Ireland Through the Centuries: A Complete Compendium of Celtic Legends* was at least 800 pages long. It would certainly do a lot more damage than *Seven Ways to Spot a Faerie Fort in the Wild* and *Banishing a Banshee in Three Easy Steps*, which were really more like pamphlets. Amy's favourite book,

Hidden Battles of the Atlantic: Where Selkies and Merrows Collide, was skulking on the bottom shelf – a safe zone – beside several copies of a shiny new book called *Myth or Madness? Searching for the Magical Kingdom of Tír na nÓg*, which Amy had never seen before. Then she noticed the name of the author.

'Gran! This one has your name on the spine! Did you really write a book?'

Liam surveyed his sister's excitement with suspicion. 'If this is a trick to get me out of the beanbag, I'm not falling for it.'

Gran chuckled from the doorway. 'Well, I spent so many years teaching my students about Irish fairytales, I thought I might as well write some of them down. I've got time, now I'm officially retired.'

Amy removed a copy of Gran's book and plonked it on her lap. 'This is *so* cool,' she said as she cracked it open. 'I bet you could knock a burglar out with it.'

After two flailing attempts, Liam managed to sit up in the beanbag to get a better look. 'I thought you said books are boring.'

'No. I said *your* books are boring,' Amy corrected him. 'This one is written by Gran. Which automatically makes it the best book in the world. And it makes me famous by association.'

To Amy, Gran had always seemed to be more of an archaeologist than a literature professor. She dug out the exciting bits of stories and mined the magic from their bones. And best of all, she believed in everything she researched – from magical sea-creatures and roaming giants to enchanted trees and wandering ghosts. For Gran, they were all real. As was the lost kingdom of Tír na nÓg.

'You know what else is famous?' she said now, with a twinkle in her eye. 'My rhubarb crumble. Come and have some before it gets cold.'

Amy surrendered her grandmother's tome of fairytales, but kept hold of her curiosity as she followed the smell of freshly baked crumble into the little kitchen at the back of the house.

* * *

'So, if Tír na nÓg exists, then how come no one's found it yet?' she asked that evening, after they had polished off dessert and were halfway through a cottage pie heaped with fluffy mashed potatoes.

'How do you know it hasn't been?' said Gran, very seriously. 'Lots of people claim to have found it over the centuries.'

'Well, lots of people say the earth is flat, but that doesn't mean it is,' said Liam, swishing his knife around.

'In fact, it's ridiculous when you consider how easy it is to prove the curvature of the—'

'Please stop blabbering on about science,' Amy cut in. 'This is a conversation about magic.'

Liam glowered at his sister. 'I thought you might want to actually learn something.'

'I do,' said Amy. 'I want to learn how to find Tír na nÓg.'

'You'll probably need an imaginary map then,' said Liam. 'Since it's quite obviously an imaginary place.'

Gran *hmm*'d as she pushed a pea around her plate. 'Perhaps it's simply hidden,' she said, skewering it with her fork. 'Sometimes places don't want to be found. And we must respect that.'

Liam snorted around a mouthful of mince. 'That's ridiculous.'

Amy's eyes flashed. '*Liam.*'

'What? It doesn't make any sense.'

While Amy loved talking about Gran's research, Liam could never bring himself to take it seriously. Writing some of her stories down in a book didn't change anything in his mind. It was quite clearly a work of 'speculative fiction', which was a fancy way of saying it was all made up.

'That's the joy of fairytales, love. They don't have to make sense.' Gran took her plate to the sink and leaned against the countertop, her gaze turning to the hinterland as she began to sing her favourite song. '*Through fields of green and mountains old, where magic glitters bright as gold* …'

A fresh hail of rain battered the window.

Amy harrumphed. 'I bet it never rains in Tír na nÓg.'

Gran fell out of her song. 'The sun always shines on Tír na nÓg. The birds there are every colour of the rainbow, and the trees are full of ancient spirits, with trunks as tall as skyscrapers,' she went on dreamily. 'The rivers sing and the wind laughs, and when the moon rises at night, it's so bright the land glows like a star.'

'That sounds way better than the Aran Islands,' said Amy wistfully. 'Imagine climbing those trees!'

Liam pulled a face. 'Imagine falling out of one. You'd break all your bones and then your arms and legs would end up like jelly.'

Amy glared at him. 'Why are you like this?'

'What?' said Liam defensively. 'You mean sensible?'

Gran smiled at them over her shoulder. 'There's a story about a little girl who found her way to Tír na nÓg many years ago.' She dropped her voice, and Amy leaned in, as if to dip her toes into the story. 'The ocean there was full of creatures that swam like seals but talked like humans. They wore seaweed all over their bodies like a second skin, so no one could tell where the sea ended and they began …'

'*Cool*,' said Amy.

Liam's chair screeched as he pushed away from the table. 'Good story,' he said, as he plonked his dish in the sink. 'But please stop encouraging her, Gran. You know it's complete nonsense.'

Amy swatted him with a tea towel.

'No offence,' Liam added hastily.

Gran turned from the window, and patted him warmly on the shoulder. 'If you ask me, I think there's a drop of truth in every story … Or sometimes an entire waterfall of truth.'

Liam looked at her in confusion. 'Er, right.'

'He'll change his tune once I find the lost kingdom,' Amy announced as she stood up. She dropped her plate in the sink with a triumphant clatter. 'I'm going to go looking for it once the rain clears up tomorrow.'

'You certainly will not.' Gran's frown was sharp and sudden. It made the temperature in the room plummet. 'They're just stories, Amy. A treat to read, but never to chase.'

'But—'

'Now then,' said Gran, clapping her hands. 'Whoever's still standing here in ten seconds gets the esteemed honour of cleaning the big pot. Ten, nine, eight …'

Liam bolted from the room, with Amy hot on his heels.

Hours later, after a movie and two bowls of slightly burnt microwave popcorn, when the fire in the living room had dwindled to its embers and the moon was a crescent hanging in a velvet sky, Amy and Liam trudged up the creaky staircase to bed. In the box bedroom at the back of the house, they returned to their time-honoured tradition of playing rock-paper-scissors for the top bunk, which Amy lost even after demanding four consecutive rematches.

She tipped her head back, her bright red hair tumbling over the edge of the bottom bunk like a tangerine waterfall. 'It'll be *your* fault if this rickety old thing crushes me in the middle of the night,' she said, sticking her tongue out at the sagging mattress above.

'I can feel that, just so you know,' came Liam's voice.

Amy listened to the wheeze of her brother's breath in the dark as he drifted off to sleep. She tossed and turned, trying to get comfortable, but the creaky slats kept her awake. She flopped on to her stomach and flung her arm down the side of the bunk. To her surprise, the back of her hand brushed against a hole in the wall. She was so used to winning the top bunk that she'd never noticed it before …

She peered over the edge and found a small hollow just above the skirting board. It was stuffed with junk: four hair bobbins and a spool of thread, a tarnished gold earring and an old tissue. *Gross.*

And wedged right at the back, a silver coin.

Amy plucked the coin free and held it up to the moonlight. She traced the wolfhound on the front, and then the harp on the back. She didn't recognise it, which meant it must be *really* old. She wondered how much it was worth, and if she might become wildly rich by selling it. Then, she could sail all the way to the Aran Islands and wave at Lily and Gita from her brand-new yacht.

She drifted off with the coin still clenched in her fist, and in that final fleeting moment between wakefulness and sleep, she swore she heard a tap at the window.

Chapter Two

THE GOLDEN WATERFALL

The following morning, Amy woke long after breakfast, ready to go exploring. Liam had deserted her, leaving his rumpled duvet and balled-up pyjamas behind him. After she got dressed in her favourite jeans and hoody, she wrangled her unruly red hair into a ponytail and pocketed the silver coin.

Gran was downstairs in the kitchen, gazing into her cup of tea. 'The rain's almost stopped,' she said, by way of greeting. 'In fact, I would say it's more of a gentle drool now.'

'Well, that's hardly enough to stop an adventure,' said Amy brightly. After she'd stuck two slices of bread in the toaster, she pulled the coin from her pocket and set it on the table. 'I found this in the wall beside the bottom bunk last night. How much do you think it's worth?'

Gran smiled at the coin, like it was an old friend. 'I thought we must have found all the sixpences by now, but still they turn up.'

'I've got a good nose for treasure,' said Amy proudly. 'This one was well hidden.'

'My sister Peggy used to collect sixpences. And I used to love sneaking a few to spend on apple drops down in the sweet shop.' Gran's smile turned sad as she curled the coin in her fist, as if to press the memory of those days back into her skin. 'I'm not sure how this one survived all these years, but seeing as we abide by a strict "Finders, Keepers" policy in this house, you are welcome to keep it.'

'I didn't know you had a sister,' said Amy.

'Oh, yes,' said Gran. 'And a mum and a dad too. But it was all so long ago that sometimes it feels like another life-time entirely.' She laid the coin gently back on the table, her shoulders deflating with a sigh. She looked smaller suddenly. Older.

'I've considered trading Liam in for a sister,' said Amy thoughtfully. 'He can be such a know-it-all sometimes.'

Gran chuckled. 'Be patient with him, love. I wish I'd been a lot nicer to my Peggy, but you don't often realise these things until it's too late.'

Amy wanted to ask Gran more questions about her sister, but a strange shadow had come over her, and she was afraid of making it worse. Then the toaster popped, and the moment broke apart. She returned the coin to her pocket and went to grab the butter from the fridge. 'I'm going to go exploring in a bit if you're up for it?'

'I'm afraid my exploring days are behind me.' Gran rose from the table, looking misty-eyed. 'And besides, I'm going to have to rescue my poor herb garden after all that rain yesterday.'

Amy ate her toast with only the sixpence for company, and thought about Peggy, a girl like her with a secret stash of oddities. She resolved to ask Gran more about her as soon as she was feeling better.

After breakfast, she found Liam in the living room, unsurprisingly reading his book.

'Hello!' She tossed a cushion at him. 'Do you want to go exploring?'

'It's raining,' said Liam, without looking up.

'Actually, it's drooling. Come on, I want to catch a frog, and I won't leave you alone until you help me.'

Liam set his book down with a weary sigh. 'All right, but only for an hour. I want to learn the Sicilian Defence today.'

Amy stared at him blankly.

'It's a chess move. I told you about it yesterday. In the car.'

Amy pretended to snore. 'That must be why I fell asleep.'

Liam grumbled under his breath as he followed his sister outside, to where Gran was on her knees tending her herb garden.

'We're off, Gran!' said Amy as she skipped past her. 'We'll bring you back a frog!'

'I don't want a frog! I have my hands full with you two!' she called after them. 'You know the rules. Don't stray too close to the mountains and keep the house in sight at all times.'

'We will!' they chorused.

And with the rules forgotten almost instantly, they followed the unruly garden down to where a trickling stream slithered into the hinterland. Amy vaulted over it, imagining herself as a fearless explorer venturing into a new world. Liam tiptoed gingerly across the stepping stones, panting as he caught up with her.

The wilderness unfurled before them in a mass of craggy peaks and rocky trails that stretched west, all the way to the ocean. Everything glistened in the freshly fallen rain, and as the sun began to poke through the clouds, it made the whole of Connemara look like a glimmering emerald.

Amy sniffed the dewy air. 'Do you know what that is, Liam? That's the smell of adventure!'

Liam pushed his glasses up his nose. 'Actually, it's called *petrichor*. It's a word scientists made up to describe the earthy smell of rain after it falls on the soil. It's Greek.'

'My explanation is better,' said Amy. 'Do you know any facts about frogs?'

Liam racked his brain. 'Did you know that when a frog sheds its skin, it eats the old one afterwards?'

'Gross,' she said, approvingly.

Neither of them noticed the yellow house disappearing from view as they wound their way deeper into the countryside, through long grass and heather and tufty fields full of wandering sheep. Amy told her brother about Peggy, Gran's mysterious sister, and showed him the old coin she had found in the wall.

'Gran says it's a sixpence, but it's old, so it's got to be worth loads, hasn't it?' she asked eagerly. 'I reckon I can buy a boat with it—'

'More like a boat key ring,' Liam said with a laugh. At his sister's look of utter dismay, he reminded her, 'And anyway, you get seasick.'

Amy shoved the coin back in her pocket. 'Killjoy.'

They set up camp beside a lake, where Liam perched on a boulder while Amy trawled through the reeds, searching for frogs. She was in the middle of chasing one when she stopped suddenly. It felt like something was watching her. The hairs rose on the back of her neck, and she looked up quickly as a shadow pulled her attention skyward. 'Hey!' she called to Liam. 'Look at that bird. It's huge.'

Liam tipped his head back for a better view. 'It looks like a hawk, only I've never seen one that colour before.'

The bird was as white as a swan. Amy stared as it circled lower and lower above their heads, its bright feathers shimmering in the fractured sunlight. After three loops, it screeched at them.

'Hello to you too!' said Amy, waving at it. 'Do you think it's trying to tell us something?'

'It's a *bird*,' said Liam, still wincing at the noise. 'It's probably after your frog.'

'But it's staring right at me!'

The hawk released another piercing cry, and then took off towards the mountains.

That bird was definitely trying to tell them something, and in that moment, Amy decided she was going to find out what. 'Come on! I think it wants us to follow it!'

'Amy, come back!' Liam shouted after her, but his sister was already off and running.

As it happened, Amy Bell was the second-fastest person in her entire school. Melissa Talbot had narrowly beaten her in the hundred-metre sprint on Sports Day, and had insisted on wearing her gold medal into school the following morning so everyone – *especially* Amy – would be reminded of her victory. She pictured Mel's swinging ponytail now as she bolted after the bird.

When Liam caught up with his sister, she was standing at the bottom of a narrow waterfall, trying to catch her breath. He took off his glasses and swept his unruly brown hair out of his eyes.

'I … didn't … know … there … was … a … waterfall … around … here,' he wheezed. 'Also … I … think … I'm … dying.'

The white hawk stared down at them with bright silver eyes.

Behind them, a slant of sunlight crept over their shoulders. It tiptoed across the river and painted the waterfall gold, until it looked a bit like drizzling honey.

Amy blinked in disbelief. 'Hang on. I think the water's going the wrong way.'

Liam crept closer, the dent between his brows deepening. Amy was right. The waterfall was flowing upside down, like it was sucking water up from the stream and carrying it over the rocks. He racked his brain for an explanation, but in that moment even science failed him. 'That's … weird.'

The hawk cocked its head, as though it were waiting for them to do something.

The back of Amy's neck was prickling again. *I think there's a drop of truth in every story*, echoed Gran's voice in her head. *Or sometimes an entire waterfall of truth.*

The bird shrieked as it took flight. It circled in the air before swooping over their heads and nosediving straight into the waterfall.

Amy flinched, bracing for the tell-tale *thwack* of feathers on rock, but there was none.

Instead, the water winked as it swallowed the hawk, leaving only the echo of its cry behind.

Liam's jaw fell open. 'Where did it go?'

'There's only one way to find out,' said Amy, as she stepped into the stream. The current flowed backwards, gently tugging her towards the waterfall.

'Amy, don't!' Liam glanced nervously over his shoulder. 'We should head back. You know Gran's rules.'

'Oh, come on, Liam. Where's your sense of adventure?'

'It's buried under my crippling fear of danger!'

Amy sighed. She suspected that her brother's cowardice was part of his genetic code, just like sparkling charm and heroic bravery were part of hers. Of course, her teacher, Miss Lennon, often referred to her as 'reckless' and 'cheeky', but Amy had always prided herself on being fearless. She wasn't afraid of snakes, spiders, aliens or homework, or even Principal Gresham's false teeth that time they fell out during Morning Assembly.

Amy's theory was that Liam spent all his time reading to try and avoid even the smallest possibility of real adventure. But really, if you lacked bravery, the best thing to do was go out into the world and *practise* it. And if that meant climbing a tree or swimming in the sea, or even punching a bear in the face, then so be it.

It was for precisely this reason that Amy went sloshing across the river bed. Before Liam could get another word out, she drew a gasping breath and ducked under the waterfall.

There was a sudden rush of wind and then—
Nothing.

'Amy!' Liam took his glasses off and cleaned them on his sleeve, but even when he resettled them on his nose, his sister was still nowhere to be seen.

'Amy?' he said again uncertainly. 'Where are you?'

There was only the pitter-patter of water to answer him. His sister had completely disappeared.

He tried to swallow the panic inching up his throat. 'If you're hiding somewhere, it's not funny! Come out!'

His heart was hammering. Anxiety tingled in his fingertips. If he didn't do something soon, it would take over his whole body and turn him into a quivering mess.

Liam waded into the stream, the water soaking his shoes and squelching between his toes. 'Amy?'

It was no use. His sister was gone. Liam wrung his hands, feeling frightened. The waterfall glinted in invitation. The clouds were inching across the sun. The golden light was fading, and Liam knew that the moment – the only one that mattered – was slipping through his fingers. He had to go after her. Before he could talk himself out of it, he scrunched his eyes shut and ducked under the waterfall.

Chapter Three

THE CURSED SUN

A my watched her brother shuffle through the thundering waterfall, feeling like her heart might burst with excitement. Liam, however, was not enjoying this new, terrifying water feature. He tried to back up but there was nowhere to go. The rock was sheer and flat behind him; it nudged him forward until he was caught, full force, in the waterfall's icy deluge.

Amy had already clambered out of the glistening blue pond. She jumped up and down now, waving her arms above her head. 'Look at the trees, Liam. They're as big as skyscrapers!'

Liam cleaned his glasses on his sleeve as he sloshed through the water, and looked up at the biggest trees he had ever seen. They were bigger than Big Ben, bigger than a Californian redwood, maybe even as big as the Eiffel Tower! But far stranger than that, the grooves in their trunks kept shifting, like there were hundreds of faces trying to peer out at them.

Amy felt like she had strayed into a daydream. She looked for the white hawk, but it had disappeared into the forest.

'What *is* this place?' said Liam as he clambered out of the water.

She turned on her heel, a smile tugging at her lips. 'Isn't it obvious … ?'

Liam shook his head in a bluster. 'Tír na nÓg *isn't* real,' he told his sister. And himself.

'Look, there! There's a nose in that trunk,' said Amy, pointing to a face in a nearby tree just as it disappeared. 'You definitely don't see that in Connemara.' She grabbed his hand and led him through the clearing. 'Come on. Let's look around. I'll find even more proof.'

The trees were huge and gnarled and twisting. Their velvety leaves looked as big and soft as pillows, and their branches were home to trilling ruby-chested robins, emerald-green larks and golden-bright starlings that flitted about like sunbeams. 'Have you ever seen birds like this back home?' she said over her shoulder.

'No …' said Liam reluctantly. 'But I've seen plenty of unusual-looking animals in my favourite nature documentaries. So, it doesn't necessarily mean—'

'*Look!*' Amy pointed to a gap between two trees, where a crimson-coloured squirrel was peeking out at them. 'I think that one's spying on us!'

The squirrel gave a little gasp before darting out of sight. Five seconds later he peeked out again, this time with just one eye.

'He's not doing a very good job,' said Liam flatly.

'Maybe he's shy.' Amy waited for another glimpse of the squirrel, then made a point of waving at him. 'He's wearing a tiny leather headband! He must be a pet squirrel!'

Perhaps it was her imagination, but she could have sworn the squirrel scowled at her before skittering away into the woods.

The branches peeled back to let them through, and they spotted a trickling river just up ahead.

'Quick and careful, if you please,
I'll lead you safely through the trees.'

Amy snapped her chin up. 'Did you hear that? I swear someone is singing.'

Liam was staring at the water, his eyes wide behind his glasses. 'I think it was …' He gulped. 'Never mind.'

The water danced and swirled at their feet, flicking droplets at them. The longer they stared at it, the brighter it became, as though it were somehow lit from within.

'*I glow where the wood is dim,*
Walk astride or come and swim.'

Amy gasped. 'It's coming from the river!'

Liam felt like he was about to pass out. 'But that's impossible,' he said weakly.

Amy smirked at him. 'I bet you've never heard a singing river in one of your nature documentaries.'

'Definitely not,' he admitted. He had watched every nature show on Netflix and read more National Geographic magazines than his dad, and not one of them had ever prepared him for *this*.

Amy smiled as she sensed a change coming over her brother. He released a long breath, his shoulders sinking as disbelief gave way to curiosity.

'All right,' he said, nervously. 'Let's go a bit further.'

They followed the winding stream deeper into the forest. Before long, a trail sprang up from the undergrowth, strewn with twigs and berries, and stamped flat with well-worn footprints. The back of Amy's neck began to prickle again.

She spun around, searching for faces in the trees. There was only the red squirrel, watching them from a nearby branch. She clicked her teeth to call him over, but he regarded her with a look of such offence, she quickly stopped. 'OK, cranky-pants. What's up with you?'

Liam suddenly stopped walking. Gran's words echoed in his head. *Sometimes places don't want to be found. And we must respect that.* 'Hang on. Didn't Gran say that Tír na nÓg didn't want anyone to find it?'

'Well, lucky for us, it changed its mind,' said Amy brightly.

Liam's frown deepened. 'But why? Don't you think that's suspicious?'

Amy could sense her brother's anxiety fizzling between them like a current of electricity. She put her arm around his shoulders. 'Look around you, Liam. We're in paradise! There's nothing to be scared of.'

Liam wrung his hands. 'I still think we need to be careful. Just in case—'

'We have fun?' teased Amy. 'Let's spend ten more minutes exploring, and then we can go back. Deal?'

'All right. Deal.'

'Great. Let me figure out where we're going.' She

stopped at the nearest tree and searched for a foothold. 'I'll climb up and get a lay of the land. You wait here, in case someone comes along.'

Amy scrabbled up the tree with remarkable ease. Every time she lifted her foot, a groove appeared in the bark to anchor her, or a branch dipped lower so she could grab hold of it. Up and up and up she went, the trunk hoisting her higher and higher until her brother was little more than a dot pacing back and forth on the ground.

'That's too high!' he shouted. 'Come back down!'

But Amy had no intention of deserting a tree that was *helping* her climb it. 'I'm almost at the top! I can't stop now!'

The canopy edged into view. She was just about to lunge for another branch when the red squirrel appeared. He squeaked angrily, like he was scolding her for climbing into his territory.

'Learn to share, fur-ball.' Amy stuck her tongue out. 'You can't have all the trees to yourself.'

The squirrel threw an acorn at her.

'Oi!' she said, as it plinked off her forehead. The tree shook like it was chuckling. Amy ignored the squirrel as she reached for his branch. She clambered on to it with both hands, and then stood up straight, throwing her arms around the top end of the trunk for balance. The leaves parted around her, revealing the crisp blue sky, and beneath it, the rolling plains of Tír na nÓg.

But Amy wasn't looking down. She was staring straight at the sun. Or rather, at the giant chain that was holding it in place. It was thick and spiked and luminous, wrapped tightly around the sun's middle as though it were trying to squeeze all the light out of it.

The rest of the chain cut a jagged line in the sky, stretching all the way north before disappearing behind a distant mountain range. It clanged faintly, like a broken wind-chime, and as Amy stood horror-stricken beneath it, a dull pain gathered at the base of her skull.

Something here was wrong. Very wrong.

Suddenly she felt sick to her stomach. Black spots appeared in her vision, and she wobbled on the branch. She stepped backwards to steady herself, but misjudged the distance and met with thin air.

The last thing Amy saw before she plummeted to the ground was the red squirrel staring down at her, wearing a matching look of horror.

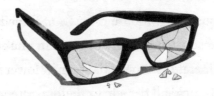

Chapter Four

THE SHADOW RIDERS

Amy shrieked as she fell, the wind whipping up around her as though it were trying to catch her. Liam's scream filled the forest as she hurtled towards him. There was a faint whistle, and then a resounding *thwack* as a branch jutted out from the tree and skewered her hood.

She came to a stop with a sudden *whoosh*, her body suspended in the air like a rag doll.

When she looked down, she was less than three metres off the ground, where her brother was standing slack-jawed.

'I'm alive!' she cheered. She twisted her neck to look up at the branch tangled in the top of her hoody. The red squirrel was perched on it, glaring at her in disapproval. A manic, hiccuping laugh bubbled out of Amy. 'The tree saved me!'

'Enjoy yourself while you can!' Liam fumed. 'Because when you get back down here, I'm going to murder you!'

With deliberate slowness, the branch lowered Amy to the ground. It tickled her cheek before retreating. The trees were still then, watchful.

Liam rested his hands on his sister's shoulders, as if he were afraid she might float away from him. 'No more death-defying stunts, *please*.'

'Well, I hardly planned it,' said Amy, as she hastily retied her ponytail. She was still trying to shake off her lingering nausea. 'I saw the sun up there, Liam. It had a huge spiky chain around it, and when I looked at it, it made me feel sick. That's why I lost my balance.'

Liam stared at her. 'Are you sure?'

Amy nodded. 'I can still see it when I close my eyes. I can *feel* it too.'

'But you can't just chain the sun.' Liam raked his hands through his hair. 'It's scientifically impossible.'

'We're not dealing with science,' Amy reminded him. 'We're dealing with magic. And it felt …' She trailed off as she searched for the right word.

'Bad?' said Liam.

'Worse.'

'Terrifying?'

Amy frowned. '*Worse.*'

'Evil?' whispered Liam.

She gulped. 'Yeah.' Maybe Liam was right to be cautious. She was about to suggest they turn back when a distant thrumming noise reached them through the trees.

Liam whipped his head around. 'What's that?'

'It sounds like thunder.' Amy frowned.

Then they spotted the red squirrel on the trail in front of them. He was stomping his tiny feet.

'He's definitely trying to tell us something,' she said uneasily.

'WE DON'T SPEAK SQUIRREL,' said Liam, slowly and loudly.

The squirrel flung an acorn at him.

'Hey!'

The wind picked up in a fierce gust. Fistfuls of dried leaves leaped into the air. Branches creaked and roots erupted from the ground, as if the trees were trying to run away.

Amy wrinkled her nose. 'What's that smell?'

'It smells like something's rotting.' Liam's freckles disappeared as he paled. 'And it sounds like something's *coming.*'

The sudden rumble of hoofs rolled through the forest.

The earth trembled, making berries fall from the trees like raindrops. The squirrel shot one last sorry look at them before scampering up a nearby trunk.

'Run!' yelled Amy.

They bolted through the forest. The drumbeat of hoofs grew louder, and when Amy looked over her shoulder she saw shadows moving swiftly through the trees. She could hear whips cracking and horses braying as they galloped, fast and hard towards them.

CRAAAAAAACK!

Th-thud! Th-thud! Th-thud!

Amy spun around, wild-eyed. The thunder of hoofs was deafening now, the crack of whips like lightning at their heels. 'They're coming this way, Liam! We need to get off the trail!'

Then she saw the riders – they wore black cloaks and leather gloves, and thick boots with silver buckles. But most terrible of all, each and every rider was headless, the stumps of their necks bleeding into shadows that shifted and swarmed like wasps' nests.

It was at that moment that Liam's foot caught on a wayward root and he went crashing down.

'Help! My ankle!'

Amy forced herself to look away from the riders as she dragged Liam to his feet. Frightened tears were rushing down his cheeks. She shouldered the brunt of his weight as she hauled him across the trail.

'Come on,' she panted. 'There's a hollow just under those roots up there!'

CRAAAAAAACK!

Th-thud! Th-thud! Th-thud!

'You g-go first!' Liam shoved Amy towards the hollow. 'I'm r-r-right b-behind you!'

CRAAAAAAACK!

Th-thud! Th-thud! Th-thud!

Amy vaulted over the ridge. She could feel her heartbeat in her throat as she crawled under the tree.

CRAAAAAAACK!

Th-thud! Th-thud! Th-thud!

The tree shook, releasing a cascade of dirt over her.

Dread roiled in Amy's stomach as she waited for her brother to join her.

CRAAAAAAACK!

Th-thud! Th-thud! Th-thud!

Liam tried to leap after his sister, but his ankle gave out and he went down hard on his knees. The rattle of hoofs vibrated in his teeth as he dragged himself towards the hollow.

He could barely see through his tears, but he knew he was close. *So close.*

Behind him, the hoofbeats slowed.

Thud. Thud. Thud.

The air was ice-cold, and it reeked of rot.

Liam's heart was hammering in his chest. If he could just haul himself over the—

Crunch! Liam screamed as a horse stamped down on his foot.

A gloved hand curled in the back of his hoody. His glasses slid off his nose as he was hoisted into the air. He hung like a puppet on a string, staring in horror at his headless captor.

The rest of the riders inched along the trail, scouring the undergrowth.

With the last ounce of his courage – perhaps the only one he had ever possessed – Liam opened his mouth and forced himself to speak. 'It's j-j-just m-m-me. I'm a-a-all alone.'

The headless horseman shifted as though it could hear him. An endless moment passed. Then the rider flung him across the horse's flank and cracked his bone-white whip. A cloud of dust kicked up and the horses took off in a stampede of dark wind, taking Liam with them.

Chapter Five

THE GREENCLOAK BOYS

Amy lunged from the hollow when she heard Liam scream but the roots tightened around her, like a seat belt. They stayed like that until the riot of hoofbeats faded to a faraway patter, and then to nothing at all.

Slowly, cautiously, the tree loosened its grip. Amy scrambled out of the ditch and hauled herself up on to the trail. Her hands were trembling and it felt like her heart was flinging itself against her ribcage. She squeezed her eyes shut and tried to catch her breath. When she opened them again, she saw Liam's glasses lying in the middle of path. She picked them up, tracing a crack with her thumb.

'Oh, Liam.' Hot tears streamed down her cheeks. It was all her fault. He'd warned her to be careful but she hadn't listened. She never listened. Now her brother was gone, and she was here, all by herself.

Amy carefully folded the glasses into her pocket. I *won't be afraid*, she thought. I *can't be*. I *have to rescue Liam*. Steeling herself, she took off in the direction the headless horsemen had gone, ignoring the prickles on the back of her neck. She could feel the forest watching her, sinuous branches jutting out from the undergrowth, as if to drag her back. She kicked them away, ignoring the furious rustle of leaves.

'I can do this,' she told herself. 'I just need to follow the hoofprints and—'

'AAAAAAAAAARGHHH!' A green blur hurtled out from the trees and barrelled into her, knocking her out of her sentence and clean off the trail.

Amy hit the ground with a bang, and groaned as she rolled on to her back, spitting leaves.

'HAAAAAALT!' The blur leaped at her. Amy flinched, expecting to be flattened. A leather boot landed either side of her elbows, and the tip of something cool and scratchy appeared at the base of her chin. 'Move and I'll gut you.'

Amy blinked. The blur had become a boy. He appeared to be no older than her, with curly black hair, swept away from his face by a leather band, brown skin and hazel eyes. They were wide and darting.

'Sorry, did that hurt?' he said awkwardly. 'I might have come on a bit strong there.'

Amy was conscious of the sword at her throat. 'Maybe just a bit.'

The boy nodded thoughtfully. 'To be honest, I've actually never done this before.'

Amy frowned. 'What? Murdered someone?'

The boy roared with laughter. 'No, acorn-brain. I'm saving your life.'

It was only then that Amy noticed the sword was made of wood. She knocked it away. 'For goodness sake,' she snapped, as she sat up. 'This is the last thing I need right now.'

'Oi! That's my sword!' The boy scrabbled to pick it up.

'Well, if it's a sword, why is it made of wood?' Amy brushed the unruly strands from her face so she could get a better look at him. He was fine-boned and at least three inches shorter than her, with narrow shoulders, a pointed chin, and a birthmark beneath his left eye that looked like a butterfly in flight. He was wearing a brown tunic with a leather belt, and a green cloak, clasped at his throat.

'Well, technically it's a *training* sword,' said the boy defensively. 'But I'll get my real one soon enough.' He flipped it around, fumbled the handle, and dropped it on his foot. 'Ouch!'

Amy raised her eyebrows.

The boy blushed as he picked it up. 'You put me off!' he complained.

They were interrupted by the arrival of the red squirrel, who skittered down from a nearby tree and hopped neatly on to the boy's shoulder.

'You're wearing the same headband,' said Amy, as she untangled a twig from her hair. 'Does he belong to you?'

The squirrel squeaked, then folded his arms in affront.

'Don't be ridiculous. Conan belongs to himself,' said the boy, before returning his sword to his belt. 'I'm Jonah, of the Greencloaks, by the way.' He swished his cloak, then raised his chin, as though he were expecting applause.

'Right. Well, I'm Amy. And I'm—'

'An interloper from beyond the veil.' Jonah rolled back on his heels. 'I know.'

Amy frowned. 'What's an interloper?'

'Someone who doesn't belong in Tír na nÓg of course,' said Jonah.

'So it *is* Tír na nÓg,' muttered Amy. 'I *knew* it.'

'It's really just a nicer way of saying *intruder*,' Jonah added. 'Extremely unwelcome intruder.'

Amy folded her arms. 'So how do you know I'm an interloper?'

He smirked. 'Well, for one thing, you're a round-top.

Your ears are a dead giveaway.' Amy noticed the pointed tips of his ears then, which were mostly covered by his headband. 'And for another, I *just* caught you trying to chase after the Dullahan. No self-respecting dweller of Tír na nÓg would *ever* do something so ridiculous. What a thistle-head!'

'The Dullahan?' said Amy. 'Are they those awful headless horsemen?'

Jonah nodded. 'You were lucky to get away in one piece.'

'But what are they? And how are they even *alive*?'

'Don't you know a curse when you see one?' He clucked his tongue. 'If you've finished risking your life, I suggest you get off your one-way trail to doom and follow me instead.' He promptly turned on his heel and stalked into the forest. 'I won't be rescuing you again today. Not on an empty stomach.'

Amy hurried after him. 'Hang on a second! I need to talk to you!'

But the boy kept marching, swinging his arms back and forth as he skipped through the trees, leaving Amy no choice but to follow him. He stopped in a mossy clearing that looked almost identical to the one they had just left, and turned around again. 'What were you saying?'

'I need to tell you about my—'

'Wait!' Jonah waved her over. 'Come a little closer. I can't quite hear you from over there.' Amy frowned as she came towards him, stopping when he held his hand up. 'That's better,' he said, furtively glancing around. 'I'm all ears.'

'It's about my brother, Liam. He— ARGHHHHH!' Without warning, a net sprang up from the undergrowth and closed around Amy. She yelled as she was hauled into the air, where she bobbed helplessly from the branch of a towering tree for the second time in fifteen minutes. She tried to wriggle free, but the net tightened, digging into her forehead as she peered out through a gap in the ropes.

Back on the ground, Jonah released a high-pitched whistle. 'I'VE GOT ONE, BOYS! I'VE CAUGHT AN INTERLOPER!'

'You tricked me!' fumed Amy.

'Sorry about that,' said Jonah, somewhat sheepishly. 'But it's kind of my job.'

Amy glared down at him.

'The Greencloaks are in charge of watching the veil between worlds,' he explained. 'And that means intercepting anything that manages to slip through it into the Elderglen. You have no idea how rare it is to catch an interloper!'

The leaves of the Elderglen forest rustled around them as a host of new faces appeared between the trees. They were all boys, as far as Amy could tell – and looked to be around her age, or perhaps a little older. They were wearing the same green cloak and leather headband as Jonah. Their ears were pointy too, and most were carrying wooden spears and swords. They regarded her warily as they edged into the clearing.

'Is she *real*?' whispered a plump, blond boy with red cheeks.

'As sure as a Selkie's tail,' said Jonah confidently. 'Just look at the ears, Owen.'

The boys crept closer. Amy offered them her most contemptuous scowl.

'Holy sneezeweed!' said Owen. 'She's a round-top! Don't get too close, boys.'

'Don't be such a bladderwrack,' snapped an olive-skinned, lanky boy with a pinched mouth, who appeared to be in a blistering mood. 'She's about as threatening as a sapling.'

He jostled the others out of the way as he stalked across the clearing.

'I'm the leader. I'll do the talking.'

'All right, Cade,' muttered Jonah. 'Who spat in your tea?'

Cade threw him a withering glare. 'The better question is, how did she get in here?'

'She came in through the waterfall,' said Jonah.

'That's impossible. The veil's sealed.'

'Not any more,' Amy piped up.

'She can speak!' someone gasped.

Amy rattled the net. 'BOO!'

Owen shrieked.

Cade took an arrow from the quiver at his back and nocked it on to his bow. 'Do that again and I'll shoot.'

'Oh, for goodness sake, I'm in a *net*,' snapped Amy. 'And I'm not your enemy!'

'Maybe not,' said Cade carefully. 'But you're a human from beyond the veil. And that's a bad sign. According to the old clock-towers, we haven't had a human here for sixty years. If Tarlock finds out about you, who knows what will happen.'

The rest of the boys looked grave.

'What are you talking about?' said Amy. 'Who's Tarlock?'

The Greencloaks exchanged nervous glances.

'He's the mage,' said Cade. 'He controls everything in Tír na nÓg.'

Amy gripped the net. 'Is he *here*?'

'No.' Cade shook his head. 'But he has spies everywhere. Even in the Elderglen.'

'Tarlock is the most powerful being in all of Tír na nÓg,' said Jonah. 'He uses dark magic to make himself invincible. He hurts people. He hurts the land too.'

'Is Tarlock the one who cursed the sun?' guessed Amy.

'He is.' Cade spat on the ground. 'He chained it to the sky to freeze time. The place has been rotting ever since.'

'And we've all been miserable,' said Owen glumly. 'We just want to grow up.'

Amy was gripping the net so tightly, her knuckles had turned white.

'It gets worse,' said Cade darkly. 'Before Tarlock sealed the veil between our worlds, he sent out his hawk, Ghost, to lure human children through the waterfall.'

Amy swallowed thickly, thinking of the hawk she had followed through the waterfall. 'What happened to them?'

'Once they reached the Elderglen, the Dullahan captured them,' said Cade. 'One managed to escape. The other wasn't so lucky. Tarlock used the interloper in his spell, and the next day, the sun got chained in the sky. It's been stuck there ever since.' His eyes darted to the sky, and Amy thought that he looked frightened. 'If the veil is open again after all these years, he must be working on a new curse.'

'So the headless riders …' Amy was feeling sick again.

'Would have taken you straight to Tarlock.' Jonah winced. 'And if an interloper ever got into his hands again, who knows what other misery he would cast on the land? Lucky thing I was here to save the day.'

A rush of dread coursed through Amy's body, knowing that at this very moment, her brother was being carted off to an evil mage who was going to use him in one of his wicked spells.

'You didn't save anything!' she said furiously to Jonah. 'The Dullahan kidnapped my brother, Liam. I was rushing after him when you knocked me off the trail.' She pulled her brother's glasses from her pocket and waved them around in proof. 'You were too late!'

Jonah's mouth fell open. 'There's more than one of you?'

Owen whimpered.

Cade's nostrils flared. 'Jonah,' he said, through his teeth. 'Why don't you explain to the rest of the Greencloaks how you managed to let an *entire human* get captured by the Dullahan?'

Jonah looked accusingly at Conan, who was sitting on a nearby branch. 'Why didn't you tell me there was a boy too?'

The squirrel gesticulated wildly. It looked to Amy like he was defending himself.

With remarkable speed, the Greencloaks descended into bickering. It was only when a horn rang out somewhere deep in the forest that they all suddenly stood to attention.

'The Fianna are back!' yelled Owen. Amy didn't miss the Greencloaks' fearful looks towards the trees.

Cade turned on Jonah. 'You'd better go and show them what you've caught. And more importantly, tell them what you failed to catch.'

Jonah's face had turned a concerning shade of green.

Up above Amy, Conan the squirrel began to chew through the net, whilst three Greencloak boys gathered underneath. The ropes gave way with a final *snap*, and she came crashing down on top of them.

She brushed herself off as she got to her feet. 'Right then. Who *exactly* are the Fianna?'

As if on cue, the war horn blared again.

'The Fianna are the bravest warriors in all of Tír na nÓg,' said Jonah, his voice showing his admiration, as well as fear. 'They are chosen by the people, and they fight *for* the people.'

'As Greencloaks, we're in training to join their ranks one day,' said Cade.

'Or at least we were,' muttered Owen. 'Until time got frozen.'

Cade peeled his lips back, revealing the glint of his canines. 'If you're feeling scared now, just wait until you meet them.'

Chapter Six

THE MIGHTY FIANNA

A my kept her eyes on the trees as the Greencloaks and their squirrel led her to a clearing full of beehive huts. She'd dismissed the idea of running away. For one thing, she might unwittingly end up in the path of a headless rider, and for another, she liked her chances with the Fianna – if they really were the bravest warriors in Tír na nÓg, then they would help her rescue her brother.

In the centre of the camp, a wild boar was roasting on a fire, the crackling flames making its tusks glow. There were at least thirty men sitting around it on logs. Amy was relieved to see they all had heads. They had pointy ears too, just like Jonah and the rest of the Greencloaks. Most of them had long stringy hair, thorny beards, and stern brows that were used to frowning. They wore dark green cloaks and black tunics, and seemed to be in possession of at least two weapons each – *real* weapons – swords and shields and whips and spears. One of them was using the tip of a dagger to pick his teeth.

Amy gulped. These were not men like her dad or her uncles, or old Mr Barlow next door, who was always hankering for a chat over the garden wall. No, these men were tough, and grizzled, and, well, a little bit scary.

Or maybe *a lot.*

The men looked up at the sound of their approach. 'The Greencloaks are back in time for dinner,' said one of the warriors, with a great booming laugh. 'Your stomachs always lead you home, lads.'

Jonah cleared his throat. 'Actually, there's, er, been an incident …'

Cade shoved Amy forward, and the rest of the boys parted to let her through. With fear hammering like a drum in her chest, she rolled her shoulders back and tried to look as brave as possible.

'Um, hello.'

The men froze.

There was a long, strained silence. The fire crackled madly, as if it were trying to break it.

One of the Fianna warriors stood up. He drew his

sword, but kept it low. 'Oscar,' he called out. 'You might want to get out here.'

At the edge of the camp, a tall, hooded man emerged from one of the beehive huts. Every man in the clearing rose to their feet. Jonah gulped. 'That's Oscar de Barra,' he told Amy. 'Don't look him in the eye.'

The leader of the Fianna – for he was quite plainly the leader – had the quiet ferocity of a prowling lion. As he moved towards the Greencloaks, Amy could feel his gaze on her face – and her *ears* – turning to dislike.

She drew herself to her full height, and told herself not to be afraid. There was already plenty to fear about Tír na nÓg, and she could not afford to spend her terror so unwisely.

Oscar's dark green cloak was trimmed in gold and, instead of a sword, he carried a long amber spear that was taller than Amy. He planted it in the ground like a flag, then removed his hood, revealing thick black hair and a matching, scratchy beard. His eyes were brown and hooded, with a ring of gold around each pupil. In place of a leather headband, he wore a gold band.

He was, Amy understood, not to be trifled with.

When he spoke, his voice was gravel. 'An interloper walks among us,' he said, more to himself than to the others. 'After all this time, the veil has shifted.' His gaze moved over her shoulder, to the rest of the Greencloaks. 'Well done, boys. Whose watch was it?' He paused, then frowned. 'Why do you look so scared?'

Jonah raised his hand. The rest of the Greencloaks were suddenly very interested in their boots. Conan was examining the end of his tail. 'I, well … you see … there's been a sort of accident … a *mistake* if you will …'

Amy almost felt sorry for the dithering boy, who seemed to shrink under the collective stare of the Fianna. If she didn't intervene soon, they would be here for hours. And for Liam, every moment was precious.

'I'm Amy Bell,' she announced, as she offered her hand to Oscar de Barra to shake. He didn't take it and Jonah seized the moment to melt back into the huddle. 'My brother's been captured by the Dullahan,' she continued, 'and I need to rescue him before he gets used in some terrible spell by this mage Tarlock I've been warned about. Will you help me?'

Oscar de Barra's left eye twitched. Once. Twice. Amy swore the trees shivered. And then the leader of the Fianna opened his mouth and bellowed so loudly that all the birds of the Elderglen scattered into the skies.

'JONAAAAAH!'

Despite her best efforts not to, Amy flinched.

Chapter Seven

THE WARRIOR'S TALE

After a trembling confession from Jonah, and a quickly scarfed meal of roast boar during which Amy couldn't touch a thing, Oscar called an immediate council of the Fianna. The warriors sat formally around the crackling fire, with the Greencloaks squishing themselves into the remaining space furthest from Oscar. Amy sat on a log, wedged between Jonah and Owen, waiting for Liam's fate to be decided.

Oscar glared at her as he stood. 'Amy Bell, you have no idea what you've done by coming here.'

Amy clenched her fists to keep her hands from shaking, but she didn't take her eyes off the fearsome leader of the Fianna as she addressed him.

'Then tell me,' she said. 'I need to know what my brother is up against.'

And what it will take to save him.

Oscar's throat bulged as he glanced around at the other men.

'Tell her,' said a tanned warrior with a stark white ponytail and a patchwork of silver scars across his left cheek. 'She should know what it means for us. For the kingdom.'

Oscar considered his words as he lowered himself on to a log, sending two nervous Greencloaks scooting on to the ground to make room for him.

'Niall is right,' he grunted, as he leaned in towards the flames. 'I am Oscar de Barra, leader of the Fianna warriors, and descendant of its founder, the war god Lug, so it falls to me to tell our tale.'

Without meaning to, Amy leaned forward too.

'*Fadó fadó* ... Long, long ago, when the world was young and the skies were starless, five ancient gods came to settle on the island of Ireland. The place you now call home,' Oscar began. 'Though by then their lives had spanned entire centuries, the gods were still young, because they were blessed with magic in their bones. When they settled in Ireland, the land and its people became blessed too. The gods had many children, who grew strong and brave and clever, and while they lived, the flowers bloomed and the animals thrived. Food was plentiful, the seasons were gentle and warm, and there was no illness. No suffering.

'But happiness breeds jealousy, and magic that bright attracts darkness. For there must be balance in all things,' Oscar went on. 'There were others who wanted the land for their own. A breed of reckless giants emerged from the silt and stones under the sea and stalked the waves, until they reached the shores of Ireland. They called themselves the Formorians, and they were not gods, but monsters. They sowed greed and chaos in the heart of the country.'

Amy shuddered, imagining the giants, drenched in seaweed and old fish guts, crashing through the ocean.

'Wherever the giants roamed, darkness followed. The trees fell into decay, the animals got sick. The crops died and the sun dimmed. Cold, rain and thunder came to Ireland and, before long, life gave way to death. The gods began to age. Their magic was leaving them, and the earth they had watered, now stamped with the footsteps of their enemies, began to weaken them. The soil of Ireland and everything that grew there became poisonous.'

'That's why we can never cross the veil into your world,' Jonah whispered to Amy.

Oscar ignored him and went on.

'The gods and their descendants fled west until the land ran out. It was there that Danú, goddess of nature and new beginnings, discovered a last whisper of earth magic that had not yet been destroyed. A waterfall that trickled backwards, as slow and golden as honey.'

Amy gasped.

Cade shushed her.

'Danú used the waterfall to tear an opening in the side of the world, just wide enough for her people to slip through. When they stepped through the crack, they found themselves in a new world, untouched by darkness. Hidden from the evils of the Formorians. They called their country Tír na nÓg, the land of the young. It was to be a place of hope. Of new life.'

Amy glanced around at the trees. They were silent as they listened.

'What happened to the giants?' she said. 'If your story is true, then why have I never seen one?' Although, she couldn't help thinking of Principal Gresham, who was surely seven feet tall and unnaturally mean-faced …

'They died out. Eventually.' The dent between Oscar's brows deepened and Amy sensed the tale was about to turn. 'The five gods watched over this kingdom for five thousand years, and when they grew weary and wished to pass to the heavens, they left the last of their magic to the earth, so the land would be forever beautiful, and its people would live long, peaceful lives. For a time, Tír na nÓg prospered under the reign of many good-hearted kings and queens, who ruled under the protection of the Fianna.'

'A band of skilled, noble-hearted warriors, as handsome as they are brave,' interjected Niall, which drew raucous laughter from the rest of the men.

Oscar shot them a warning look. 'The Fianna was originally founded by Lug,' he went on. 'The first warriors were trained by the god of warriors himself.'

'So *lucky*,' said Jonah wistfully.

'We roamed these lands in large numbers, protecting it from rebellions, keeping the Selkies content, and sowing peace throughout the towns and villages. There was no one who could match our strength, or threaten our existence ...'

Amy sensed a 'but' coming.

Oscar sighed. 'Until Tarlock.'

The men swore under their breath, while the Greencloaks shifted uncomfortably.

'Tarlock is the last living son of the goddess Danú,' said Oscar, his lips twisting. 'He stole the final drops of her magic when she was on her deathbed and used it in secret for his spells. Soon he became the most powerful being in the kingdom, sustained by magic that no one – not even the Fianna – could defeat. We could only wait for time to end him. But when Tarlock grew old and withered, and the thread of his life was finally fraying, he didn't want to die. So he created a spell that would stop time.'

'He cursed our sun,' growled a warrior called Manus who was missing most of his front teeth. 'And the rest of us along with it. Now the sun is angry. It gets inside our heads and gives us no peace. It makes our bones heavy. Our hearts too. We have forgotten how to be happy. How can we be, when there is no tomorrow?'

The rest of the men nodded grimly, their shoulders slumped. In that moment, Amy realised that despite their bravado, they were shadows of the great warriors they had once been, haunted by the memory of their glory days and the man who had stolen them.

'So Tarlock really chained the sun in the sky just to stop his own death?'

Oscar nodded. 'For a spell that would stop time itself, Tarlock needed ingredients so poisonous, they didn't exist in this place. He needed to use something from the land of the Formorians. Or rather, some*one*.'

'So that's why he needed a human child,' muttered Amy.

'When the Dullahan brought the child to his tower at Silverstone Castle, Tarlock ordered his blacksmith to forge the strongest chain imaginable, and then, when it was ready … he used the child to complete his wicked spell.'

Amy trapped a whimper on her hand. 'Were they really killed?'

'Worse,' said Oscar. 'Tarlock bound the child to the sun. The interloper became its anchor. A living sacrifice, every last breath and blink and thought used to sustain the mage's curse.'

Amy sucked in a breath. That did almost sound worse.

'At least the other interloper got away,' said Jonah, trying to brighten the tale. Then his face fell. 'But before they could return with help, Tarlock sealed the veil between our worlds.'

Oscar scrubbed a hand across his jaw, trying to hide the pain on his face. 'Once the chain ritual was complete, the sun was bound in the sky and the land of Tír na nÓg was frozen in time. Without our nights, even our stars are gone. Our gods can no longer watch over us.' He stood abruptly and began to pace back and forth. 'Now, after all these years, Tarlock has opened the veil again. Which means he's up to something.'

'I'd bet my best sword it's to do with the sun curse. The chain clangs and creaks in the wind. It's crumbling in parts … weakening,' said Niall. 'Which means his power must be weakening.'

'The druids of Blackthorn Wood talk of Pookas there who have turned back into people,' said Manus. 'And down in Butteroak Village, a farmer's crop of wheat has begun to grow again. All by itself.'

'Do you think the mage might really die?' said Jonah hopefully.

'I don't know,' said Oscar uncertainly. 'But he must be worried.'

The warrior beside Niall – Ultan, who had wild red hair and bits of boar meat in his beard – grunted. 'We should be the ones worrying now that he's captured the boy.'

'We've got the girl though.' Manus pointed across the clearing. 'What do we do with *her*?'

The Fianna warriors and the Greencloaks turned to stare at Amy. She tried not to cower.

'We could send her back through the waterfall,' reasoned Niall.

Amy's jaw tightened. 'I'm not going home without my brother.'

Oscar stopped pacing. 'Fine. We either keep her, or kill her.'

'You can't be serious!' Amy burst out.

Oscar drew his amber spear, acting as if he hadn't heard her. 'I call a vote. Weapons up for killing her.'

Amy looked around the clearing – frantically counting thirty-seven grumpy warriors, who now stood between her and death. To her horror, a slew of them raised their swords at once.

'Nothing personal,' said Manus evenly. 'If we kill you, the mage won't be able to get his hands on you.'

'But you'd be murderers!' said Jonah angrily. 'You can't kill someone who's done nothing wrong!'

Conan squeaked ardently in agreement.

Amy gulped.

Oscar's fingers twitched around his spear as he counted the votes in favour of Amy's demise. 'Sixteen,' he announced. 'Right. Weapons up for keeping her.'

Eighteen weapons went up, slower this time.

Jonah clapped his hands together. 'Saved by two.'

Amy blew out a breath.

'Hang on,' said Oscar, as he finished the count. 'That only makes thirty-four. Who didn't vote?'

'I didn't,' piped up an older, bald warrior who hadn't said a thing all council. 'I would have liked more time, but I'll add my spear to the first vote – she's too dangerous to keep.'

Amy's throat tightened. That narrowed it down to just one vote in her favour. Then something awful happened. Ultan stood up.

'I will do the same,' he said, but he dipped his chin, too ashamed to look Amy in the eye.

Now, it was eighteen to eighteen. The vote was tied.

'No,' whispered Jonah.

Amy couldn't breathe.

Oscar turned his spear in his hand. 'It's been long years since we've seen a tied vote,' he said, more to himself than to his men. 'It falls to me to break it.'

He hesitated, a muscle moving in his jaw as he deliberated, and at that moment Amy knew that if she didn't say something, she was done for.

She leaped to her feet. 'You're supposed to be heroes!' she cried. 'I came to you because I needed help. If you kill me, then you're no better than the mage. And isn't that why you exist?' She looked around at each of them, staring into their hardened faces and daring them to look away. 'To be better than him? To protect people from him?'

Oscar's nostrils flared. 'We do not debate while a vote is in progress.'

'You're voting on whether to murder me or not!' shouted Amy. 'I should be allowed to defend myself.'

Oscar spun his spear, the sharpened tip coming to rest less than six inches from her throat. 'Sit,' he spat through his teeth.

Amy sat.

After what seemed like an eternity, Oscar spoke again.

'My decision is that we should spare the child,' he said evenly. 'For now, we will keep her under our supervision.'

Amy nearly fainted with relief. A tear squeezed out but she quickly scrubbed it away.

Some of the warriors began to grumble, unhappy with the decision.

Oscar raised his spear, silencing them. 'The Fianna rides to defend innocents, not kill them, no matter where they're from.' He looked hard at his men. 'We will not start today. Not under my command.'

Jonah patted Amy on the knee, and gave her a subtle thumbs-up. She returned the gesture, doing her best to ignore the warriors who were glowering at her through the flames.

'As for the remaining interloper,' Oscar went on, 'we must decide whether to go after him or leave him to his fate. Whatever that may be.'

'Of course we have to rescue him!' said Amy, before Oscar could stop her. She hopped up on to the log and raised her voice to make sure she was heard. 'Liam doesn't deserve any of this! He's smart and clever and kind, and—'

'QUIET!' bellowed Oscar.

Amy's heart sank at the men's stony faces. They seemed utterly unmoved.

'Indeed it would be reckless to allow the Dullahan to take your brother to the mage.' Oscar spoke with authority. 'But still, we must vote. All those in favour of rescue, raise your weapons.'

Much to Amy's relief, the vote landed in Liam's favour by a margin of twelve weapons.

'We'll leave for Silverstone Castle at once,' said Oscar. 'If we're fast, we may catch the Dullahan before they reach Mount Arrigal.'

'And if you don't?' Owen piped up nervously.

'Then we'll have to storm the castle,' said Oscar, like it was the simplest thing in the world.

Amy clamped her lips shut. She was alarmed at the simplicity of Oscar's plan. How many soldiers did the mage have inside the castle? The Fianna were strong and brave, but they were only thirty-seven men. There was no way they could do it alone!

Niall came to stand by his leader, clapping a supportive hand on his shoulder. 'Tarlock doesn't know about the girl. And he doesn't know that we know about the boy either. He won't be expecting us to strike.'

'That doesn't mean he won't be prepared for us,' said Ultan. 'He has spies all over this kingdom. The skies belong to him, and so do most of the towns. He might try to pick us off on the way.'

'We'll travel by the outskirts and keep our heads down,' said Oscar, undaunted. 'We've been evading Tarlock for sixty years.'

'Not very well,' said Manus boldly. 'We've lost far more men to the Dullahan than we have left. The Fianna are not what we once were, Oscar. If we run into the mage's army, we'll be hopelessly outnumbered.'

Oscar looked solemn. 'Every warrior here fights with the strength and speed of twenty men, Manus. We are used to being outnumbered.'

'What if there are *thousands* of Dullahan?' challenged Manus.

Oscar's eyes flashed in warning. 'Then we will have our work cut out for us.'

'And what about Tarlock?' said Manus, refusing to be cowed. 'We only suspect that he's weakening. We don't know anything for certain yet.'

'DO YOU CHALLENGE ME?' boomed Oscar, the sudden explosion of his rage bringing a swift and deadly silence with it.

Manus shrank back. 'No. I'm simply saying—'

'The decision has been made. It is not for *you* to question it. If you cannot square yourself to the task, then you are free to stay behind with the Greencloaks.'

Manus pressed his lips together, his fists clenched as

he swallowed the order. 'Of course I'm going.'

Oscar waved him away, and Manus went, like a chastened dog.

The Fianna broke apart, the men splintering across the clearing to collect their things and ready themselves for the journey ahead.

'When do we leave?' Amy asked Jonah, as she hopped off the log.

Oscar stepped in front of her. '*You* are not going anywhere, little *sionnach*. We are leaving you in the care of the Greencloaks until we return.' He jabbed his finger at Cade and the others. 'Do *not* let her out of your sight.'

'There's no way I'm staying here!' Amy folded her arms in defiance. 'This is as much my fight as it is yours. And just so you know, I'm extremely brave and I'm the second-fastest runner in my school.'

A few of the nearby Fianna looked up from their preparations at this, and one or two began to laugh.

Oscar was not laughing. The vein in his temple was bulging.

Amy had had her fair share of run-ins with teachers over the years, not to mention one or two long-suffering babysitters, but she had never been glared at the way Oscar de Barra was glaring at her now. It looked like he was trying to incinerate her with his eyes.

'We do not ride with children. And besides, *you* are a girl.'

'So?'

'So, the Fianna do not ride with girls.'

The warriors guffawed, the sound echoing through the forest until it sounded like the trees were laughing at her too.

Amy blushed violently. 'Why not?'

'Because the fellowship of the Fianna is exactly that,' said Oscar impatiently. 'A *fellow*ship. It's right there in the name. Let me show you, little girl.' He raised a hand to stop her interrupting, and Amy swallowed her retort. When he spoke again, it was not just to her but to everyone in the clearing. 'It has been this way since the dawn of Tír na nÓg, when the warrior god Lug founded the Fianna. We are hunters and fighters, fearless in all we do. We live on the edges of the kingdom, travelling the wilderness until we are called upon to fight for our people and defend our values.'

An answering rallying cry went up around him.

'And what's all that got to do with me?' said Amy, as the Fianna went back to their business.

'Nothing. Which is exactly the point.'

Before Amy could protest, he stalked back to his hut. 'Finish your preparations, then saddle up the horses,' he called to his men. 'The Dullahan have a long start. We leave within the quarter-hour.'

While the Fianna warriors busied themselves, the Greencloaks descended on the last of the roasted boar, their ravenous hunger making them forget all about Amy.

She hovered at the edge of the camp with Jonah.

'I don't want to stay here,' she grumbled. 'It's not fair.'

'Don't feel bad, Amy. You did your best.' He patted her shoulder encouragingly. 'And hey, at least they didn't kill you. That's a silver lining, right?'

She threw him a withering look. 'I don't want to be your prisoner.'

'Sorry.' Jonah looked at his boots. 'This whole mess is my fault. If I could make it right, I would.'

Amy pictured Liam's face in her mind, pale and frightened. She wouldn't give up on him just because one very tall, very cranky man said so.

'Jonah. Where are the horses kept?'

'Why?' he said warily.

'You said you would make it right if you could. Well, you can. You can help me rescue Liam.'

Jonah's eyes went so wide, Amy could see her reflection in them. 'Yeah … that's not really what I meant.'

'I thought you were supposed to be brave,' she said pointedly. 'Don't you want to help me?'

Jonah took a step backwards. 'You're asking *me*, a member of the Elderglen Greencloaks, to go against the command of Oscar de Barra of the Fianna, steal one of his horses, and then embark on a doomed adventure across the cursed plains of Tír na nÓg to help a thistle-head who clearly never learned the word "please" in her life? No way! We'd be killed or kidnapped or boiled before you can say "Dullahan".' He glanced around, before dropping his voice. 'Or we'd be turned into ruddy *squirrels!*'

Conan, who had been sitting on his shoulder, squeaked in affront.

Jonah grimaced. 'Sorry, Conan. I didn't see you there.'

'I don't care how dangerous it is.' Amy's eyes darted towards Cade, who was busy wrenching a tusk from the boar's head. 'I'm not staying behind twiddling my thumbs in some forest with a bunch of immature boys while my brother's life hangs in the balance. One way or another, I'm going to find Liam and get us home to Connemara. If you're not brave enough to help me, I'll do it on my own. Just tell me how to get to the castle.'

Jonah narrowed his eyes. 'Are you trying to manipulate me?'

'Is it working?' said Amy hopefully.

'Kind of,' he sighed, and looked at Conan.

Conan gave three pointed squeaks.

'But she's a *girl*,' said Jonah. 'And we don't even know her.'

Another squeak.

'I am NOT *scared*. It's not about that.'

Conan began gesturing wildly.

'I know you don't regret it, but we can't just ignore the fact that you are now a—'

The squirrel gasped, then raised a little finger in warning.

'OK, sorry,' said Jonah sheepishly. 'All right then. Fine. I said *fine*.' He turned to Amy. 'We'll help you,' he said, somewhat begrudgingly.

Amy was so relieved she threw her arms around both of them. 'Thank you, thank you, thank you! You won't regret this.'

'I already do,' muttered Jonah, but Amy was too busy working out the next part of her plan to hear him.

While the rest of the Greencloaks engaged in an impromptu tusk-flinging competition, Jonah grabbed Amy's hand and pulled her into the trees. 'This way. Hurry,' he hissed. 'And by the way, after this, we're even for the whole kidnapping-you-in-a-net thing.'

Amy crept after him, crouching low so the rest of the Greencloaks wouldn't see her. 'I suppose that's fair. Hey, why did Oscar call me "little *sionnach*" back there?' she said, pronouncing the word the way he had said it: *shun-uck*.

'It means "little fox",' said Jonah. 'Probably something to do with your red hair.'

'Oh. I thought it meant something much worse.'

'Well, he hates foxes with a deep and burning passion,' added Jonah as an afterthought. 'One nibbled his ear lobe off when he was a boy. Ever since then, he can't stand the little rascals.'

Amy's face fell. 'That does make more sense.'

After a while, they reached the edges of the Elderglen forest, the trees becoming more spindly and sparse before petering out into a meadow. Most of the Fianna were already there, tying supplies to their grazing horses and fixing weapons to their belts and their boots and their backs and anywhere else they could fit one.

Amy stepped out of the trees, and stumbled. A strange heaviness settled around her, as though she were suddenly wearing a cloak made of lead. Every time she tried to move, it was like wading through quicksand. And worse still, her head was pounding awfully. 'Ugh,' she groaned. 'What's happening to me?'

Jonah threaded his arm through hers to steady her. 'That's the sun curse, I'm afraid. There's no shelter from it out here. You'll get used to it.'

Now that they were out of the Elderglen, Amy could see the sun again for the first time since she had climbed the tree. It was choking in the sky, the chain clanging violently as it held it in place.

'I can't believe you've been living like this for so long,' said Amy.

Jonah shrugged, but there was a sadness in his eyes. It was the shadow of a life permanently set to pause, the whisper of a future that was always just out of reach. Conan was sitting glumly on his shoulder, his little head drooped so low, she couldn't see his face.

If they rescued Liam, she'd be going home to grow up and *be* someone. But Jonah and Conan would never have that chance. So Amy promised herself that after she got to Silverstone Castle and saved her brother from Tarlock, she'd make it her mission to break that awful curse once and for all, so they could grow up too.

Then she clenched her fists and walked determinedly into the meadow.

Chapter Eight

THE LAST-MINUTE BARGAIN

The fact that most of the Fianna warriors were already sitting on their horses drastically decreased Amy's chances of stealing one. But she'd come too far to turn back now, and she could hardly go after her brother on foot. She spotted a horse that was grazing apart from the others, right by the treeline. It was a magnificent white mare with a wheat-coloured mane, but – more importantly – it was still waiting for its rider.

'I wouldn't do that if I were you,' said Jonah, seeing what she was thinking. 'That's Arrow. She might look sweet, but she's as temperamental as anything.'

'Well, she's the only one I've a chance of taking before the Fianna stop me,' said Amy, without breaking her stride.

But when they reached the horse, she realised it was far too tall for her to simply clamber on.

'Quick, give me a boost.'

'But that horse belongs to—'

'Scaredy-cat.'

'I'm not, it's just that —'

With a frustrated huff, Amy turned back to the horse. 'Please let me up,' she whispered. 'I'm on a very important mission.'

Arrow took a long look at her, sizing her up.

Amy's eyes darted sideways. The sudden silence of the Fianna meant they must have noticed her. She was just about to sneak back into the forest, when the horse tossed her head and gave a low whinny. Arrow bent her front legs and dipped towards the ground. With a rush of gratitude, Amy clambered on to her back. She threw her arms around the horse's neck and buried her face in her mane as Arrow stood up again. 'Thank you, Arrow. You're the best!'

Arrow whinnied, as if to say, *You're welcome.*

When Amy looked up, *all* the men were staring at her. So too were the horses.

Jonah had backed away several more paces, his mouth hanging open in a perfect O. On his shoulder, Conan was frozen in shock.

Niall – the warrior with the white hair – was the only

one smiling. 'Well, knock me down with a feather.'

'What have I done?' said Amy.

'In all the years of her life, Arrow has never yielded to anyone but Oscar.'

Oh. Arrow was Oscar's horse.

Amy's triumph was short-lived. She felt like a warrior sat so high, but the sight of Oscar stalking out of the forest towards them, with his spear clenched tightly in his fist, suddenly made her want to shrink.

He stopped dead in his tracks when he saw Amy sitting on his horse.

The other warriors shifted uncomfortably.

'Nice knowing you,' muttered Jonah, slinking away to hide behind Niall's piebald horse.

Amy waggled her fingers at Oscar. 'Hi.'

His left eye twitched.

She swallowed the quiver in her voice. 'I told you I wanted to come, and I meant it.'

'How did you get on my horse?' Oscar turned his accusing gaze on the rest of the Fianna.

'Don't look at us!' said Ultan, holding up his hands in a display of innocence. 'We didn't even know she was here.'

'I got up by myself,' said Amy, enjoying the look of surprise on his face. 'If you let more girls into your little club, that wouldn't surprise you one bit.'

Jonah flinched. 'Amy.'

But now that Amy was on Arrow, with Oscar below her, she realised she was the one in charge here and it gave her confidence.

'If you don't take me with you, I'll ride away on your horse and give myself over to the Dullahan instead, if that's the only way to find my brother,' she threatened. 'Then you'll have lost *two* interlopers.'

There was a long silence. Amy could feel her heartbeat in her ears. She gripped Arrow's reins. 'Even your horse wants me to come. Doesn't that count for something?'

Just when she thought Oscar was going to make a grab for her, he turned his attention on Jonah, who was still cowering behind Niall's horse. 'And what do you have to say for yourself?'

Jonah crept out from his hiding place. 'Well, if you're going to ride to Silverstone Castle to face Tarlock, I don't see why she can't go along too. After all, that's where her brother will be, and he's family. It's only what the Greencloaks would do for each other if one of us was kidnapped. It's what *you* would do.' Conan was nodding resolutely on his shoulder. 'And since it's my fault that her brother got taken in the first place, I'm going to help her.' Jonah placed a hand on his heart. 'It's a matter of honour.'

Amy blinked in surprise. This Greencloak boy was a lot braver than she'd given him credit for.

Oscar remained unimpressed. 'It's too hard a journey, Jonah.'

'Do you really trust the Greencloaks to keep me here?' Amy asked. 'See how easy it was for me to sneak away just now? I bet the others haven't even noticed I'm gone.'

Oscar sighed through his nose. 'We don't have time for this.'

Amy patted the horse. 'We can discuss it on the ride.'

This time, to her amazement, Oscar gave in. He muttered angrily as he rummaged around in his saddlebag. Then he pulled out a scratchy brown cloak and flung it at her. 'Put this on. If you're spotted, we'll have every bounty hunter in the kingdom tracking us. Not to mention the Dullahan.'

Amy shrugged the cloak on, her face disappearing inside the gaping hood. 'You won't even know I'm here.'

'Good. And for my sanity, keep the talking to a minimum, little sionnach.'

While Jonah clambered up on to Niall's horse with the warrior's help, Oscar fixed his spear to the saddle, before vaulting on to Arrow's back in what Amy had to admit was a *very* impressive leap. He landed with a thud and yanked the reins from her grip without another word.

She looked at him over her shoulder. He was close enough now that she could see the white hairs in his dark beard, and the lines around his eyes. 'That was really cool.'

'Remember what I said about talking?' said Oscar, as he urged his horse into a gallop.

The sun beat down on them as they left the enchanted forest behind. Far from the protection of the Elderglen, the curse grew stronger. It pressed down on Amy's shoulders and gathered between her ribs until her breath grew shallow and her neck ached. It rolled around inside her skull like a marble. But every time the pain flared, she scrunched her eyes shut and thought of Liam.

* * *

For a long time, all Liam had heard was the steady *th-thump* of hoofs and the panicked staccato of his own breath as the shadow riders carried him fast and far from the forest. He sat wedged in front of the leader, a burlap sack tugged roughly over his head, while his hands were fastened to the horse's reins. At first, he bucked and struggled, shouting until his voice ran out, but it was no use. There was no one to help him.

I *should have been quicker*, he scolded himself. I *should have been smarter*.

For Amy.

His annoying little sister, who was now all alone without him.

He pitched forward on the horse, trying to see out of the bottom of the sack. If he could at least get an idea of what direction they were taking him in, maybe he could find his way back. The ground whipped by in a blur, the horses galloping so fast their hoofs barely touched the ground. They were as unnatural as their riders, faster than cheetahs in the savanna, faster even than a high-speed train.

When the thrum of hoofbeats changed to the silent shifting of sand, the stench of rotting seaweed reached Liam on the wind. He couldn't see the ocean, but he could smell it drying up – the stink of dead fish and congealed seaweed baking in the hot sun. It stuck to the inside of his nostrils, making him gag.

Then abruptly the ocean was gone, the trail winding inland like the body of a snake. The horses thundered onwards, barely stopping to rest. No one fed Liam, but he wasn't hungry anyway. He was too frightened to think about food. Every so often, he tried to plead for his freedom, but his rider sat unmoving behind Liam, his barrelled chest heaving steadily against his back.

Eventually, Liam nodded off in the saddle, his neck straining as his head lolled back and forth. More hours passed in fitful jerking between waking and sleeping, and a new kind of dread took root inside Liam. At first he swore he was imagining it, but as the day wore on and on, and night never came, the bad feeling inside him grew. The sun in Tír na nÓg wasn't setting, which made it impossible to tell the time.

And then he remembered what Amy had told him about the sun being chained in the sky, and he began to wonder if perhaps time didn't move at all here. If perhaps Tír na nÓg was cursed. And now, he was too.

Chapter Nine

BLAGGARD'S KEEP

Amy and the Fianna passed through acres of farmland, where the fields were surrounded by neat stone walls. The crops were burnt and blackened, and some weren't growing at all. Most of the animals were curled up on the ground, barely breathing. In the distance, something let out a terrible, keening groan.

'Are the animals OK?' Amy asked Oscar, over her shoulder.

He shook his head. 'They're sick. Half dead, and half alive. It's no way to exist.'

Amy's heart clenched. 'Poor creatures.'

When they passed through sleepy villages nestled deep in the countryside, Amy peeked out through a gap in her hood, watching the people of Tír na nÓg run out of their homes to meet the Fianna. They all had the same pointed ears, and wide, frightened eyes. Whispers of Tarlock followed them on the breeze. Even though the mage was far away, Amy could see they lived in fear of him, and what horrible curse he might cast next.

The Fianna didn't stop, only nodded their heads as they passed, urging their horses onwards, through town after town. Sometimes children would run after their horses, begging to go with them, but the steel-eyed warriors never looked back.

When Amy's legs had gone numb and her back was stiff from riding, they came upon a mighty oak tree standing alone in a field. Its trunk was thick and gnarled, and had a knot so large, Amy could see it from all the way across the field. It looked like the face of a shocked owl.

Without slowing Arrow, Oscar drew his spear and pulled his arm back. 'Duck if you want to stay in one piece.'

Amy had barely lurched to one side when he let the spear fly. It whistled through the air like an amber comet before perfectly skewering the middle of the owl-shaped knot.

'Good shot,' she said breathlessly. 'But why are you showing off all of a sudden?'

'Watch and learn, little sionnach.' Oscar urged Arrow on faster. 'Yah!'

They galloped towards the oak tree, just as the air around it began to shimmer. Amy gasped as everything on the other side of the tree turned wavy, like a watercolour painting. And then fell away completely.

Oscar flung his arm out, yanking the spear from the trunk as they passed, then pulled back hard on the reins. Amy screamed as Arrow reared up, bringing them to a sudden stop. Behind them, the rest of the Fianna halted too.

When Arrow's hoofs hit the ground, Amy took a second to gather her breath, then blinked hard. They were hovering at the top of a valley that definitely hadn't been there a moment ago. She whipped her head round in amazement, but no one else looked the least bit surprised.

'What is this place?'

'Welcome to Lug's Valley,' said Oscar, as he nudged Arrow down the steep slope. Rocky hills rose up on either side of them like crests in a wave. The air changed as they descended, the long shadows of the hills hiding them from the sun's ever-present glare. Amy's headache dulled, and the weight of the curse shifted just a little. She sighed as her shoulders relaxed.

'Lug used to train his warriors here long ago,' Oscar went on. 'Legend says he was faster and stronger than all of his men put together. A god of war *and* victory. He wouldn't settle for anything less.'

Amy got the sense that Lug was Oscar's hero. He spoke about him the same way Liam talked about David Attenborough – with awe, and a little bit of envy.

She looked over her shoulder, to where the mighty oak tree now peered down at them. 'But it just appeared out of nowhere.'

'Lug cloaked this valley before he passed on,' said Oscar. 'Only his spear can reveal it.'

Amy glanced sidelong at the amber weapon. 'You have his *spear*?'

'It's one of the oldest relics in Tír na nÓg,' said Oscar, with a hint of smugness. 'Passed down through the Fianna, from leader to leader. Through all the changes that have befallen our kingdom, one thing remains true: the Spear of Lug will always find its mark.'

Amy couldn't help but be impressed. 'So you just fling it at the big tree and hope it hits the bullseye?'

'It never misses,' said Oscar, the gold of his eyes shining as though he were telling her a secret. 'And neither do I.'

The horses gingerly picked their way down into Lug's Valley, where they followed a stream to the ruins of an old stone keep. There were trees dotted around it, and though it was wincingly bright and unavoidably summer everywhere else they had been, deep in the Valley a secret autumn had been perfectly preserved. The air down here was cooler, and the leaves on the trees were crimson and amber.

'This is Blaggard's Keep, training ground and safe house of the Fianna Warriors.' Oscar hopped off the horse and stalked ahead of the others, his words flying over his shoulder. 'We'll be leaving you and Jonah here for safe keeping, while we ride on to Silverstone Castle. But first, we must rest.'

Leaving her here? In this dilapidated pile of stones? Had that been his plan all along? She realised she'd been tricked!

Amy scrabbled off the horse and ran after him.

'I'm not staying in this crumbling-down place while you go off to fight the mage! I told you I want to go to Silverstone Castle, and I meant it.'

Oscar ignored her.

Inside the crumbling walls of Blaggard's Keep, the Fianna lit a fire and sat down to eat. Amy lingered on the outskirts of the circle, glaring at Oscar with all the fury she could muster.

'You can scowl at him all you want, but it's not going to make him change his mind,' said Jonah, drifting over to join her. 'I knew he wouldn't let us go all the way to Mount Arrigal.'

'If he thinks he can just leave us in the middle of nowhere, he's wrong.'

'He's the head of the Fianna,' sighed Jonah. 'He can do whatever he wants.'

We'll see about that, thought Amy.

Jonah held out a chunk of bread and a bright red apple. 'I found some food, if you're hungry?'

Amy's stomach grumbled loudly in answer. She hadn't eaten a thing since she'd arrived in Tír na nÓg. She had no idea how much time had passed since then, but her stomach had never growled like a tiger before, so it must have been ages.

'Thanks.' She snatched up the bread and bit into the thick crust.

'Before you eat that, I really *should* warn you—'

'UGH, YUCK!' Amy spat it straight out. 'It tastes like dirt!'

'As I was *about* to say ...' said Jonah. 'The bread is rotten.'

'You tricked me!' Amy shoved the rest of it into his chest. 'Why would you do that?'

'It's not a trick. All the bread in Tír na nÓg is rotten,' Jonah explained. And then he did something even stranger – he took a bite of crust and gobbled it down, barely wincing as he swallowed it. 'Except the stuff in Silverstone Castle, of course. But I doubt we'll be dining there any time soon.'

Amy stared at him in horror, as Conan climbed up on to his shoulder and presented her with a nut. When she didn't take it, he smashed it against Jonah's wooden sword. It broke in half and a maggot wriggled out.

Amy shrieked.

The nuts were rotten too!

She reached for the apple, just as a worm poked through the waxy red skin.

Amy dropped the fruit. It rolled away, coming to a stop under a warrior's boot. He picked it up and devoured it in two bites.

Her stomach flipped, the ravenous gnaw of hunger congealing into nausea.

'The curse is in everything here. Tír na nÓg might look nice on the outside, but it's rotten at its core,' sighed Jonah, as he handed the rest of the bread to her. 'It's not so bad. After a while, you get used to it.'

'Stop saying that. You shouldn't *have* to get used to it,' said Amy angrily.

But she soon realised she had no choice but to eat what there was. She nibbled gingerly at the crust before washing it down with Jonah's flask of stagnant water.

On the other side of the campfire, Oscar and Niall had set aside their food and were having what looked like an important conversation. Amy edged closer to eavesdrop.

'… need to know what the mage is up to,' Niall was saying. 'Filly's not too far from here. My sister still lives there. I could drop in on her. See what I can find out.'

Oscar stroked his beard, nodding as he listened. 'Be quick about it, Niall. We can only spare a short break here. I wish it were longer.'

'I can slip away now?'

'Not yet. Wait until the others are asleep,' said Oscar. 'I don't want anyone getting any ideas …'

Fed, watered, and exhausted from an endless day of riding, the Fianna settled down for a quick nap.

Amy sidled back to Jonah, who was nestled in a corner, trying to get some shut-eye.

'Oi.' She nudged him with her shoe. 'What's Filly?'

He cracked an eye open. 'A town full of tongue-wagging gossipers. Half of them are probably in Tarlock's pocket. Why?'

'No reason.' Amy sat down beside him, and pulled her hood over her face. 'We should get some sleep.'

After about fifteen minutes, a cacophony of snores

was rattling through the stone keep. Jonah's head lolled against Amy's shoulder, his breath snuffling out of him in little whistles. Oscar was all the way on the other side of the keep, curled on to his side like a lumbering sack of potatoes. He was facing away from Amy, but she could tell by the steady rise and fall of his back that he was asleep. *Good.*

She stayed perfectly still, watching through a gap in her hood as Niall rolled to his feet, donned his cloak and crept away without so much as a backward glance.

She silently counted to sixty, then carefully removed Jonah's head from her shoulder and got to her feet. She scurried out of the keep, with all the stealth of a cat-burglar—

And ran straight into Conan.

The squirrel folded his arms and gave her a hard look.

Amy raised a finger to her lips.

Conan shook his head in disapproval, but Amy didn't have time to explain herself. The people of Filly might know if Liam was OK, and if she lingered for too long, she wouldn't be able to follow Niall to find her way there.

'Excuse me,' she hissed, as she stepped over Conan, and hurried on down the valley.

Niall had already mounted his horse and was clambering up the slope. Amy jogged over to where the rest of the horses were sleeping, but Arrow opened one eye to look at her and firmly closed it again.

'Please?' said Amy desperately. 'Won't you help me again?'

But it was clear Arrow wanted her sleep and had no intention of helping her sneak away.

Niall was halfway up the valley already, his silver ponytail getting further and further away. Amy panicked. There was nothing else for it. She would have to chase after him. On foot. She broke into a run, huffing and panting as she climbed up the hill. Sweat beaded on her forehead and pooled underneath her cloak, until it felt like her lungs were filled with cotton wool, but she didn't dare slow down.

By the time she dragged herself over the top of the hill and on to flat land once more, she thought she was going to be sick.

At the towering oak tree, there was no sign of Niall anywhere. He had galloped away to Filly, and she had no idea in what direction he had gone.

Amy was alone in a field that looked like all the rest of them, the cursed sun beating down on her without mercy. Almost at once, her head began to pound.

A tear slipped down her cheek as she collapsed on the grass, utterly spent.

'As far as daring escapes go, that one was pretty useless,' came a voice from behind her. Amy looked over her shoulder, to find Jonah stalking towards her, his dark hair still mussed from sleep. Conan was scurrying alongside him.

She threw him a filthy look. 'Squealer.'

The squirrel blew a raspberry at her.

'Don't blame Conan,' said Jonah, as he offered her his hand to help her up. 'I knew when you asked me about Filly that you were up to something.'

'I thought I'd be able to make it there by myself. I want to know if anyone's seen Liam.'

Jonah snorted. 'Filly is miles away, acorn-brain. You can't just jog over to it.'

'You seem to know a lot about it,' fished Amy. 'Why don't you show me the way?'

'Shall I just remove my head and hand it to Oscar, while I'm at it?' scoffed Jonah. 'If you know what's good for you, you'll come back to the keep before he wakes up and notices you're missing.'

'No can do.' Amy pointed behind him, past the oak tree, to where the land had resettled into an expanse of flat, green grass. The valley had disappeared, and they had no magical spear with which to open it again.

Jonah groaned. '*Great.*'

'Since we're already in trouble, we may as well make the most of it.' Amy tugged his sleeve and dragged him away from the tree. 'If you take me to Filly, I promise I'll never ask another favour ever again.'

Jonah's lips twisted. 'Why don't I believe you?'

She offered him a sheepish smile. 'Come on. It'll be an adventure.'

He relented with a sigh. 'Fine. But we're not going on foot.'

'Suits me,' said Amy. 'The horses are back in the valley. How are we going to—'

She yelped, as Jonah brought two fingers to his mouth and released a piercing whistle.

There came a far-off rumbling.

Amy stiffened, thinking for a terrifying moment that the Dullahan were coming. But then two gigantic creatures tore out of the distant trees and came charging towards them.

She leaped behind Jonah. 'What on earth are those?'

'Wilderbulls,' he said, with unnerving calmness. 'Haven't you seen one before?'

'No!' said Amy, as the earth began to rattle at her feet. 'We don't have them in Connemara!'

'Huh. Then you've been missing out.'

One wilderbull was brown and the other was white, both of them sporting humongous, spiralling horns that glittered in the sunlight. They were far larger than any cow Amy had ever seen, with curly wool sprouting around their shoulders as if they were wearing shaggy winter scarves. Even though their legs were short and stocky, they were thundering towards them at remarkable speed, their horns looking bigger and sharper and—

'Why aren't they slowing down?' cried Amy. 'They're going to flatten us!'

'Not if we gain their respect,' said Jonah, far too confidently.

'What's that supposed to mean?' said Amy, in rising alarm.

'SHOW NO FEAR!' Jonah sprinted towards the charging bulls and flung himself into the air. He landed on the brown one with a resounding *Oof!*, his legs swinging wildly as he dug his fingers into its shaggy wool and dragged himself up on to its back.

Amy charged headlong at the white wilderbull, fear ratcheting up her throat and bursting into a rallying cry. 'AAAGGGGHHHHH!'

Just as the bull was about to skewer her, she flung her arm out and grabbed on to its horn, kicking off the ground, and landing on its back with a bone-rattling thud. She threw her arms around its neck, burying her fingers in its fluffy white wool.

When she looked up, Jonah was galloping alongside her, Conan clinging on to his cloak for dear life. 'That was pretty impressive. Especially for a girl!'

Amy stuck her tongue out at him, her triumph momentarily banishing the pain in her head. 'You haven't seen anything yet!'

'Then I suppose you'll have no trouble keeping up with me!' Jonah smirked over his shoulder as he pulled ahead.

Amy urged her wilderbull into a thundering charge, a burst of laughter flying out behind her as they took off for Filly, like twin streaks of lightning.

Chapter Ten

THE TOWN OF FILLY

Amy took to the wilderbull like she had been riding it her entire life. She vaulted over winding streams, cresting humpbacked hills only to thunder down them again, until finally a town appeared in the distance.

'There! Do you see it?' said Jonah, who was keeping pace alongside her. 'Isn't it magnificent?'

Filly was far bigger than the other towns and villages they had passed on their way to Blaggard's Keep. It sprawled across the horizon like a rainbow. Tall, narrow houses of blue and yellow and green and pink huddled side by side along white-cobbled streets, their copper chimneys piping silvery smoke up into the sky. There were market stalls and taverns, each one bedecked with a huge, overhanging awning to shelter the townsfolk from the sun.

'It certainly looks pretty,' she agreed, as they approached, but she couldn't ignore the air of heaviness that lingered over Filly, like an invisible mist clinging to its steeples. As they drew closer still, she was able to make out the townsfolk. They were wearing the same drab, worn-out tunics as the others Amy had seen on her travels, and were drifting through the streets like zombies, stopping every so often to rub their eyes, or yawn.

Amy and Jonah left the wilderbulls to graze by a river, before adjusting their hoods and hurrying over a bridge that marked the entrance to the busy town of Filly.

An elaborate stone fountain welcomed them. In the middle of it stood a statue of a short, plump man with a smiling face, pointed ears and a generous swoop of hair. He was posing with his quill in the air. His mouth was wide open, like he was mid-sentence, and from it, water erupted in a perfect spout and pooled in the basin at his feet.

'That's Ogma, the god of art and artists,' said Jonah. 'When he was alive, he built this town as a tribute to creativity.' The ghost of a smile passed over his face. 'Filly used to be one of the happiest places in the kingdom. People danced and sang in the streets, and wore rainbow dresses and sparkling tunics and enormous silly hats.' He threw his arms out wide to show her the size. 'The musicians were so good, people travelled from miles around to hear them play, and the bards' stories were so brilliant, the clouds would float down to listen in.'

Amy stared up at the statue and felt curiously sad.

She turned away, only to notice a figure in a long grey robe skulking on the other side of the fountain. Jonah grabbed her hand. 'Don't say anything else,' he hissed, out of the side of his mouth. 'Keep your head down and walk with me.'

Amy glanced over her shoulder as Jonah led her away from the fountain. Though the figure's face was hidden in the shadows of his hood, she glimpsed the silver pinprick of his gaze, and felt the hairs rise on the back of her neck.

'Who was that?' she whispered.

Jonah waited a full minute before responding, their quickened footsteps clacking on the cobbles. 'That was a warden.'

'What's a *warden*?' She knew the answer wasn't likely to be good.

'A rotten snitch, that's what. The wardens are Tarlock's spies. You can tell them by their grey robes and creepy silver eyes. They lurk in towns and villages, keeping watch over everyone. They don't sleep, or even *blink*. The mage has spelled them to be that way so they're on constant alert. They carry spelled dust in their pocket, and if they ever spot anything against Tarlock's rules, like a stray Fianna warrior, say, or an *interloper* –' Jonah's eyes darted fearfully – 'they send up a bright red flare that can be seen for miles. And then—'

'The Dullahan come?' guessed Amy.

Jonah nodded.

She swallowed. 'Do you think that one knew—'

'No.' He shook his head. 'It didn't send a flare. But there'll be more of them. We need to be careful.'

Amy drew her cloak tighter, making sure her ears were well hidden. She would have to be careful asking questions about Liam – she didn't want to give herself away.

Jonah led her down another cobbled street. 'If anyone here knows anything about your brother, it will be the traders,' he said, as though he could read her mind. 'They're the biggest gossips in Filly.'

They ducked down a bustling lane, where market stalls heaved with freshly baked bread, enormous wheels of milky cheese, and bowl after bowl of roasted nuts and fresh fruit. There were steaming pies and tarts too, and little pots of jam and honey. Amy knew it was an illusion –

that the food here was as rotten as the bread back at Blaggard's Keep – but that didn't stop her stomach from grumbling.

She stuck her hand into her pocket, tracing the rim of Liam's spectacles before settling on Peggy's silver sixpence. She pulled it out as she drifted towards the first stall.

Jonah yanked her back by her cloak. 'Put your human money away before you bring the wardens down on us!' he whispered urgently. 'You might as well announce yourself as an interloper with that thing!'

'Sorry,' mumbled Amy, as she stowed the sixpence away.

'Anyway, Filly isn't that sort of town. The money here isn't coins, it's *stories*. Gossip is even better, if you have it. Let me show you.'

They drifted over to a wooden stall, where Jonah pointed to a wedge of cheese the size of his own head. 'One of those, please.'

'What's your story?' said the woman, behind the stall. She had a long, droopy face and flat grey hair, and her chin was almost as pointed as her ears.

Jonah cleared his throat. 'Do you know the one about the Salmon of Knowledge?'

'Heard it four times today already,' said the woman, in a bored voice.

His face fell. 'What about Queen Maeve and the Wild Cattle Raid?'

The woman yawned. 'Know it like the back of my hand.'

'The legend of the Blackthorn Giant?'

The woman's sigh whistled through her nose. 'Got anything new?'

Jonah's cheeks flushed.

'How about a joke?' suggested Amy.

The woman cocked her head. 'It's been ages since I've heard one of those.'

Amy's thoughts turned to her brother. If the joke inside a Christmas cracker were a person, it would be Liam. Over the years of his life, he had amassed the corniest collection of jokes on the planet. Perhaps she could use some of them to get the information she needed.

'What sits at the bottom of the sea and twitches?'

The woman licked her lips, waiting.

'A nervous wreck,' said Amy sheepishly.

'Oh.' There was a beat of silence, and then the woman threw her head back and laughed. It was so loud, it sounded like she was screaming.

Amy stared at her in alarm.

Beside her, Jonah was doubled over with laughter.

'Wow,' Amy muttered.

Even though the joke was bad, and a part of her was embarrassed for telling it, she felt a prickle of pride at making them both laugh so hard. The woman's smile completely transformed her face. It was like someone had switched the light on behind her eyes.

So far, the plan was working.

Amy edged closer. 'Do you want to hear another one?'

'*Oh?*' The woman arched a grey brow.

Amy suddenly felt like she was walking on a tightrope.

She had to be clever with her next joke. And she had to be careful too.

'What did the headless horseman say before leaving the party?' Amy didn't wait to deliver the punchline. 'I'll beheading off then!'

This time, the woman didn't laugh. 'That's not funny,' she said with a frown. 'The Dullahan just passed by our walls earlier, and both my children hid under their bed. Smelt them from a mile away, they did.' She suppressed a shudder. 'I only caught a glimpse of them myself, and it made me sick to my stomach.'

'You mean you saw them with your own eyes?' said Amy, far too eagerly.

Jonah squeezed her wrist. *Careful.*

'Aye.' The woman wrung her hands. She looked up, to

where the cursed sun was trying to burn a hole through the awning of her stall. 'A band of 'em passed right by the outer wall. They were in an awful hurry.'

'So are we, come to think of it,' said Jonah, attempting to pull Amy away.

She tried to shake him off.

'Why were they in a hurry?' she said, her voice hitching. 'Did they have someone with them?'

Jonah dug his fingers into her wrist, but Amy didn't budge.

The woman leaned in, and so did Amy, her hood slipping as they bent their heads together under the awning. 'There's a rumour going around …'

Amy held her breath.

'The leader was riding with an *interloper*,' whispered the woman.

Amy's heart stuttered in her chest.

'Now I don't know about that, but they had something scrawny and wriggling bundled up in a sack – I saw that much.'

Liam was still alive. Still within reach.

'Which way did they go?' She had to ask. She couldn't help herself. She leaned across the stall, her hood falling away completely. 'What road did they take?'

Jonah tried to save her, tugging her hood back over

her head, but the woman was already staggering back-wards.

Her eyes narrowed.

'What makes you so curious?'

'Nothing,' said Amy, quickly. 'What do you call a pony with a cough?'

The woman blinked.

'A little hoarse!' announced Amy.

She watched the joke spark in the woman's eyes, the cobwebs of suspicion falling away as a laugh wheezed out of her.

'Quick.' Jonah nudged her. 'Tell another one.'

'What did one plate say to the other?' said Amy, without missing a beat. 'Dinner is on me!'

This time, the woman shrieked in amusement. There was a guffaw from somewhere over Amy's shoulder, and from her other side, a small, tittering laugh. The townsfolk had caught wind of the jokes and were huddling around the stall to hear more.

'Why wouldn't the shrimp share his treasure? Because he was a little shellfish!'

More laughter rang out. People began to crowd in on Amy, their eyes wide, hungry for more. With dawning horror, she realised she was making a scene. Which was the exact opposite of what she was supposed to be doing!

'Thanks for the chat, but I have to go now.' Amy waved to the woman. 'Bye!'

Jonah dragged her through the gathering crowd, ducking and weaving until they were safely out of the market.

'I meant *one* more joke,' hissed Jonah, as they hurried for the bridge. 'What were you thinking, drawing attention to us like that?'

'Sorry,' huffed Amy. 'I didn't realise I was so funny!'

'Easy crowd. These people haven't heard a joke in sixty years!'

They were almost back at the bridge when out of nowhere a tall, grey-hooded figure stopped them dead in their tracks. He loomed over them, pinning them with his bright silver gaze. A warden!

'Jonah,' she said, in a trembling breath.

'It's all right,' said Jonah, raising his hands. 'This is just … a misunderstanding, that's all.'

The figure didn't send up a flare. He didn't say anything either. He simply took their wrists in a vice-like grip and dragged them back into Filly.

'Don't make a fuss,' said Jonah out of the side of his mouth. 'If we run, he'll call the Dullahan.'

The warden marched them past the marketplace and through the town square. Jonah and Amy looked at their feet to avoid rousing further suspicion, while Conan remained hidden in the folds of Jonah's cloak. Even so, Amy could feel the stares on the side of her face, and hear the whispers that followed them down the cobbled streets. The rumour-mill of Filly was already hard at work.

When the warden turned a corner and led them towards a spindly purple house that looked out over all the streets of Filly, Jonah snapped his chin up.

'Oh no,' he groaned. 'Not Violet Mistwhistle.'

Amy looked at him blankly. 'Who?'

'The Town Whisperer,' he explained. 'She sits on all the rumours of Tír na nÓg, like a goose guarding golden eggs. She knows the comings and goings of everyone in the land.'

'But why does she want to see us?' said Amy warily.

'Because Tarlock got to her some time ago.' Jonah gulped. 'Now she's the Head Warden of Filly.'

Chapter Eleven

THE TOWN WHISPERER

Violet Mistwhistle, the highest-ranking warden in Filly, was sitting in her armchair when Amy and Jonah were prodded into her living room. Their chaperone returned to the hallway, leaving them hovering uncertainly by the door. It slammed shut behind them, sealing them in.

Violet was petting a furry grey cat whose face was as wide and flat as a pancake. Instead of a long grey robe, she was dressed all in black, and wearing a funereal veil over her face. In the firelight, Amy could just about make out the silver glint of her eyes.

'Jonah, of the Elderglen Greencloaks,' Violet announced in a deep, plummy voice. 'It has been some time since you visited us here in Filly.' She turned to Amy.

'And you have brought a friend with you. I welcome you both to the House of Whispers. Please, take a seat.'

Amy didn't want to sit – she wanted to run – but she forced herself to stay calm. They would have to be on their guard if they wanted to get out of this in one piece.

Jonah sank into a green velvet armchair near the door, Conan peering out fearfully from beneath the folds of his cloak. Amy drew her hood tighter as she perched on the armrest. Her eyes took in the crackling fireplace and the fancy-looking desk beside it, which was piled with ledgers and maps. She wondered if there might be one of Silverstone Castle.

'You may tell the squirrel that Ralph is not going to eat him,' said Violet, as she stroked her cat. 'He is not allowed to feast on Pookas.'

'Thank you, Madam Mistwhistle,' said Jonah, in what Amy assumed was his most polite voice. 'We appreciate the warm welcome, but I'm afraid we really must be on our way.'

'Oh?' said Violet curiously. 'And where precisely are you going?'

'Nowhere,' said Jonah quickly. 'We only came for a brief visit, but the other Greencloaks will be missing us.'

Violet pointed a spindly finger at Amy. '*She* is not a Greencloak.'

Amy winced.

'She's visiting from Butteroak Village,' said Jonah smoothly. 'We're distant cousins.'

'*Very* distant,' squeaked Amy.

'Butteroak,' purred Violet Mistwhistle, and from her lap, the cat's gaze seemed to sharpen. 'Is that where you learned your *hilarious* jokes?'

Amy felt like she was straying into a trap, but she could hardly refuse to answer. She tried to avoid the question instead.

'Well, I only know a few.'

'And yet somehow you've remembered them,' said Violet, with the same idle curiosity. 'Even though everyone else in this land has forgotten jokes ever existed.' She sat back in her chair, drumming her bright purple fingernails along the armrest. Amy's gaze darted back to the desk, her fingers itching to rifle through those maps. 'And here I was, thinking you might have come this way because you are chasing the boy. The one who rides with the Dullahan.'

Amy whipped her head around, causing strands of red hair to tumble out of her hood. She hastily stuffed them back in.

Violet's teeth winked at her from behind the veil. 'Isn't he the one you were asking about down in the marketplace?' The silence swelled. 'In between your little jokes, that is.'

Amy forced a laugh. 'Oh, I was just gossiping. It was the trader who brought him up.'

'She couldn't stop herself,' added Jonah. 'We only wanted to buy some cheese.'

Violet Mistwhistle chuckled coldly. 'You came all the way to Filly for cheese?'

Amy and Jonah nodded. 'Yeah.'

'So, you are not interested in the interloper then?'

Amy's heart was clattering in her chest. She badly wanted to ask what Violet Mistwhistle knew.

'The boy is an *interloper*?' Jonah did a little gasp. 'Well, that's the first we've heard of it!'

'And you a Greencloak,' said Violet flatly. 'I find that hard to believe.'

Jonah shrugged.

Ralph arched his back and released a drawling *miaow* before hopping off Violet's lap. Conan shuffled about inside Jonah's cloak as the cat prowled across the room and began sniffing around the ends of Amy's cloak.

'Shoo, *shoo*,' she said, trying to push him away.

'And what of the poison in her pocket?' said Violet. 'I suppose that has slipped past you too.'

Amy froze. It suddenly felt like Peggy's coin was burning a hole in her jeans.

Jonah's eyes flitted towards the door. 'I don't know what you're talking about.'

Violet licked her teeth. 'It's not of this world. I can *sense* it.'

And so could Ralph.

Oh no!

Amy shot to her feet. 'I'm afraid we really have to go. We'll be late.'

'For what?' Violet stood up. The black lace of her dress trailed after her as she crossed the room in three easy strides. She was at the door before them, blocking their way. Her hand shot out, tugging Amy's hood back.

Amy gasped as it fell away, revealing her long red hair, freckled cheeks and round-top ears.

'Well, well, well,' said Violet smugly. 'What do we have here?'

Amy dodged around her and wrenched the door open, but Violet Mistwhistle grabbed her by the shoulders and pinned her against the wood. Her eyes flashed, and in them Amy glimpsed a hint of desperation. 'How many of you are there, interloper?'

Amy tried to shake her off. 'Leave me alone!'

Violet tightened her grip, her fingernails digging into her skin. 'Why are you travelling with a Greencloak? Tell me the truth, interloper. Are you riding with the Fianna?'

Jonah stiffened.

Amy blinked. 'What's the Fianna?'

'More lies,' Violet hissed. She turned on Jonah. 'Where is Oscar de Barra?'

'Don't ask me. You know the Fianna don't share their plans with the Greencloaks.' Jonah's chuckle sounded forced. 'And besides, why would they go anywhere with an interloper? That's like *asking* the Dullahan to attack you!'

The warden's silver gaze narrowed. 'Oscar de Barra knows precisely how valuable interlopers are. Especially now that Tarlock is dying—' She stopped abruptly, her bright eyes widening.

This time, Jonah's gasp was real. 'So it's true? The mage really is dying?'

Violet barked a laugh, but Amy could see the fear in her eyes. She had said too much. 'Only until he fixes the sun chain. Which he will. Very soon!' She tried to force another laugh, but it was interrupted by a high-pitched squeal, and then the scrabble of tiny paws. Conan had leaped from Jonah's cloak and was leading Ralph on a wild chase around the sitting room, the cat squalling every time he lunged for his bushy tail.

Violet's grip on Amy loosened. 'RALPH WHISKERSHINS, FOR CRYING OUT LOUD, WOULD YOU GET A HOLD OF YOURSELF!' she shouted, in a completely different voice. Gone was the plummy lilt of her curiosity, replaced by a high-pitched caterwaul that reminded Amy of the Sunday food market in Galway City.

She yelped as her foot snagged on the end of her dress. She fell to her knees, struggling to rip the veil from her face. 'Stupid veil, I can't see a thing!'

Amy rushed to the desk and grabbed a stack of maps, just as the cat vaulted on to the couch, swiping his shiny claws at Conan. She picked up a paperweight, flinging it at the cat as she hurried back across the room. The squirrel leaped at Jonah. The Greencloak caught him easily, and the three of them bolted through the open door.

The warden who had delivered them to Violet Mistwhistle chased them down the hallway. Jonah drew his wooden sword and slammed it into his stomach. He doubled over with a pathetic wheeze, then Jonah struck again, slamming the hilt into his shoulder and knocking him to the ground.

'Nice!' huffed Amy, clutching the maps to her chest as she kicked the front door open.

Jonah bounded out after her. 'See? It has its uses!'

They thundered through the town of Filly, ignoring the excited whispers trailing them on the wind. It didn't matter who spotted them now – they had already been discovered and the sooner they got away, the better.

They reached the bridge as a distant *pop!* rang out. Behind them, Amy saw a bright red flare shoot up from Violet Mistwhistle's chimney. It exploded in the sky like a firework, sending sparks crackling out in every direction.

'Holy sneezeweed!' panted Jonah as they vaulted over the bridge. 'The Dullahan are coming!'

Amy gasped a breath. 'Keep going!' she yelled. 'And don't look back!'

* * *

Amy and Jonah didn't speak again until they were back on the wilderbulls, several miles away from Filly. After charging at a thunderous pace, the bulls now slowed to a canter to catch their breath.

'That was close!' panted Jonah, as they rode side by side.

'At least we got out with these,' said Amy, removing the maps from where she had bunched them under her cloak. 'With any luck, one of them will show us Silverstone Castle. *And* we know that Tarlock is dying. That's good, right?'

He frowned. 'But now Violet knows about you too.'

'Let's forget about that part,' said Amy, changing the subject before fear got the better of her again. 'What's a Pooka? Violet mentioned it, and back in the Elderglen, the

Fianna were talking about them too.'

'It's what we call an animal or bird who used to be a person,' Jonah explained. 'Tarlock has a vicious temper. He turns anyone who stands up to him into a Pooka.'

Amy paled at the thought. Then she looked to Conan, who was sitting on Jonah's shoulder. 'Is that how you became a squirrel?'

The squirrel nodded, and began to mime an elaborate sword-fight.

Jonah interpreted for Amy. 'Back when Tarlock first opened the veil between our worlds, Conan was the one who first discovered the pair of interlopers wandering in the Elderglen. The Fianna were training at Blaggard's Keep, and we had no weapons to fight the shadow riders when they came, but Conan's always been the bravest of all of us. He couldn't help himself. He tried to help the humans escape.'

Jonah fiddled with the wilderbull's curly mane. His cheeks were going red, and Amy got the sense he was a little ashamed. Not of his friend, but of himself.

'He got one of them out, but when the other got caught, so did Conan. Tarlock was so angry that he made an example out of him, right there in the Elderglen. As a warning to the rest of the Greencloaks, who were hiding in the trees.'

Amy had never imagined she would ever find herself in admiration of a squirrel, and yet here she was. 'That was very brave of you, Conan. I'm only sorry how it all turned out.' She leaned across the space between their wilderbulls and offered him her finger. The squirrel puffed his chest out and shook it with both paws.

To Jonah she said, 'And it's very brave of you to come and help me rescue my brother. Especially knowing how it might turn out.'

Jonah idly traced the birthmark under his eye. 'I sometimes think that if I had been braver that day – that is to say, if all of us had been braver – things would have turned out differently for the kingdom. But fear has a way of coming at you like a wave, and if you're not careful, it can sweep you away.'

Conan nodded glumly.

Amy's heart ached for the little squirrel. 'Nothing is forever, you know.'

'Except here,' sighed Jonah. 'Here, everything is forever.'

'Hey,' said Amy softly. 'Why do bees have sticky hair?'

They both looked at her expectantly.

'Because they use honeycombs.'

Jonah's face split into a grin, and Conan squeaked in amusement.

Amy began to rifle through the maps, tossing aside the ones she didn't need. She was just about to lose hope when she saw the words *Silverstone Castle* on the second to last parchment.

'Jonah, look!' she said, waving it about. 'It's a map of the castle!'

'Thank the gods!' Jonah clapped his hands in triumph. 'Maybe now Oscar won't kill us.'

Still grinning to herself, Amy carefully folded the map and stowed it back inside her cloak. She felt one step closer to Liam already.

A short while later, the mighty bough of the knotted oak tree appeared in the distance. Beyond it, a rail of dark mist moved in from the north. The sky, once blue and blisteringly bright, clouded over in an instant, and the sun disappeared behind a veil of grey shadow. The rain came fierce and violent, the thunder growling so loud, Amy had to shout over it to be heard.

'I've never seen the weather change so quickly!' she said, as they galloped hard and fast towards the tree. 'And I'm from the west of Ireland!'

'It's been doing that a lot lately,' shouted Jonah. 'The king must be throwing a tantrum!'

Amy glanced at the sky, just as a fork of lightning tried to split it in two. The earth shook, and she felt a deep trembling in her bones. She didn't miss the glare of the cursed sun, but she wasn't sure this storm was any better. 'Are you being serious?' she shouted back. 'And why haven't I heard of the king before now?'

'I was getting round to it,' yelled Jonah, through a mouthful of raindrops, but the rest of their conversation was abruptly cut short. Through the spitting rain and skulking clouds, a figure was waiting for them underneath the oak tree. The amber glint of his spear told Amy exactly who it was.

She could also tell that Oscar was fuming.

In that moment, she couldn't decide what was worse – the storm overhead, or the one waiting for them at the entrance to Lug's Valley.

Chapter Twelve

THE HOWLING DARK

Liam travelled with the shadow riders of Tír na nÓg until the stench of death clung to every inch of his skin, until his back screamed and his throat ached. His fear worsened with every mile, the horses galloping so fast, sometimes it felt like they were flying.

He knew the further they travelled from the enchanted forest, the less hope Amy had of ever finding him again. The longer they rode, the more sure Liam was that he was going to die.

He tried to imagine what Amy would do in his position. She would be brave, certainly. But most of all, she would fight, right until the bitter end. In the back of Liam's mind, a voice whispered to him: *If you're going to die, why are you making it easy for them? Why don't you go down swinging?*

Liam dipped his chin, examining the binds around his wrists. They were still tied to the reins, his skin raw beneath them. Either the rope would snap on his dismount, or his bones would, but wasn't escape worth a try? Isn't that what Amy would do?

He took a deep breath. It was now or never.

Just as he was about to fling himself off the horse, the animal slowed. Liam snapped his chin up, the back of his head flopping against his rider's chest as they were carried through a narrow, rocky pass. The sack was tugged off his head, revealing a jagged grey mountain that speared up towards the sky. A castle had been cut into the side of it, its turrets rising and twisting into the mist. Without his glasses, everything was blurry, but Liam thought it looked a bit like a tombstone, peering out over Tír na nÓg.

'*Oh*,' he whispered, with some surprise.

The horses gathered at the bottom of the mountain, where the trail turned steep and rocky. Liam's rider slipped silently to the ground, untied him from the reins and dragged him off the horse. Liam squeezed his eyes shut, wishing he could unsee the headless warrior that carried him up the mountain – the barrelled chest heaving with phantom breath, the stump of a neck bleeding into darkness. His boot buckles clinked with each stride.

Sunlight blared behind Liam's eyelids, and a terrible pain gathered in his skull. It felt like there was a creature trapped inside it, trying to pound its way out.

Clink. Clink. Clink.

When Liam opened his eyes again, they were approaching a pair of towering black gates. The headless horseman dumped him on the ground before them, and turned on his heel. He was gone in a breath of cold wind, leaving Liam whimpering and alone on the craggy grass.

Act first. Think later, he told himself.

He started to scrabble back down the mountain on his hands and knees, trying not to put too much weight on his injured ankle, which had been trodden on back in the forest.

Somewhere over his shoulder came the crunch of new footsteps. Liam didn't stop crawling. Not when the footsteps sped up, nor when an angry voice shouted after him.

But then a soldier appeared, standing squarely in his way. He wore black armour emblazoned with a golden sun, and a matching helmet with an open visor.

Liam could see the situation was hopeless, but still he tried to go round.

The soldier blocked Liam's path again. He was tall and

brutish and scowling, and though Liam was frightened of him, he was also relieved to see that he possessed a head. The very existence of ears meant there was a chance he could be reasoned with.

Liam staggered to his feet. 'I'll just … be on my way,' he said, unsuccessfully.

The soldier scooped him up.

'Put me down!' huffed Liam, but he was too weak to struggle. The soldier carried him back up the mountain, as easily as if he were a sack of potatoes.

Without his glasses, the world was smudged around the edges, but Liam did his best to study it. Towers wound up and out in every direction, green-and-silver banners rippling from their spires. The tallest of them rose up from the middle of the castle, like a finger pointing at the sky. It was a clock-tower, with a moon-white face and a tick-ticking black hand.

The soldier's armour was cool against Liam's cheek. 'There's been a mistake,' said Liam, as he pushed against it. 'I'm not supposed to be here.'

The soldier grunted as he ferried him through the black gates and into the bowels of the castle. They descended a stone staircase, spiralling down, down, down into the darkness, until the damp settled on Liam like a second skin. The only light flickered from a lone sconce on the wall. It bounced off the soldier's armour, making it look like the sun was burning. There was a keening creak, and then Liam was lowered on to a hay-strewn floor. A key turned with a sickening *click*. When he looked up, squinting without his glasses, he noticed the iron bars.

'Wait!' Liam flung himself at the bars. 'Where am I? What's going to happen to me?'

But the soldier was already plodding away. 'Mind the Banshee if you want to stay in one piece,' he said, over his shoulder. And then he was gone.

Liam tried to squeeze through the bars. 'Wait! PLEASE!'

His voice echoed back at him.

PLEASE!

'YOU CAN'T JUST LEAVE—'

A bloodcurdling shriek rang out as a creature came skittering out of the darkness. Liam leaped backwards, just as she curled her bony fingers around the bars of his cell. The Banshee's face was impossibly wrinkled. Her milky eyes were unseeing, and her toothless mouth was open so wide, Liam could see the blackness of her throat. He also saw there was a key swinging from her neck.

'Please, don't eat me!' he cried.

The sconce on the wall went out. The Banshee didn't move, but he could feel her cloudy eyes on him as he huddled at the back of his cell in a loose scattering of hay.

Liam scraped his hands through his hair, trying to calm down, but everything was crowding in on him again – fear and confusion and horror, and hopelessness.

Just breathe.

But suddenly that seemed impossible. Everything inside him felt too tight – his skull, his throat, his ribcage. It was all closing up, like the bellows of an accordion.

He remembered the last time he'd had a panic attack. Six months ago, right before a piano exam. His insides had closed up then too, and Liam had flapped about the kitchen, gasping for air. Amy had come running in from outside, laying her hands on his shoulders as she helped him count out the seconds of every breath until his cheeks stopped prickling and he could breathe properly again.

Liam tried that now, breathing in for five seconds. Out for five seconds. Again, and again, and again, until the world stopped spinning. Then he curled up into a ball, and buried his head in his hands to shut out the darkness.

He hoped Amy was OK, and that maybe – just maybe – she was coming to rescue him.

Chapter Thirteen

THE WELL OF WISHES

Oscar didn't say a single word to Amy and Jonah when he met them at the oak tree, but he served them with a glare so blistering, Jonah whimpered. The leader of the Fianna uncloaked Lug's Valley with his spear and marched them back to Blaggard's Keep, muttering angrily under his breath. Amy caught certain words, like 'disobedient' and 'reckless', and got the uncanny sense that speaking would only make everything worse for both of them. So, with great effort, she bit her tongue.

At the keep, with the rest of the Fianna gathered around them, there was no avoiding the calamitous truth of what they had done.

'Speak,' Oscar ordered them. 'Tell the men what you did.'

Amy summoned her courage, and said, 'I went to Filly to get information about my brother—'

'Which was *my* job,' interrupted Niall, who had managed to make the same journey and return before them, without causing an unholy fuss.

'I didn't want to wait,' said Amy. 'I wanted to see for myself.'

'And to go with a Greencloak, who was still wearing his *green cloak!*' said Oscar, looking accusingly at Jonah. '*You* should have known better.'

Jonah stared at his boots. 'Sorry,' he mumbled.

Amy cleared her throat. 'There's more.'

Oscar bit off a curse. 'Of course there is.'

Without looking at any of the Fianna, she told them about Violet Mistwhistle in one hurried breath, scrunching her eyes shut when it was done.

There was a long, painful silence.

'So … Tarlock knows about you,' said Manus, in a low voice.

Amy nodded.

'And Jonah.'

Again, she nodded.

'Which means he likely knows about us too,' said Ultan.

'But did you hear the part about Tarlock dying?' said

Amy, trying to focus on something helpful. 'It means you were right! This is the perfect time to strike! And, we've got this too.' She pulled out the map of Silverstone Castle and waved it under Oscar's nose. 'It's a map of the castle!'

Oscar snatched it from her, his gaze narrowing as he studied it. 'You're not completely useless then,' he muttered, as he tucked it inside his cloak. 'But I'm not trusting you to keep this safe when you can barely look after yourself.'

He turned away from the huddle. 'Tarlock will be sending his riders this way,' he said, as he stalked back to the fire. 'We need to go. Before we end up trapped in this valley like sitting ducks.'

'What about Liam?' Amy called after him.

'We've missed him by some time,' said Niall, relaying the information he had gleaned from his sister on his scouting mission. 'The Dullahan were much faster than we thought. The curse doesn't drain them, the way it does us. It *feeds* them. They've likely reached Silverstone Castle by now.'

The world spun around Amy, and she thought for a second she might faint. 'Liam really is in trouble.'

'There's still time to save him,' said Niall. 'Tarlock's not at the castle. I've heard he's gone to the Wailing Wastes to gather ingredients for his new spell. He has not yet returned to Mount Arrigal.'

Amy jolted into action. 'Then maybe we can beat him back. Let's not waste another second!'

'You're staying here,' Oscar said sternly, flinging his full satchel over his shoulder. 'Both of you. When this business is over, we'll come back for you.'

Amy shook her head. 'I've come this far. I'm *not* staying behind now.'

'If she goes, I go,' said Jonah, and not for the first time, Amy could have hugged him.

'And if you try to leave us here, the Dullahan will find me,' she threatened.

Oscar scrubbed a hand across his face. Beside him, Niall looked equally conflicted. 'That's true,' he muttered. 'Thanks to their performance in Filly, the Dullahan will make camp by the entrance way as soon as they get here.'

A sigh whistled through Oscar's nose. 'And that little sionnach is just arrogant enough to try and sneak past them.'

'Yes,' said Niall disapprovingly.

'Uh-huh,' agreed Jonah.

'Yup,' said Amy.

And so it was decided. The Fianna would go to Silverstone Castle, and Amy and Jonah would go with them.

The storm had passed by the time they set off again, and they were back to blinding sunshine once more. Oscar watched the sky as they galloped northwards.

'Doesn't that hurt?' said Amy, who was hiding from the sun's glare beneath her cloak.

'Not as much as getting ambushed will,' said Oscar tightly. 'After the stunt you pulled, we have to be even more careful. And these skies are full of spies.'

'I wish I had a weapon or something.' Amy looked longingly at Oscar's spear, which was glinting in the corner of her eye.

'Don't even think about touching it. That spear will split your finger at the slightest touch.'

This only doubled Amy's interest. 'What else can it do?'

'Lug's Spear was fashioned from the dying rays of sunset by the warrior god himself. It makes its wielder quick on his feet. Cunning in battle. It's light as a feather, but stronger than steel. It can block dark magic, and turn curses back on themselves. And of course, it never misses. Do you know what that means?'

Amy looked at him blankly.

'It's not for little girls.'

She scowled. 'What if you ever need me to save your life?'

Oscar barked a laugh, then broke off suddenly as the sun chain screeched overhead.

Without warning, a luminous sliver of metal fell away from it and drifted to the ground like a feather. When it landed on the trail in front of them, it scorched a hole in the earth.

'Tarlock really is growing weaker,' said Oscar, more to himself than to her. 'We have no way of knowing when he'll be back from his travels, but let's hope we get to him before he gets to your brother.' He gripped the reins and urged Arrow onwards. '*Yah!*'

The next landmark was the Dabberlock River. It cut across the land like a grey belt, and as Amy watched the currents leap over each other, she could have sworn she spied a face skulking in the waves. It disappeared in a ribbon of froth, leaving her to wonder if she had imagined it.

The river was fast-flowing, but they found a bend that was shallow enough for the horses to wade through. As they sloshed towards the other side, Amy spied a circular, stone well up ahead. The air around it was shimmering, just a little, as though it were encased in a soapy bubble.

'What's *that* thing?' she marvelled.

'That's the Well of Wishes,' said Oscar. 'It's made from old magic.'

Amy stiffened. 'You mean it can grant wishes? For real?'

'It can *show* you things,' said Oscar, a note of caution in his voice. 'But it no longer works as it should, which is why we must take care to—'

Amy leaped off Arrow and landed with a flailing splash. The water lapped against her chest as she waded towards the riverbank, her fingers curling in the long reeds as she pulled herself up.

'Oi! Get back here!' shouted Oscar, but she was already off and running. By the time she reached the well, the horses had come to a stop in the reeds, and their riders were staring at her with varying degrees of annoyance.

'Amy!' shouted Jonah, as he slipped off Niall's horse and hurried after her. 'Why are you so bad at following orders?'

Amy ignored him and leaned over the well. The water at the bottom was turquoise. The bubble of magic stretched around her, and the pain in her head eased.

'This is *wonderful*,' she sighed, her voice echoing back at her from the depths.

'Wonderfully *dangerous*.' Jonah's glowering face appeared beside hers. 'If you don't get back on the horse, the Fianna are going to ride away and leave us here.'

'This will only take a minute.' Amy reached into her

pocket, her fingers brushing against Liam's cracked spectacles as she fished out Peggy's sixpence. 'I just want to find out where *exactly* my brother is.'

'AMY, STOP!' Jonah shouted as she dropped the coin. It whistled as it fell, and then landed with a *plonk!*

Amy blinked at him. 'What's wrong? It's just a coin.'

Jonah raked his hands through his hair. 'That coin is from *your* world! That means it's poisonous here! It's going to break the—'

He was interrupted by a loud gurgle.

Amy froze. 'Uh-oh.'

The well belched. Then trembled. The water churned, faster and faster, and then, with a giant heave, it spat the coin back out. It whizzed up, up, up past their ears, and without thinking, Jonah shot his hand out and caught it.

'ARGH!' he screamed, as it sizzled against his palm.

Amy grabbed it from him and stuffed it in her pocket. 'Sorry, sorry, sorry.'

Jonah rushed back to the river to soak his burning hand, leaving her feeling like a monumental fool. She was about to trudge back to the waiting Fianna – who were angrier than ever – when Conan scampered across the grass, dragging a small brass horn behind him. He hopped up on to the well, took one look at Amy, and then scrabbled down into the water, where he filled the horn with a single mouthful of liquid. When he returned to the top, he passed the horn to Amy, and she understood exactly what she was supposed to do.

As she drank the mouthful, her head swam, becoming light as a balloon until she thought she might float away. The well began to ripple, and from its depths, she heard the faintest lilt, like the water itself was singing:

'Wish, wish, wish on me.
Tell me what you long to see.'

'Liam Bell,' whispered Amy. 'Show me where my brother is.'

The water stilled. The silence swelled …

And then the darkness swept in. The water turned murky and black, and in it, Amy glimpsed her brother. He was curled up in a ball on a stone floor somewhere. In the quiet of the Well of Wishes, she heard Liam whimpering. The sound was like a fist closing around her heart.

'Liam!' she cried out. 'Liam, it's me! Don't worry! I'm coming to save you!'

But Liam was a world away, and the louder Amy shouted, the quieter his whimpers became. The darkness pooled around him, his hunched figure getting further and further away, until Amy glimpsed the rising turrets of Silverstone Castle. They were teeming with wardens in long grey robes, the mage's court keeping careful watch over the courtyards, while soldiers in black armour marched about doing drills. The vision expanded and Mount Arrigal shifted into view, its peak as sharp as a knife. At the bottom, hundreds of headless horsemen spread out like a shadow, making an unbroken line for as far as the eye could see.

Amy recoiled, but the well pulled her back. It was not yet done with her. The water began to rise. There was a bright flash, and then a new figure appeared. Beneath the folds of his hood, Amy glimpsed an impossibly creviced face. A long nose, a thin and twisting mouth, and a pair of luminous silver eyes. They snared her, like a trap, and when she tried to look away, she found she couldn't.

The water hissed and churned, and in its thrashing, Amy heard a low voice. '*Show me the girl.*'

'No!' she screamed, as the air twisted around her like a rope. It tugged her into the well, her feet scrabbling for purchase as they lifted off the grass.

'*Ah.*' The mage's laughter echoed around her. 'I can sense *you.*'

The air was a weight on Amy's shoulders, pushing her down, down, down, towards the water. She lost her grip on the stone rim. The darkness was rising up to swallow her. And then, suddenly, she was hauled backwards with a yelp.

She lay on her back a moment, trying to catch her breath, as the mage's laughter echoed through her mind.

Then Oscar's face appeared above her. Unsurprisingly, he was scowling. But instead of scolding her, he said, 'What did you see in the well, little sionnach?'

'I saw Tarlock.' Amy scrunched her eyes shut. 'I think he saw me too.'

Another head appeared beside Oscar's. It was Niall. 'How did he look? Weak? Tired? Scared?'

Amy shook her head. 'None of those things. He looked … happy.' She swallowed thickly. 'He was laughing.'

Around her, the Fianna were silent.

Jonah returned from the river, cradling his hand against his chest.

Amy sat up. 'I'm really sorry, Jonah. I didn't think about the coin. I should have been more careful.'

He held up his hand, where blisters bubbled between his fingers. 'Now you know why none of us have ever crossed the veil into your world, so you can forget about inviting me to dinner when this is all over. Did you at least see your brother?'

Amy nodded, but her mood was sombre. 'He's alive, but he's frightened. I think they're keeping him in a dungeon.'

'Good,' said Oscar, as he turned for the horses. 'That will narrow down our search once we get to the castle.'

'Wait.' Amy scrabbled to her feet. 'There's … something else.'

The Fianna listened in grave silence as she told them about the castle spilling over with soldiers and wardens, and the hundreds upon hundreds of Dullahan standing sentry at the bottom of Mount Arrigal.

As she spoke, she made a quick count of the men before her. There were thirty-seven warriors, one Greencloak, an interloper, and one brave-hearted squirrel. She offered Oscar a pitiful look. 'I think you're going to need more warriors.'

Oscar folded his arms. 'We're the best Tír na nÓg has to offer. Saving the kingdom has always been *our* destiny.'

A distant rumbling alerted them to another oncoming storm. Amy glanced at the darkening sky. 'Well, I think it's time to share it.'

Chapter Fourteen

THE GIRL KING

Deep in the dark belly of the dungeon, Liam kept track of the time by counting his meals. A bowl of gloopy porridge marked the morning, while another arrived around what he supposed to be lunchtime. Dinner was cold broth that smelt like old bathwater. It tasted that way too. He ate it to keep his strength up, holding his nose as he swallowed. He wished he could do something about the darkness, but in the dungeon, the blackness was constant.

The Banshee flitted around the dungeon like a bat, her toenails scrabbling against the stone as she kept a wary eye on him. Given the creature was quite clearly his keeper, Liam had come to suspect that the key around her neck must be the one to his cell, but she never came close enough to the bars for him to try and swipe it. And even if she did, he was not quite sure he was brave enough to try.

Every now and then, a soldier ducked their head around the door to the dungeon to check on him. Most of them vanished in the same instant, content to see him still curled up in his cell, but there was one who lingered a little longer, crept a bit closer. Once, she came down without her helmet on, and smiled at Liam, but when he leaped to his feet to talk to her, she hurried away, as if she were afraid.

Though there were no windows in the dungeon, the roar of thunder still reached Liam through the walls. The storm made his fear worse, so he tried to drown it out by singing. He plucked one of Gran's songs from his memory, his voice getting louder and louder until he couldn't hear the clash and clamour outside.

'Through fields of green and mountains old,
Where magic glitters bright as gold …'

By the time he stopped singing, so too had the thunder, and he managed to doze off for a while.

Between storms, the door to the dungeon swung open, and a sliver of light crept in. A soldier came hurrying down the stone steps, the same one who had smiled at him before. She had dark brown skin, brown eyes and short black hair, which revealed the pointed tips of her ears.

'Hello, songbird,' she said, as though the two of them were friends and Liam was not, in fact, a terrified prisoner. 'I hope the Banshee hasn't bitten you yet. And I do mean that quite literally. She has been known to chew on people's fingers.'

Even though it wasn't the conversation he'd have chosen, Liam was relieved that she was talking to him at all. It felt like ages since he had spoken to another person. He scrabbled to his feet. 'What time is it?'

'Who knows?' said the soldier, with a shrug. 'Between you and me, it doesn't matter all that much.'

'Of course it matters,' said Liam. 'Where am I?'

The guard cocked her head. 'You're at Silverstone Castle. Hasn't anyone told you that?'

'No one has said anything to me since I got here.'

She clucked her tongue. 'Always leaving it to me to do the explaining,' she muttered. Then: 'Between you and me, I had hoped we were done with the whole stealing-children-away-from-their-families-and-using-them-in-wicked-world-altering-curses thing, but here we are again.'

Liam flooded with alarm. 'Please don't hurt me.' He quickly glanced around, checking they were alone in the dungeons. Apart from the Banshee, who was snoring loudly in the corner, there was no one else in sight. 'If you just let me out, no one will even—'

'Let you out!' said the guard. 'And what would Tarlock do to me then? I'd be a squirrel by morning. And a squirrel can't feed a family of five.'

Liam frowned. 'Who's Tarlock?'

The guard cleared her throat, her own eyes darting. 'The less said about him, the better.'

'You're the one who brought him up.'

'And in any case,' she said evasively. 'You're an official prisoner of Silverstone Castle. You can't talk your way out of it, no matter how sad and hopeless you make yourself look.'

'But I'm only *eleven!*'

'Enough dilly-dallying.' She opened Liam's cell and tugged him out by his sleeve. 'We need to get you to the throne room before another storm kicks up. The king has requested music. And I have a feeling one of your tunes might help calm things down a bit.'

'But my ankle's injured. I can't even walk.'

'You look like you're standing just fine to me.'

Liam frowned as he stepped out of his cell, surprised to find that his ankle wasn't hurting any more. It must have healed whilst he slept. 'That was quick,' he muttered.

Too quick.

The guard's hand fell heavy on his shoulder as she steered him up the staircase and into the heart of Silverstone Castle. The vaulted hallways were adorned with plush red carpets that swallowed their footsteps, and the walls were hung with colourful tapestries depicting ancient battles. Liam could make out every single strand.

'Hang on. I can *see* again.' He traced the bridge of his nose to make sure his glasses hadn't somehow magically re-sprouted on his face. 'But that's … *impossible.*'

'You're in Silverstone Castle now, interloper. There is nothing broken here that cannot be fixed.' The soldier dropped her voice. 'Unless Tarlock *wants* you broken. I'm afraid that's another matter entirely,' she said uneasily.

There was that name again. 'What do you mean?' asked Liam. 'Does it have something to do with those awful headless riders?'

'Shh!' she hissed. 'Keep your voice down. I'm not even supposed to be talking to you. If the mage found out, he'd have *my* head!'

A suit of armour craned its neck as they passed, and Liam got the sense that he was being watched by more than just the guard. In fact, Silverstone Castle was swimming with people. Apart from the harried-looking servants, there were several figures swanning about in grey robes. Liam felt their eyes on him as he shuffled down the hallway, the hairs on the back of his neck rising. Outside, the sky was rumbling again, the first droplets of a new storm plinking against the arched windows.

Escaping was going to be difficult. And that was without counting the soldiers stationed at every doorway. If he wanted to get out of here in one piece, then he couldn't simply bolt for the nearest exit. He would have to go about it in a different way.

'I'm not *just* an interloper, you know,' he said. 'My name is Liam, and I'm turning twelve next month. I've got a mum and a dad and a gran back at home, and at school my best friends are called Jakub and Alex. I've got a sister too, and she's the bravest person I've ever met. She's not scared of anything.'

'Well, I hope she wasn't foolish enough to cross the veil too,' said the soldier under her breath. 'Because if she ever sets foot on Mount Arrigal, the mage will snatch her up faster than you can say, *Oh look at that! More interlopers for my evil spells.*'

Outside, a bolt of lightning flashed.

The soldier quickened her steps. 'Hurry up before these blasted walls start to shake again. We lost three chandeliers in the last one.'

'What's *your* name?' said Liam, hurrying to keep up.

The soldier waited for two more robed strangers to

pass by before she answered. 'Kit,' she said, in a low voice. 'Though I'm really not supposed to tell you that.'

Another bolt of lightning struck, this one closer than the last.

The rain was bucketing down with a vengeance now.

'It's nice to meet you, Kit.'

Kit threw him a warning look. 'I know what you're doing. And it's not going to work. I can't be your friend.'

'I might grow on you,' said Liam hopefully. 'Like a rash?'

But Kit kept her lips firmly pressed together.

At the end of the hall, they came to a set of heavy oak doors that stretched all the way to the ceiling. A deafening shriek rang out from the other side, followed by the sound of glass breaking. Kit glanced at Liam as she pressed her hand against the door. 'Get ready to duck.'

The door swung open to reveal a sprawling marble throne room, where everything was bright and white and blinding. The ceiling curved into a magnificent glass dome that revealed the cloudy sky beyond. Towering statues of kings and queens looked down on Liam with blank stares as Kit prodded him towards a marble dais at the other end of the room. There, a golden throne sat haloed by a crescent window. It trembled in the grip of the rising storm.

There was a little girl sitting on the throne, but before Liam could make out very much of her, a teapot went whizzing past his left ear. It shattered against a statue behind him. 'Not enough mint!' she shrieked. 'And it's too hot! Much too hot!'

'Who is that?' said Liam, as he ducked to avoid a flying teaspoon.

'That's the king. And as you can see, she's in a *foul* mood.'

Liam was about to ask why the King of Tír na nÓg was a little girl when a saucer sailed over his head, and clipped a servant in the cheek. She fell to the ground with a howl.

'I need you to sing,' said Kit urgently.

Liam blinked. 'What? Now?'

'Yes! Quickly! Do the one you were singing in the dungeon,' hissed Kit, as she shoved him towards the throne. 'And whatever you do, don't look her in the eye!'

There came another hair-raising shriek, followed by an almighty crash of thunder, the lightning so close it felt like it was coming from inside the room.

'Gods above, hurry up, boy!'

Liam took one look at Kit's terrified face, then opened his mouth and began to sing:

'Through fields of green and mountains old,
Where magic glitters bright as gold …'

His voice was scratchy at first, the words uncertain as he tried to untangle them from his own confusion. But he caught the tune well enough, and as the thunder growled, he sang it louder, belting out his gran's favourite song until the sound of breaking glass stopped.

The room stilled as Liam slipped into the second verse. He closed his eyes and thought of Gran, standing in her kitchen, with her arms open, and the smell of rhubarb crumble wafting in the air. His heart swelled as he returned to the chorus. The last notes echoed in a sudden silence. To his surprise, the thunder had stopped, and the rain had dissolved into a shaft of glorious sunlight. It slipped in through the dome in the ceiling and scattered golden pinwheels along the floor.

The little girl was silent as she watched him, her face lost in a halo of light.

'I *knew* it would work,' whispered Kit. 'I haven't heard a song like that in a very long time.'

The little girl crooked her finger at him. 'You. Come here.'

With his heart in his mouth, Liam shuffled up the aisle towards her.

The King of Tír na nÓg looked more like a doll than a person. Her long brown hair was shot through with strands of copper, and it was all braided into an elaborate fishtail plait. Her skin was pale as porcelain, and her eyes were bright silver. She was wearing a purple velvet dress with lace frills around the collar, and white socks that came up to her knees. On her head sat a crown that was far too big for her. It came down to cover her ears, framing her eyes like a heavy golden brow.

'You really are a girl,' said Liam, with some surprise.

'Girl *king*,' she corrected him, swinging her legs back and forth.

Liam looked around the throne room, expecting the *real* King of Tír na nÓg to jump out from his hiding place. 'But kings can't be girls. Or ... Well, girls can't be kings.'

The girl king stuck her tongue out at him. 'If you think that, then I'm afraid you don't know very much at all.'

Liam was beginning to think she might be right.

'Do you have a name?' said the king.

'It's Liam.' He cleared his throat. 'And what should I call you, Your, er, Majesty?'

The little girl flashed two rows of small pearly teeth. 'Since you sang so beautifully just now, you may call me Gilda.'

All around the room, soldiers in heavy black armour stood watching them. There were grey-robed people lurking in here too, and although their faces were hidden inside their hoods, Liam could feel their gazes on the sides of his face. Some servants had even stopped work to listen to them.

Now that the king had finished her tantrum, Liam seized his opportunity to plead with her. 'Gilda, there's been an awful mistake. I'm not supposed to be here. I stumbled into Tír na nÓg by accident, and then the headless horsemen captured me, and now I'm here in the dungeon and I haven't done anything wrong and I did try to explain but no one will listen. There are people back home waiting for me and if I don't return soon, they are really going to worry—'

He was interrupted by a high-pitched giggle. 'Goodness! I don't think I've *ever* heard someone talk so fast in my whole life!' said the king gleefully. 'I'm not sure I caught a single word of it!'

Liam stared at her.

She blew a strand of hair from her face. 'Have you got anything else to say? It's been ages since we've had any visitors.'

'I'm not a visitor,' said Liam. 'I'm a *prisoner*.'

The king's silver eyes narrowed. 'And what do you expect me to do about it?'

'You're the king! You can let me go!'

'I can't! It doesn't work like that. But, I know! We'll

have some tea, and you'll feel better then.' She clicked her fingers and two servants came bustling in with a tray full of iced buns and a new pot of steaming tea.

Gilda leaped off the dais. She was a full head shorter than Liam, and now that her mood had brightened, she preferred to skip instead of walk. Liam followed her to the tea-table, trying to figure out how to interest her in what had happened to him.

She hopped on to a chair and sank her teeth into an iced bun. 'What are you waiting for?' she asked, bits of crumbs flying out of her mouth and landing on Liam's hoody. 'It's not rotten, you know. And even if it were, you're already stuck here, so you'd have to just get used to it.'

Liam lowered himself into a chair, and nibbled at the edges of a bun. 'Why can't you just let me go? You seem like a perfectly nice girl.'

Gilda slurped her tea. '*King.*'

'King.' Liam set his bun down. 'I don't think anyone would think badly of you if you just—'

Gilda began to laugh. It wasn't the trilling giggle from before; this time it was a cold and hollow sound that didn't reach her eyes. When it was done, she slumped in her chair as if she were suddenly exhausted. 'If I can't rescue *myself* from this place, what chance do you think *you* have?'

Liam's cheeks began to prickle. He glanced around, at all the people in the room: the robed watchers in the corners, the soldiers stationed at every door. Kit was still hovering nearby. 'Do you mean you're stuck here too?' he said, in a low voice.

The king nodded. 'Can't you hear that?'

Liam frowned. Now that she mentioned it, there *was* a faint clanging coming from somewhere above them. He tipped his head back and looked up through the sun dome, to where the clouds were finally parting. Whilst Amy had told him what she'd seen of the sun from the top of the trees, this was the first time Liam had witnessed it for himself. He gasped. Amy had not been exaggerating! And the longer he stared at its half-choked form, the more his head began to pound, until he had the horrifying realisation he was about to pass out.

'You shouldn't look right at it. It will give you a blinding headache.' When the king looked at him again, her eyes were bleary. She rubbed them with her fists. 'Lately, all it does is make me feel tired.'

Liam leaned across the table. 'What happened to the sun, Gilda?'

'*Tarlock*,' whispered Gilda. That name again! It sent a shiver down Liam's spine. 'He's the most powerful sorcerer in Tír na nÓg, and when he returns from the Wailing

Wastes, he'll be the one to decide your fate.' Her words began to slur, her lids turning low and heavy. 'So you see, we're all stuck. You, me and everyone else in this cursed kingdom.' Her nostrils flared as a yawn bubbled up. 'I can't help you.' She stretched her arms out wide as it took hold of her. 'No one can help you.'

By the time Liam opened his mouth to reply, the king was already fast asleep.

Chapter Fifteen

THE SELKIE PRINCE

After another storm that soaked Amy to the bone, the sun returned to full brightness, following them west across the plains towards the ocean. She knew the Dullahan would be hunting her, but she tried not to look over her shoulder or listen for the distant rumble of hoofs on the wind.

Under Oscar's direction, the Fianna avoided the towns and villages dotted along the horizon, and instead made for the sleepy fishing village of Weatherglass, on the edge of the Western Sea.

Weatherglass was tucked beneath a limestone cliff that curved over the ocean like a jagged mouth. The sea wind howled as they raced along the sand towards it, and

Amy grimaced at the sudden sour taste on her tongue.

The coast should have been beautiful, but it was a far cry from the golden coves of Connemara. Here, the water was rancid. There were dolphins floating listlessly on their sides, seagulls wailing in the sky, and a dead whale baking on the sun-bleached rocks.

'That *smell*,' said Amy. 'It's getting worse. What *is* it?'

'Death,' said Oscar grimly. 'Try to bear it.'

'And if I can't?'

'At least stop complaining about it.'

Amy turned to scowl at him, then spotted something else in the water. A round, pale face was watching her from the waves. Its eyes were black and wide as moons, and its hair was the greenish brown of lank seaweed. In fact, it *was* seaweed. Amy blinked, and the face disappeared, but she soon spotted another out of the corner of her eye – gone as quickly as it came. She whipped her head round, searching the waves for more.

'Selkies,' said Oscar, whose gaze was still pinned to the fishing village ahead of them. It was little more than a mass of thatched huts and rudimentary fishing boats, all huddled together beneath the white cliffs. 'Don't stare at them. They'll get aggressive.'

'I saw one in the water by the Well of Wishes,' said Amy, staring harder than ever.

Oscar poked her. 'Why do you *never* listen?'

'There are *loads* of them.' Every time Amy thought she spotted another mass of seaweed, a head popped up from underneath it. The Selkies were swimming alongside them, tracking the Fianna across the cove. They were *almost* human-looking, save for their hollow black eyes and flat, slitted nostrils. Amy spotted one leaping over a wave and squealed at the sight of his flapping brown tail.

'They're like seals!'

'Stop talking about them,' hissed Oscar. 'You're going to ruin everything.'

'Ruin what?'

But the warrior didn't respond. Amy could tell she was not going to be trusted with important information. She folded her arms and stewed in silence, yet she couldn't help the traitorous flick of her gaze every so often.

When they reached Weatherglass, the men dismounted and went to join the figures who had come out of their huts to welcome them. The fisherfolk of the Western Sea had long been allies of the Fianna and, according to Oscar, some of them were even family. While the men indulged in a brief reunion and picked up more supplies, Amy went to stretch her legs. It was only when she stared up at the cliffs from below that she noticed the stone figure that protruded from them. It was a carving of a Selkie – a woman with lashings of seaweed hair and a tail that curled neatly beneath her. On her head, she wore a five-pointed crown, and though she was only a sculpture, it looked to Amy like she was staring out to sea.

'That's Manann, goddess of the sea,' said Jonah, appearing at her side. 'These were her cliffs and this was her sea. By the end of her life, she spent more time in the ocean than out of it.'

Amy pointed to her tail. 'Well, that makes sense.'

'Selkies only take the form of seals when they're in the water,' said Jonah. 'On land, they shed their tails and take on human form, and when they do, they're fierce.' He gnashed his teeth. 'Or so we're told. Ever since Manann and the rest of the gods left, they've kept more and more to themselves.'

Even though they were far up the beach, Amy could feel the Selkies watching them. She didn't like it. 'How long are we stopping for?'

'Not long. Oscar's going to ask the Selkie Prince for help against the mage.'

Amy's eyebrows rose. 'He *is*?'

Jonah looked just as surprised as she was. 'I think you spooked him back at the well. But don't tell him I said that.'

When they turned around, Oscar was marching down to the water. The strand spread out into five narrow peninsulas, like a golden hand reaching through the waves. He trod along the thumb, his spear held tightly in his fist. A host of new faces rose to the surface, and Amy could barely contain a sudden flush of excitement. She wondered which of them was the Selkie Prince.

She didn't have to wait long to find out. Oscar returned less than ten minutes later, stomping through the sand like a child in the middle of a tantrum. When he reached Weatherglass, he stabbed his spear into a half-cooked fish and tore the skin off with his teeth.

Amy rushed over to listen.

'… slippery, self-serving, cowardly bladderwracks, the lot of them,' he fumed, between mouthfuls. 'They'd rather drift out to sea and abandon their own kingdom than entangle themselves with the mage. I don't know why I expected anything different.' He threw a withering glance at Amy, like it was *her* fault. 'Prince Tristan is nothing but a spineless jellyfish.'

'The Selkies have always looked out for themselves,' said Niall calmly. 'They live in a sea full of predators. It's what they're used to.'

'I've a good mind to get them used to my spear.' Oscar's grimace was so severe, it made him look like a cartoon. 'Now is no time to flee from responsibility. The fate of Tír na nÓg balances on a knife edge. If we do not strike soon, we may never strike again.'

'I don't understand,' said Jonah, with mounting dismay. 'Did Prince Tristan really just say *no*?'

'Worse than that.' Oscar grabbed another fish straight from the flames. 'He said nothing. He didn't even come to the surface.'

The Fianna stiffened in affront. Some of them palmed their weapons, as if they were thinking about going down to the sea and dragging the Selkie Prince out of there by his tail. Amy, for her part, was keeping a clear head about it all. 'Well, how did you ask for him? Were you polite about it?'

Oscar glared at her. 'I used the formal greeting appropriate to my rank and his.'

'Uh-huh. It's just that you've kind of got an attitude,' she went on, delicately.

Oscar bit the head off the fish and chewed it with his mouth open. 'What is *that* supposed to mean?'

'It *means* that I'm guessing you forgot to say it nicely ...'

'Warriors don't have time for niceties.'

'Well, maybe they should make time,' said Amy, as she rolled to her feet. 'My gran always says you catch more flies with honey than with vinegar.'

'Flies won't help us fight the mage, you acorn-brain,'

said Jonah, with a chuckle. 'Those things are *tiny*.'

'Never mind,' sighed Amy. 'If none of you are going to make a proper effort, I'll have to go and talk to the prince myself.'

Oscar snorted. 'Be my guest, little sionnach. Prince Tristan would sooner eat his own tail than present himself to a mouthy interloper like you.'

Amy resisted the urge to stick her tongue out at him. 'You haven't seen me turn on my charm.'

'I wouldn't waste my time,' said Niall wearily. 'We've lost enough of it already.'

'Let the cowardly prince hide in his kelp forest. Leave us to save the kingdom,' added Manus.

'Or die trying,' said Amy pointedly.

The men were silent.

'Right then,' she said, as she dusted her hands. 'I'll be back.'

Amy took off across the beach. She could feel the Fianna watching her as she stalked towards the shoreline, but her mind was firmly on Prince Tristan.

Faces bobbed up from the sea as she neared it, but she couldn't tell if the prince was among them. She waded into the surf until the waves lapped against her ankles and the rotting stench of seaweed slammed into her like a truck.

Without any real semblance of a plan, Amy addressed

the first creature she saw. 'Hello, I'm looking for Prince Tristan. Are you him, by any chance?'

The Selkie laughed in her face.

A blush rose in Amy's cheeks. She could see why Oscar had marched away in such a huff. She moved on to the next Selkie and waggled her fingers in greeting. 'Could I speak with Prince Tristan?' Another hissing laugh. Amy sighed, and tried again. And again. And again. Until it sounded like the entire sea was laughing at her.

She had a horrible feeling that the Fianna were laughing at her too.

With her confidence quickly waning, Amy folded her arms and addressed the whole putrid, baking ocean and all the taunting faces floating about inside it. 'PRINCE TRISTAN, I AM PRINCESS AMY BELL FROM THE KINGDOM OF CONNEMARA, AND I HUMBLY REQUEST YOUR ESTEEMED PRESENCE ON THIS BEACH!' She paused, then thought to add a very loud, 'PLEASE.'

This time, the sea was silent.

She brushed the frizzing strands away from her face and tried to make herself look as regal as possible.

Then the waves drew back, as if the ocean were taking a breath. The sand began to tremble. The sea parted, and out of it walked a creature so tall, Amy had to tip her chin back to take him in. There was no mistaking Prince Tristan as he waded towards her, the shore shivering with each thudding step. He was a beast – broad-shouldered and thick-muscled, with a crop of green seaweed growing from the middle of his head and snaking all the way down his spine. There were legs where his tail had just been, but they were covered in wreaths of trailing seaweed that made it difficult to see where the sea ended and the prince began.

His torso was as pale and shiny as a pearl, and with each step towards her, Amy glimpsed a new scar – there was an angry red crescent along his ribs, and another wide slash below his collarbone. The sea had taken several bites out of the Selkie Prince, but he had lived to tell the tale. He did not, however, look too happy about it. His eyes were wide and black, his fanged teeth glinting menacingly as he opened his mouth to speak.

'Who *dares* summon me from the depths of the sea?' His voice was exactly like the sound a wave makes when it crashes against a rock. Amy found herself swept up in a tide of anger.

She stood her ground, even as she trembled. 'I think you already know who summoned you, Prince Tristan. After all, you are looking straight at me.'

The prince took another step towards her, and all

along the beach, half-dead crabs flipped off their backs and scuttled away from him.

'An *interloper*,' he hissed.

'My name is Amy.' Prince Tristan was wearing a necklace full of shark teeth. Amy wondered briefly how many he had fought and, if this meeting didn't go well, whether he might think about ripping her teeth out too. In any case, one thing was certain – this prince would make a fearsome ally in battle.

'I've come to you for an important reason. I'm afraid it can't wait a minute longer. The future of this kingdom – if there is to be one – depends on it.'

The Selkie's nostrils flared. 'The fate of Tír na nÓg has little to do with me.'

Amy folded her arms. 'Are you really so afraid of Tarlock?'

Prince Tristan bared his teeth, and behind him, the Selkies screeched in offence. 'There is a difference between fear and common sense.' He took another step towards Amy, casting her in his considerable shadow. The droplets on his skin began to sizzle in the sun. If the curse was causing him pain, he was careful not to show it. 'The mage has left the Wailing Wastes. He journeys now to Silverstone Castle to prepare for the new sun ritual. You are too late.'

'It's *not* too late.' Amy balled her fists and raised her chin in defiance. 'I'm going to rescue my brother and put an end to the mage's hold on this land, once and for all. And I'm not going to do it alone.' She gestured over her shoulder. 'The warriors up on that beach are riding to Mount Arrigal to save Tír na nÓg. They're risking their lives for the fate of their people, their land. The question is, Prince Tristan, what are *you* going to do?'

The prince's smile was mirthless. 'The Selkies are going to do what they should have done a long time ago. We are going to swim away from this land and find a new home. The ocean belongs to us after all. Why would we cling to the shelf of a place that has been cursed for an endless eternity?'

Amy took a step towards him. 'If that were true, you'd already be gone.' The prince's eyes flashed, and she saw the moment of weakness. 'You're still here though. Why? You must be waiting for something.'

The Selkie chuckled. It sounded like he was choking. 'Perhaps I was waiting to see the one who would dare stand against Tarlock, the last son of the gods.' He brought his face close to Amy's, the hot stench of his breath bringing tears to her eyes. 'And now I have, I am not impressed.'

Amy stumbled backwards, trying to put some space

between them. 'So, you're just going to *leave*?'

'I see doom in your eyes, interloper,' said the prince. 'I won't wait to see it come to pass.' He took a step away from her, away from the land. 'Time and tide is against you. You have my respect for your bravery – foolish as it is – but you do not have my army. We are bound for bluer waters.'

Amy balled her fists as the waves rushed in to claim their prince. The sea rose quickly, past his knees and to his waist, until she had to back up to keep it from taking her too. He turned from her then, his seaweed-covered legs morphing into a tail before her eyes, and before fear and defeat could get the better of her, Amy raised her voice and called after him. 'Leave us then. But you should know the curse will still find you.' She dragged her finger back and forth, pointing at all the faces in the waves. 'All of you. You can't outswim it or outlive it, no matter how far you go. When the land is good and rotted through, without any hope of saving it, the sea will start to rot too. It already has.'

Prince Tristan froze in the water, a webbed ear pricking up.

'The coral and the kelp and the fish and the whales will all die, until there's nothing left but stinking seaweed and the Selkies who swam away from their kingdom when it needed them most. And when that day comes, there will be no one left to save you, Prince Tristan! Only this reminder ringing in your ears: when Oscar de Barra came to ask for your help, you turned him away. You turned your back on Tír na nÓg, and doomed it with your selfishness. You can cradle that thought tight when the curse rots you.' She narrowed her eyes. 'Then again. Maybe it's already done that too.'

Prince Tristan twisted his head, looking at her with one glassy eye. The rest of the Selkies stilled in the water.

'Manann would fight!' shouted Amy. 'If your god were still here, she would never desert her kingdom. When you leave these shores, you're leaving her too.' She flung her arm over her shoulder, pointing at the magnificent white-stone carving. 'If she saw you now, she would be ashamed of you.'

Silence came on a brisk wind. Goosebumps erupted on Amy's arms as the sea watched her. But her eyes were fixed on the prince, both of them staring at each other across the shore, daring the other to look away.

Prince Tristan's nostrils flared. When he spoke, it was not to Amy. 'The interloper is right,' he said, in a low voice. 'Manann would fight.'

The sea hissed, but Amy couldn't tell if it was in anger or agreement.

'Even so.' The prince turned back to Amy. 'The road

ahead is long and dangerous, and we won't risk our lives lightly.' A pause. Then: 'But in the name of Manann, I will make you a deal.'

Amy sucked in a breath, waiting. H*oping.*

'If you make it to Mount Arrigal, the Selkies will join you in your fight against Tarlock.'

Amy ignored the note of doubt in his voice. 'Is that a promise?'

Prince Tristan flashed his razor teeth. 'It is a pledge.'

'Thank you.' She backed away from him, before he could change his mind. After all, an ally who arrived late was better than no ally at all, and Amy knew with every fibre of her being that she was going to make it to that mountain – no matter who or what got in her way. 'See you at Mount Arrigal! Don't be late!'

The sea rushed in and claimed its prince. The waves folded over him as he disappeared, the Selkies following one by one, until the surface was glassy and still, the sun bouncing off the water and making her wince.

Amy hurried back up the beach. Oscar extended a hand to her, and she took it. 'Well?' he said, as he hoisted her up on to Arrow's back.

She told them the deal.

When she finished, Oscar snorted. 'A Selkie's pledge is as slippery as its tail.' He looked at Amy piteously, like she was a fool for taking it seriously. Even Jonah didn't seem excited.

'Well, I believe him,' she insisted. 'You weren't down there. You didn't hear him. He still cares about Tír na nÓg. I know it.'

'Then you are more naive than I thought,' said Oscar dismissively. 'I'll believe Prince Tristan's word when I see him at Mount Arrigal, and not a second before.'

Amy tossed a glare over her shoulder as she gripped the reins. 'Then what are we waiting for? Let's go!'

They set off from Weatherglass, leaving the sea and its Selkies far behind them. They were so distracted by what had just happened that no one noticed the white hawk circling in the air above them. By the time they heard its piercing cry, it had already disappeared over the cliffs.

Chapter Sixteen

THE MAGE'S TOWER

Liam paced his cell, trying to muster up the dregs of his courage. He didn't know how much time had passed since he'd seen the girl king, only that he'd eaten little and slept even less. One way or another, he had to escape Silverstone Castle before Tarlock returned.

Just do it, he scolded himself. *You have to try.*

Because there was someone – or rather some*thing* – at Silverstone Castle, who he suspected held the key to his cell.

Finally, before he could second-guess himself any more, he curled his fingers around the bars and screamed at the top of his lungs.

The Banshee came skittering out of the darkness, her

face barely an inch from his as she screamed right back.

Liam reached through the bars and pulled her towards him.

The Banshee screeched into Liam's ear, and made to grab him.

He leaped backwards and, as he did so, he ripped the key from around her neck. He gave a triumphant gasp. His eardrums hadn't burst and all his fingers were still intact. It had worked! The key was curled in his fist.

And better yet, the Banshee hadn't even noticed it was gone. She just hovered there wailing until, eventually, she gave up and pottered away into the darkness.

Liam threaded his arm through the bars and carefully slotted the key into the lock. He held his breath, hope rising in his chest as it turned with a faint *click*. It fitted!

He went very still, listening for the Banshee.

Silence.

He eased the door open and slipped out of his cell, before crossing the dungeon and tiptoeing up the stone staircase. He followed a slant of sunlight to where a narrow door opened out from the turret on to a familiar hallway. He pressed his forehead against the wood, and conjured a map of the ground floor in his mind. On his way back from his visit to Gilda, he'd taken note of every exit, especially the ones that led out to the courtyard, where there were nooks and crannies he might be able to hide in. Liam had worked out a route in his head. With a little stealth and patience, he might be able to escape while the guards were changing posts.

And if that didn't work, he'd engage Plan B and make a run for it.

He made to step through the door … and froze. Footsteps. Two figures in grey robes were coming his way! He ducked back into the tower, and crouched in the darkness. The footsteps got louder, closer. If they opened the door to the tower, he was done for.

He leaped to his feet and began to climb, following the winding staircase all the way up to the top.

To his relief, there was a room tucked away up there.

It was full of books – dusty old tomes with yellow pages huddling along shelves that stretched up to the cobwebs in the rafters. At one end of the room was a wooden desk scattered with papers. Liam crept towards it. The shelves behind the desk were filled with dead animals; a stuffed fox caught mid-leap, a spotted fawn curled up in sleep. There were three dead squirrels tied together by their tails, and a vase of white swan feathers. A peacock had been mounted on the wall, its magnificent tail spread out like a stained-glass window.

Liam clapped his hand over his mouth as he

examined the desk. The papers were full of incantations –
spells and chants scribbled in spidery black ink. Fear
swelled in his throat as he studied the one on the top of
the pile. It was a drawing of the chained sun.

And there were words underneath:

> Foreign bones, freshly ground,
> A young king newly crowned,
> Will bind the chain and freeze the hour,
> For the sun's curse to yield new power.

Beneath the spell, there was a list of peculiar ingredients:

- Beak of an Elderglen robin, mid-song √
- The beard of a Blackthorn druid √
- One thimble of Selkie blood √
- One bloodied wolf fang √
- Seven tears from the Wailing Wastes
- Two interlopers, still squirming

Liam stared in horror at the last line. *Two interlopers, still
squirming.* Wasn't that what Kit had called him? An *interloper.*

His stomach churned, and for a brief moment, he
thought he might get sick. And then another terrible
thought struck him.

If I'm one interloper, then where is the other?

Liam stiffened. Amy! The mage wanted his sister for his wicked spell. No. He *needed* her. And that meant that wherever she was, she was in danger too.

There came a sudden ripple of wind, and then the sound of wings flapping against the window.

Liam dived underneath the desk and curled into a ball, just as a familiar white hawk ducked inside. The bird launched off the ledge and landed on the desk, disturbing a stack of papers. They fluttered to the floor around Liam. Outside the office, the tower stairs creaked under the weight of new footsteps. Liam squeezed his eyes shut and imagined himself turning invisible as the door flew open.

'Ghost, you clumsy little fool,' snapped a familiar voice. 'Stop disturbing your master's things!' Liam watched a pair of boots stomp across the floorboards. The bird shrieked as it took flight, its mighty wings knocking jars off the shelves and sending papers flying across the room as it returned to the window.

Kit shut it out, slamming the window with a rattling thud.

Liam curled into the shadows, digging his fingernails into his palms as he waited for the soldier to leave. Instead, she turned back to the desk, her armour chinking as she came towards it.

'GOTCHA!' Her face appeared upside down in front of him. 'Tricksy little interloper. I *knew* you'd hide under here.' She clucked her tongue. 'Really, it's *so* obvious. Why didn't you go for the cabinet in the corner?'

Liam flinched. 'How did you know I was here?'

'Well, for one thing, you're not in the dungeon any more,' said Kit drily. 'And for another, this castle is crawling with wardens – far too many for you to ever make it out in one piece. Also, you're a real mouth-breather, did you know that?'

Liam crawled out from under the desk. 'Kit, I don't want to die. Please help me.'

'I don't know what you're talking about,' said the soldier stiffly. 'And I certainly don't want to find out.'

'But it's a new sun ritual,' said Liam urgently. 'He's going to do something else to the sun. And he's going to use me to do it! Wouldn't that just make things even worse here, Kit?'

'It would.' The soldier's expression faltered, and for the briefest second, Liam thought she looked frightened. He fished the drawing of the chained sun off the floor and shoved it against her chest.

'If you stop this, you could save me,' he pressed. 'You could save Tír na nÓg.'

Kit's eyes flickered to the spell. They went wide, and

this time Liam saw her fear as plain as day.

'I can't talk about this right now,' she whispered. 'And anyway, I don't even know what I could do about it.'

She quickly put the paper back on the desk.

'Please,' said Liam desperately. 'Maybe we can plan something?'

'Not up here we can't. I need time to think. But in the meantime, there's only one place for you, boy, and I'm afraid that's the dungeon. Now, hurry up before that awful hawk comes back and sees you.'

She grabbed Liam by the arm and marched him back down the tower. As they passed the entrance to the heart of the castle, Liam glimpsed a rising commotion. The servants were running about in panic, while the wardens – as Kit had called them – were gathering on both sides of the hallway, as if they were expecting a parade to pass through it at any moment.

'What's going on?' he said, craning his neck as they continued down.

'Tarlock is returning,' said Kit grimly.

Back in the dungeon, she swiftly locked Liam in his cell and confiscated the key. He slumped against the wall, feeling more hopeless than ever. He was crying before he realised it, tears pooling underneath his hoody.

Kit lingered a moment at the bars. 'It's not me who

can help you,' she said, in a low voice. 'At least, not the way you need to be helped. If you truly want to make it out of here alive, you should be appealing to the king.'

'But when I asked Gilda for help, she said she couldn't and fell asleep,' said Liam.

'Then try again. You have more in common with her than you might think,' said Kit, as she retreated into the darkness. 'With any luck, she'll figure that out before it's too late for both of you.'

Chapter Seventeen

THE GRAVEYARD OF THE GODS

After several hours of riding inland, Amy finally couldn't smell the rotting sea any more. It was only a mild improvement on her comfort levels. The muscles in her legs were aching and her heart was sore from worry. The sun's curse was still thudding behind her eyes, so when a grey cloud moved in front of it and the rain came – slow and pattering – she tipped her head back and welcomed it.

'The king is weeping,' murmured Oscar. 'I wonder why.'

Amy was too distracted by what Prince Tristan had told her about Tarlock's spell to give it much thought. Up ahead, a pair of flagstones marked an entranceway between two lumbering hills. Beyond it, the land was dry and barren. It looked like a dead meadow, where five hulking stone tombs squatted between thousands of scattered bones. Oscar pulled back on the reins as he called to his riders. 'We'll make our final camp here. To rest for a short while and plan our attack before we reach Mount Arrigal. The gods will keep us safe for a few hours at least.'

As they passed between the stones, Amy was struck by a sudden chill in the wind.

'What is this place?' she whispered. 'It feels weird.'

'Show some respect, little sionnach.' Behind her, Oscar's head was bowed. 'This is the Graveyard of the Gods.'

After they dismounted Arrow, Amy found Jonah standing with the rest of the horses, stretching his arms above his head. 'I have to say, I don't *love* the idea of napping in a graveyard,' she said, by way of greeting.

'That makes two of us,' he said, through a yawn. 'Though I did once fall asleep in a swamp, and that was *far* worse. I had a lizard living in my hair for ages.' He chuckled to himself. '*So* embarrassing.'

Amy stared at him.

'Oh, don't act like it's never happened to you,' he said defensively.

'What's the deal with all these animal bones?' She

gestured around them. The graveyard was littered with old skeletons and still-decomposing carcasses, stray rib bones and skulls and tusks all strewn about like confetti.

'Oh, yeah, those,' said Jonah, like he had only just noticed them. 'Back before the sun was cursed, when the animals of Tír na nÓg got old or sick, they often made their way here to die next to the tomb of Cernunnos, the god of all wild things. I suppose it made them feel at peace.'

Amy wrinkled her nose as she stepped over a pair of antlers.

'We'll be all right here for a bit, as long as we don't trespass inside the tombs,' said Jonah.

'Why? Is it bad luck?'

'No. It's just really rude.'

Amy studied the five stone tombs, arranged roughly in a circle. They looked like building blocks, made of huge grey slabs piled haphazardly against each other to create a narrow tunnel that led to a tucked-away chamber. They reminded her of the Stone Age cairns she'd seen in one of Gran's history books.

Across the graveyard, most of the Fianna were reclining in the shelter of the largest tomb. The top stone was just wide enough to stave off the worst of the rain.

'That's Danú's tomb,' said Jonah, following her gaze. 'Remember? Goddess of nature and new beginnings – the one who carved the pathway from your world into Tír na nÓg.'

'What about these other skeleton houses?' said Amy, as they wandered around, tracing the designs etched on the front of each entrance. She stopped at a tomb that bore the outline of a harp.

'This one belongs to Ogma,' said Jonah. Amy remembered his fountain in Filly. She wandered inside the dark tunnel.

Jonah grabbed her and pulled her out. 'What did I *just* say about trespassing?'

'Sorry, I got curious.' Amy hurried on to the next tomb, which was inlaid with seashells and shining pearls. It didn't take an expert to work out it belonged to Manann, the Selkies' goddess. 'That top stone is massive. There'll be more than enough shelter for both of us.'

Jonah glanced warily at the sky. 'Unless the king decides to throw another thunderstorm at us.'

Amy sat down and propped her back against the stone. 'Like I told you, I'm from Ireland. I can deal with a little rain.'

Jonah sat down beside her. On his shoulder, Conan curled his bushy tail around himself and used it as a pillow. Both of them fell asleep within minutes.

Amy scrunched her eyes shut and tried to nap, but

the grass was scratchy and with the Fianna at rest, the graveyard was eerily quiet.

I'm almost there, Liam.

When she finally nodded off, Amy dreamed she was back in Connemara, helping Gran in the kitchen. There were chocolate chip cookies baking in the oven, and music wafting from the radio on the window sill. Gran was singing along with gusto, Amy swinging her legs from the countertop and tracing the feathery clouds through the window. The sky was sapphire blue, and even though she couldn't see the sun in it, she felt happy. Safe.

Then Gran stopped singing. 'Do you hear that, Amy?'

Suddenly, Gran didn't look like herself any more. Her skin was made of shadows and her head had disappeared. Amy leaped off the countertop and bolted into the garden as the headless rider came after her. Overhead, a swarm of grey clouds swallowed up the blue, and the rattle of thunder sounded somewhere in the distance.

Amy woke up in the graveyard with a scream trapped in her throat. In the distance, the sound of thunder was getting louder.

How weird to have thunder, but no rain, she thought.

The earth trembled beneath her.

Then she realised. It wasn't thunder.

It was hoofbeats.

The kind of hoofbeats she'd heard only once before in her life.

She shook Jonah by his shoulders. 'Get up! Quick! I think the Dullahan are coming!'

Jonah snapped his eyes open, took one look at her horrified face, and jumped to his feet. On his shoulder, Conan did the same.

'How did they even find us here?' said Amy, as they raced across the graveyard.

'I bet it was Ghost,' said Jonah. 'He was watching us back in Weatherglass. Or, maybe the Dullahan picked up our scents in Filly and are tracking us.'

'But they don't even have *noses*!'

'Their horses do,' he reminded her. 'Big gaping ones.'

They ran into Oscar halfway across the graveyard. There was a wildness about him; his eyes were darting and his hair was mussed. Lug's Spear was clutched tightly in his hand. The rest of the Fianna were on their feet too, their weapons drawn as they looked west, towards the shadow on the horizon. It was getting bigger and bigger.

Oscar brandished his spear at Amy. 'Hide! Quick! They're here for you!'

Jonah drew his wooden sword, but Oscar shook his head and nudged him towards the tombs. 'You too, Jonah. It's too dangerous.'

Jonah heeded the order and bolted for the tombs, pulling Amy after him.

'I thought Oscar said we'd be safe here!' she huffed.

'Usually they won't come near here,' panted Jonah. 'The ground is blessed. It weakens the Dullahan.'

Somehow that only made Amy feel worse. 'They must be really desperate to get their hands on me!'

Jonah pushed her into the first tomb they came to, before finding his own shelter in Lug's, the darkness swallowing him in one bite. Amy retreated into her own darkness, following the carvings of leaping stags into the belly of Cernunnos's final resting place.

She winced at the sound of her footsteps. There were animal bones everywhere, cracking and crunching in the dark.

Outside the tunnel, she heard the slow thud of the Dullahan as they entered the graveyard.

Amy squinted out at the dead grass. Oscar marched past the entrance, brandishing his spear. 'BE GONE FROM HERE, CURSED DULLAHAN,' he bellowed. 'THIS GROUND IS HALLOWED. YOU HAVE NO POWER HERE.'

The Fianna spread out at his back with their weapons drawn.

The Dullahan clopped onwards through the

graveyard. The sudden stench of death prickled in Amy's nose and made her stomach twist. Their leader, towering and headless and wreathed in smoky shadows, stopped before Oscar.

As tall as Oscar was, he barely reached the muzzle of the rider's black horse.

But if he was afraid, he didn't show it. 'You do not scare us, Dullahan. We are the riders of the mighty Fianna and if you don't heed my warning, I'll run my spear through your chest. There are ways of killing you, and we know them all.'

The shadows that surrounded the leader of the Dullahan twisted themselves into the familiar face of a withered old man. It grew until it loomed over the Fianna like a terrifying spectre.

Amy stiffened. *Tarlock.*

Black smoke billowed from the spectre's mouth, and an eerie voice echoed through the graveyard.

'*Oscar of the Fianna,*' it hissed. '*I am the one true ruler of Tír na nÓg. Give me the interloper, and I will spare you from the wrath of my Dullahan.*'

Oscar didn't even flinch. 'The Fianna does not bargain with curse-makers.'

'*This is your last chance. If you do not hand over the girl, then we will cut you to your knees.*'

'The answer is no! And besides, you cannot hurt us here.'

'*Do not be so sure,*' threatened Tarlock. '*You have chosen a terrible fate …*'

The face disappeared, the shadows regathering around the headless rider as he drew his sword and brought it crashing down. Oscar met the blow with Lug's Spear and an ear-splitting crash reverberated through the graveyard. He twisted away from the sword, and swung his spear like a baseball bat. It slammed into the rider's shoulder and knocked him off his horse, but he was on his feet in half a heartbeat.

Amy gasped as he charged full-force at Oscar.

With a rallying cry Oscar struck again, but this time, the shadow rider dodged the blow. He leaped over the warrior and landed on the grass behind him. He turned then, lightning-quick, his hulking sword flying out and nicking Oscar in the arm.

Oscar cursed as he leaped backwards, spinning his spear until it blurred to a pinwheel of amber. He lunged, and another screech rang out – metal meeting metal for the second time.

This time, the shadow rider faltered. He stumbled as he absorbed the blow, forced to his knees on the ground.

Amy's heart leaped. Jonah was right! The Dullahan

did seem weaker here. The graveyard was helping the Fianna, *protecting* them. All they had to do was stand their ground.

As Oscar bore down on the leader of the Dullahan, the rest of the Fianna and the headless riders joined the fray. The clash and clamour of fighting filled the air.

But two of the headless riders took advantage of the chaos and broke away from the battle. Unseen by the Fianna, they began to search the tombs, one steering his horse towards Manann's grave while the other came straight for Amy's hiding place.

Amy felt its shadows reaching towards her like tentacles. She shuffled backwards, sliding over tusk and bone until the tunnel widened into a small chamber that housed a stone coffin.

Upon it, a simple inscription flickered in the darkness:

Here lies Cernunnos,
God of all things wild and free.

On the other side of the tomb, a bone crunched.

Amy gulped as a black stallion stuck his muzzle into the tomb and sniffed the air. She held her breath, but it was too late. The creature had picked up her scent. There came an ominous thud as the headless rider dismounted, then the shuffle of boot on bone as he inched down the narrow passageway towards her.

Crunch.

Crunch.

Crunch.

The stench of death came with him.

Amy grabbed the silver sixpence from her pocket, and got ready to throw it.

The rider stopped to trace a leathered finger along the coffin's inscription, as if he could read it. Shadows swarmed above his neck, and for a terrifying heartbeat, Amy thought they were going to swoop down on her. She was just about to fire the coin at him when a noise from outside stole his attention away – something small and hard *plink*ed off the stone. The horse whinnied in the passageway. Another *plink*, this one closer than the first. The horse stomped its hoofs in warning. When another *plink* rang out, the rider turned on his heel and stalked away.

Amy huddled in a ball at the back of the tomb, with the sixpence in her fist, until the clamour of battle died down. Then she crept out. She spied a handful of nuts lying around the entrance way, and smiled. It could only have been Conan who threw them, to distract the Dullahan from finding her.

Outside in the graveyard, the rest of the Dullahan

were retreating, too weak to continue fighting. The Fianna were on horseback, chasing them over the hills. Oscar had stayed behind and was scouring the tombs for stragglers, but the graves were eerily quiet and the rotten stench had moved on.

Amy released a sigh of relief. She spied Jonah in the tomb next to hers, his narrow face peeking out from the darkness.

She waved at him and mouthed the words, 'You OK?'

He nodded, but his face was ashen. Conan was peering out from between his legs, clutching an acorn to his chest, like he was afraid he might have to launch another one.

A shout startled all three of them. At the other end of the graveyard, a Dullahan rider had crept out from the shadows of Danú's tomb. Oscar was caught completely unawares. The rider cracked his whip, the spine wrapping around Oscar's ankles. The spear flew from his grip as he landed on his back.

'OSCAR!' Jonah broke into a run.

Amy went after him, running faster than she ever had at school. Oscar's men were half a mile away. Only she and Jonah could help him now, but the Dullahan rider was picking up speed too, dragging Oscar behind him like a wagon. The warrior dug his fingers into the earth to try and slow the horse, but the grass was too brittle to anchor him and there were only bones to hang on to. He was swept through the graveyard, twisting and shouting as he went.

Amy grabbed a wilderbull horn from the grass as she outpaced Jonah. It was heavy in her hand, hard and sharp and perfectly curved. She fired it like a frisbee. It whistled through the air, spinning faster and faster and faster, until it cut right through the shadows swarming above the rider's neck.

He shuddered violently. Then grasped helplessly at the space where his head had once been. Though he didn't make a sound – in fact, he couldn't – Amy thought that he looked panicked. Frightened, even. Sensing his rider's distress, the horse reared up.

The strike bought Amy precious seconds. She swiped Oscar's spear from where it had fallen, surprised at the sudden spring in her steps. The weapon was much lighter than she expected. Instead of weighing her down, it doubled her speed.

The Dullahan rider took off again, but this time it was too late. Amy drew her arm back and sent the spear spiralling through the air. It made a faint whizzing sound as it went, and even though she had aimed too high, and slightly to the left, the spear righted itself. It flew straight as an arrow at the space between the rider's shoulder blades and skewered him in one sickening *thwack*.

The black horse skidded to a stop, and the headless rider slumped to one side, before falling to the ground in a heap.

By the time Amy caught up with Oscar, he had managed to untie the whip from around his ankles. He leaped to his feet and went to retrieve his spear. It lay amidst a bundled black cloak on the ground. The rest of the rider had turned to ash, and they watched as every last bit of him was swept away in a gust of wind.

The black horse took off with a frightened whinny, galloping hard and fast towards the hills.

Amy let it go. 'Wow,' she said, through gasping breaths. 'You weren't kidding when you said the spear always finds its mark.'

Jonah barrelled into the space between them. 'I thought you were a goner, Oscar,' he heaved. 'It's a good thing Amy was here!'

Oscar was looking at Amy like he had never truly seen her before.

Amy tossed her ponytail. 'The words you're looking for are *thank you.*'

His lips flickered, and for the briefest moment Oscar of the Fianna very nearly *almost* smiled. 'I won't forget what you did here today. I owe you a debt.'

Amy grinned. 'I'm always happy to save your life at short notice.'

Oscar clapped her on the shoulder, and though the force of it nearly knocked her sideways, her heart ballooned with pride.

When the rest of the Fianna returned, Oscar told them the tale of his rescue. Afterwards, the men lined up to clap Amy on the back and shake her hand. She felt like a true warrior then, as tall and proud as any of them, and as they gathered their supplies and prepared to leave the graveyard behind, she knew that now she had defeated her very first Dullahan rider, she could take on anything that awaited them beyond the horizon.

The good cheer was short-lived, however. As the Fianna saddled up the horses and prepared for their final trek north, Niall pulled Oscar aside.

'Tarlock knows how close we are to Mount Arrigal now,' he said in a low voice, but Amy, who was well-versed in the art of eavesdropping and was skulking behind Oscar's horse, had no trouble hearing their conversation. 'He'll be watching the North Road. We should tread east, and cut a trail through the Fang-lands instead.'

Oscar nearly choked. 'That's Culann's territory. His wolves won't just stand aside and let us pass. We'd be safer hitching a ride with the Dullahan.'

'It's been long years since you and Culann last saw each other, Oscar.'

'That's because the last time we spoke, he nearly tore my head off.'

'Ancient history,' said Niall mildly.

'There is no history here any more. Only the present.' Oscar rubbed the back of his neck, and Amy noticed a faint white scar below his left ear, in the shape of a crescent moon. 'The Fang-lands are too risky.'

'If we take the North Road, we take on double that risk,' countered Niall. 'The Dullahan who found us today are just a whisper of Tarlock's power. They'll be waiting for us. And you heard what the girl saw in the well. We're outnumbered, and we can't rely on Tristan. The simple fact is we need more men.'

'And women,' muttered Amy.

'And women,' added Niall.

She looked up, over the horse's flank, to find both warriors staring at her.

'We know you're there,' said Oscar flatly.

'Oh.' Amy blushed. 'Well, I was just—'

'Eavesdropping,' said Niall good-naturedly. 'We know.'

Amy swallowed. 'Well, do you want my opinion?'

'No,' said Oscar.

'Please,' said Niall.

'Well, I think we should go through the Fang-lands,' said Amy confidently. 'Whatever they are.'

'Of course you do,' sighed Oscar.

'If there are people there who might help us, then it's worth asking them.'

'My thoughts exactly,' said Niall, with a satisfied smile.

'And if there are people there who might *kill* us?' said Oscar pointedly.

'Seems like there are people who might kill us everywhere,' Amy felt compelled to point out. 'So we may as well avoid the ones we know for sure.'

Niall chuckled. 'Wise as ever, little sionnach.'

That seemed to settle the matter.

The Fianna mounted their horses, the sun shredding the last of the rain clouds as they left the Graveyard of the Gods behind. When they had settled into a familiar rhythm, Amy asked Oscar about the Dullahan. It troubled her that no matter how fast and far they rode, or how they had looped and twisted their way around the edges of Tír na nÓg, the headless riders had still managed to catch up with them.

'It's no wonder really,' Oscar told her. 'The riders of the Dullahan were once riders of the Fianna. We fought and journeyed together as brothers.' His voice darkened. 'The ones you saw today were unlucky. Somewhere along the way, they got caught by Tarlock. Captured and carted away, and then turned into something else. Something *cursed*.'

'So if that rider in the graveyard had succeeded in taking you …?'

'Then I would have become the same as him, yes.'

Amy paled. 'Tarlock doesn't just turn people into animals then.'

Oscar shook his head. 'He's too clever to waste our years of training. When he catches a Fianna warrior he makes them into something that will work for him. That way, we end up fighting each other if we try to get to him.' A sigh whistled through his nose. 'It's an extra burden on us.'

Amy glanced at the disintegrating sun chain. Even in the last few hours, it had become thinner, like a glittering snake slowly shedding its skin. The curse was still weakening. Tarlock was dying, but for how long? 'Do you really think you'll be able to kill him this time?'

'I don't know what lies beyond that horizon, little sionnach, but I know this is the only chance we have to make Tír na nÓg whole again, so you'd better believe we'll give it everything we've got.'

So will I, thought Amy solemnly. *No matter what.*

'Hey, look!' cried Jonah, as Niall's piebald horse drew level with them. The Greencloak was pointing over his shoulder. 'What does that mean, do you think?'

Amy followed his gaze to where a stag was lumbering

after them. Behind it, seven deer were peering out from a thicket of trees. There were foxes scampering nearby too, five badgers and at least twenty squirrels, though Amy suspected there might be more moving in the branches. Overhead, an owl soared with a flock of starlings, and when she snapped her chin down again, she glimpsed a family of moles poking their heads out of the ground. It was like the nearby forest had been turned upside down and shaken, until all of its animals fell out.

'What on earth is going on?' said Amy.

Conan smacked his forehead with his fist. Then he pointed emphatically to his own chest.

'Oh! How stupid of me!' said Jonah, with great delight. On his shoulder, Conan was jumping up and down in excitement. 'They're Pookas, that's what! They've come to *help*.'

Amy blinked, and saw what she had missed the first time. These weren't ordinary woodland creatures. They were steely-eyed and determined, a motley crew of warriors on a mission of their own. 'You mean they're coming with us to fight Tarlock?'

'Looks like it.' Niall smiled at the gathering of Pookas. 'Courage is rooted in the soul, no matter what you look like on the outside.'

Amy's heart lifted at the thought. Alone, they might

be small and insignificant, but together, they were shaping up to be quite an army indeed. 'We're all very glad you're going to join us!' she called out. 'Let's go and save Tír na nÓg together!'

Oscar tugged the end of her cloak, pulling her back into her seat. 'Easy on the enthusiasm,' he said, through his teeth. 'Let's just make it through the Fang-lands first.'

Chapter Eighteen

THE LIVING LAKE

When Tarlock returned to Silverstone Castle, the sky split open and the rain fell like tears over the mountain. Not long after, Gilda summoned Liam. Though he was glad to get out of the dungeon, he was surprised she remembered him at all, given she had fallen asleep during their last meeting.

The rain was a dreary grey mist by the time he was hauled into an outdoor courtyard by two burly soldiers, neither of whom were interested in talking. Gilda was sitting at a chessboard, waiting for him. Behind her, a glassy lake mirrored the rocky peak of Mount Arrigal. Swans glided on the water, staring forlornly at their reflections.

The king waved him over. Her crown was sparkling, but beneath it, her expression was sour. 'Well, there you are,' she said impatiently. 'Don't take all day about it. Can you play? It doesn't matter, because I'll beat you anyway.' She moved her pawn before Liam sat down, and even though he was good at chess – in fact, at school he was on the chess team – he let her win. Twice in a row.

This put Gilda in a very good mood indeed. The mist cleared and the sky brightened, and soon Liam could feel the sun's curse pounding behind his eyes again. He tried his best to ignore it. After all, it was better than shivering in the cold, dark dungeon, waiting for Tarlock to use him in his wicked spell. At least out here, freedom felt possible. He had taken Kit's words to heart – if anyone could help him, it was Gilda. *You have more in common with her than you might think.* Liam just had to figure out what that common ground was, and how to use it to his advantage.

Gilda sat back in her chair and looked past him, towards the lake. Sunlight picked out the copper strands from her hair and made them shine. Liam was reminded of Amy with a sudden, sharp pang. The light caught in the king's eyes too, making the silver gleam so brightly Liam had to look away. 'I'm hungry,' she said, to no one in particular. 'I want honey and bread.'

No sooner had she demanded it than two heaped

plates of honey-drizzled bread appeared before them, along with two mugs of warm milk. The sight of it worsened his heartache. His expression must have said as much, because Gilda was looking at him oddly.

'Don't you like honey and bread?' she asked.

'My gran makes this for me and my sister all the time when we stay at hers,' he said, in an effort to make conversation. 'It just made me sad thinking of her. Do you have anyone like that in your life? A mum or a sister or a brother or—'

'No.' The king shook her head. 'And if I did, I don't remember them. There's only me here.'

'What about Tarlock?' Liam fished. 'Isn't he like a kind of dad?'

'Of course not!' Gilda looked frightened. 'What a wretched thing to say.'

In the distance, thunder rumbled. The sun chain began to clang.

'Sorry.' Liam tried to push his glasses up his nose – a nervous habit – before realising they were no longer on his face. 'I didn't mean to upset you.'

Gilda pushed away from the table, her chair falling backwards in a clatter. 'I want to go for a walk.'

Liam took his slice of bread and followed her towards the lake. The swans raised their heads to watch them. Liam glanced nervously at the mage's tower, sure he saw a shadow moving in the window. He couldn't shake the feeling that there were other things watching them too.

'How did you come to be the king of this place?' he asked. 'You seem very young …'

'I've been very young for a very long time,' said Gilda. 'I don't remember the specifics. It's hard to remember anything at all here, to tell you the truth. I only know that Tarlock chose me.' She frowned then. 'I don't think I was very happy about it. Whenever I try to remember, I get the most horrid pain in my chest …' She trailed off, her eyes glazing as she lost focus.

Liam stayed silent. If Tarlock had chosen the ruler of this kingdom, then he must be very powerful indeed. But then why didn't he make himself king? That way he could be a mage *and* a king, and he would have the castle all to himself.

Gilda took off her shoes and socks and sat down on the edge of the lake. 'Have you ever thought about being a swan?' she said, as though their previous conversation had never happened. Or perhaps she had simply already forgotten it. She swung her legs into the water, disturbing the floating lily-pads. 'I sometimes wonder what it would be like to glide around all day, ruffling my feathers.'

Liam lowered himself down beside her, but he didn't

dip his toes in the lake. Upon closer inspection, the water had a strange tinge of brown, and it smelt a bit like a sewer.

'I'm not sure these swans are enjoying themselves very much.' He gestured to one nearby, whose head was drooped so low its beak grazed the water. Its feathers were grizzled and half plucked, and there were black smudges under both its eyes, like two teardrops frozen in place. 'In fact, they all look miserable.'

The swan raised its weary head like it had overheard them. Liam tossed it a piece of his honey bread to try and cheer it up. The swan swiftly gobbled it down.

'You should keep your food for yourself,' said the king disapprovingly. 'I doubt they feed you very well in the dungeon.'

I *doubt they feed these poor creatures at all*, thought Liam, but he was careful not to say so. The sky was finally settling again, and though the clouds brought relief from the sun, he didn't want to attract any unwanted attention by bringing down another thunderstorm. He waited until Gilda was looking the other way, and then chucked another piece of bread at the swan.

'Can't they fly?' he asked. Liam didn't know much about being a bird, but he thought if he had to be one, he would spend his time in the air, not starving and sulking in a stagnant lake.

'They do at the start,' said the king. 'But then they give up. The sun burns their feathers and chars their beaks. And anyway, where is there to go?'

'Well, when you put it like that, it doesn't sound very appealing.' He glanced around, furtively, to see how far he'd make it if he decided to run. There were soldiers in every corner of the courtyard, and those strange hooded wardens were drifting about too.

He was startled by a sudden, high-pitched squawk. Across the lake, a bedraggled-looking swan with greying feathers was flapping about in a panic. It squawked again.

And then, in the blink of an eye, its wing disappeared and became an arm – a *human* arm!

It tossed its head and suddenly its beak was a nose.

Oh!

Another squawk and the rest of its body changed, until quickly – impossibly – it became a little boy, splashing about in the water.

Liam trapped his shout on the back of his hand as four soldiers hurried towards the little boy. 'Pooka reversal in the Living Lake!' one of them shouted. 'Alert the mage at once!'

A pair of wardens rushed back into the castle. The other swans surrounded the poor squawking boy and spread their wings, as if they were trying to protect him.

Liam craned his neck, trying to see over the barrier of feathers.

'Don't just stand there,' yelled Kit, who came sprinting across the courtyard. 'Fish him out!'

'Oh dear,' said Gilda, in a sudden fright. 'This will put Tarlock in a terrible mood.'

Liam watched in muted horror as the soldiers launched themselves into the water, beating back the swans to fish the little boy out of the water. He wailed for his mum as he was hauled into the castle, the rest of the swans looking after him in silent dismay.

'What on earth just happened?' said Liam.

'The mage's power is weakening,' said Gilda. 'His spells are breaking apart.'

'Do you mean those swans …'

'Are not really swans at all. Or at least, they weren't always swans.' She shook her head. 'They stuck their beaks where they didn't belong and now they're Pookas. Cursed to live out the rest of their days as animals. That's why we call this place the Living Lake. It's a sort of torture, I suppose. To live in a body you weren't meant to be in, knowing what you once were. What you can't be ever again.'

'What about that little boy?' said Liam, with rising alarm. 'What will become of him now?'

'I expect Tarlock will turn him back into a Pooka. Something smaller. A dragonfly, perhaps. And if he can't, then I suppose he'll think of some other way to silence him.' She bit her lip.

Liam's stomach turned as he looked at the rest of the swans. 'Can't *you* turn them back?'

'*Me?*' The king splashed him. 'You don't know anything, do you? Tarlock put the curse on them. So only Tarlock can undo it. That's how it works.'

'But you're the king. Don't you have any kind of power here?'

Gilda shook her head, so vigorously the crown slipped down over her ears. 'Just this silly old thing,' she said, as she fixed it back into place.

But Liam was struck by something else now – something he had only just noticed. 'Your ears,' he whispered. 'They're round. They're like mine.'

You have more in common with her than you might think, echoed Kit's voice in his head.

Liam's heart thundered in his chest. Could the King of Tír na nÓg possibly be an interloper too? Someone just like him? He was about to ask when the tear-stained swan lunged towards them, snapping at their bread. Gilda splashed it in fright. 'Get back, you sneaky thing! Don't you dare come near us!'

Liam grabbed her wrist. 'Stop that. It's only hungry.'

Gilda gasped, as though Liam had struck her. His fingers tingled around her wrist. It felt like there was a current of electricity passing between them. When she turned her head to look at him, her cheeks were dappled with pink and her eyes were a bright, blazing blue.

They were Amy's eyes. His eyes.

'I feel quite strange all of a sudden,' she whispered.

Liam leaned towards her. 'Who are you? Where did you come from?'

Gilda's brow furrowed, trying to remember. Liam held her tighter, as if he were afraid she would float away and take the truth with her.

'I remember a yellow house,' she said slowly.

'What else?' said Liam urgently. 'What else do you remember?'

Gilda glanced around, her face clouding with fear. The air around them had fallen too still, as though the wind itself were listening in. 'There was a bird,' she confided in him. 'A white bird.'

'Yes,' whispered Liam. 'Go on.'

Gilda stared at her hand in his. 'It came to the house and tapped on my window. I was afraid of it at first. But I was curious too. So I followed it.'

'Did you go through the waterfall?'

She nodded slowly.

'By yourself?' pressed Liam.

Gilda shook her head, her frown deepening. 'There were two of us.' Her bottom lip began to tremble. 'The bird showed us where to go. We found a forest more beautiful than anything we had ever seen. It was like stepping into a fairytale. And then—' Her expression turned fearful suddenly. She glanced up at the mage's turret, her voice so small, Liam had to lean in to hear it. 'And then *he* came.'

'Tarlock?' Liam knew they were being watched, possibly even being listened to, but this was the only time he had – the only chance to get through to Gilda. If he could figure out how she'd got here in the first place, then perhaps he might find a way for them to escape too.

'I'm frightened,' she whispered. 'I'm not supposed to remember.'

Liam squeezed her hand. 'It's all right, Gilda. I'm here. I want to help you.'

Above them, the sun chain creaked.

'Tarlock *stole* me.' Gilda's eyes were so wide, Liam could see his reflection inside them. 'The bird and the waterfall – it was all a trick. It was a doorway into the darkness, only we didn't know that until it was too late. The horses came and brought me here. Tarlock needed a king for his spell. So he chose me.'

'To rule?'

Gilda wiped a tear from her cheek. 'To *curse*.'

All at once, the swans began to screech. More wardens came drifting out of the castle. Liam pulled the king close. 'We've got to escape, Gilda. You and me. We can do it together. We can go back home, to the yellow house.'

She shook her head. 'I can't go anywhere with you.'

'I don't mean right this minute,' said Liam. 'But we can make a plan. We can—'

'No!' she burst out, and as she did, the sun chain twisted on itself. 'You don't understand. I'm not just cursed. I *am* the curse.'

Liam stared at her in shock.

'The King of Tír na nÓg is a sacrifice.' She clinked the crown on her head, and high above them, the chain clinked too. 'The sun chain is tied to *me*. It uses my strength and my mind, until I don't have room to remember anything else. And now that it's getting weaker, I am too.' Her face crumpled. 'I won't ever be free unless it's broken, but Tarlock would never do that. He'll never give up his immortality. His *power*.'

In the course of one conversation, everything had suddenly become much more complicated. Liam squinted up at the sun chain, and tried to imagine a weapon that could sever it. 'Has anyone ever tried to break it?'

Gilda snorted, mirthlessly. 'How *on earth* would they do that? The sun chain was forged with magic, which means it will take magic to destroy it. And there's not a whole lot of that going round any more.' She blew out a breath, and with it, the last morsel of hope. 'I can't help you, Liam. I can't even help myself.'

Before Liam could think of anything to say – for what can you say to a living curse who knows their own terrible destiny? – Gilda pressed her fists against her eyes and began to wail.

Thunder rumbled overhead. Dark grey clouds came skulking over the mountain top.

Liam grabbed her by the shoulders. 'We can help each other. You just need to calm down and listen to me.'

'I c-c-can't c-c-c-alm down,' hiccuped Gilda.

'Yes, you can,' said Liam, as the first raindrop landed on the tip of his nose. 'I think you're having a panic attack. I get them sometimes. It feels a bit like swallowing a tornado.' He glanced at the darkening sky. If he didn't do something about her worsening mood, they might soon be *in* a tornado.

The girl nodded. 'Yes. Yes, it feels like I've eaten one of those.'

'Can you count backwards in threes from five hundred and ninety-seven?' he said, in a bid to distract her.

She blinked. 'What on earth are you talking about?'

'Or do you want to try a handstand instead?'

'A handstand?' she cried incredulously.

'Never mind. Let's try breathing then. In and out. But slowly. I'll count for you.'

Gilda did as he directed, slowly breathing in through her nose and out through her mouth until her shoulders stopped shaking. She scrubbed the tears from her cheeks with the sleeve of her dress, and just like magic – for that's what it was – the sky cleared up. When she looked at Liam again, the silver sheen had returned to her eyes.

Kit's hand fell heavy on Liam's shoulder. 'On your feet. *Quick.*' She dragged him up from the lake and steered him swiftly away from Gilda. 'The mage is coming.'

Liam left her staring forlornly at her own reflection, the sun chain clanging above her as it wiped away every word of their conversation.

By the time he made it back to the dungeon, his thoughts were reeling. He should have figured it out sooner. After all, the king's moods rattled the sky. They brought the clouds and the rain and the thunder. When she smiled, the sun shone on Tír na nÓg, even if it hurt. Gilda was tied to this kingdom by the chain itself – she was part of the curse, and that meant she was bound to this castle, to this mountain.

But the truth was, she came from Connemara. That was where she truly belonged.

As he crouched in his cell, listening to the footfall overhead, Liam resolved to find a way to save the girl king of Tír na nÓg. After all, how could he leave her behind now, knowing what he knew? Gilda had come from the yellow house, just like him and Amy. It was up to him to bring her home again.

Chapter Nineteen

THE FANG-LANDS

Amy was so busy inspecting the Pookas behind her that she didn't notice the landscape change. In the blink of an eye, it slipped from blistering summer into a cracked and barren winter. The earth hollowed out into a steep bowl, helmed by rugged hills and dense pine forest sprinkled with powdery white snow. A brisk wind raised the hairs on her arms as they descended, the horses' hoofs sliding over loose shale and crumbling rock. The Pookas picked their way down after them, into the unknown. The sun was less strong in the Fang-lands, and dark shadows snapped at their heels as if to chase them away. They kept on, treading a steady pace as they wound deeper into the silence.

Somewhere in the distance, a wolf howled.

Amy knew it for what it was – a warning.

Oscar stiffened, a flicker of fear passing over his face, as he gripped his spear. Amy desperately wished she had one of her own, but she knew as long as she stuck with Oscar she would be all right.

'So who lives in this place anyway?' she asked him.

'The Fang-lands belong to the Wolf-riders of Tír na nÓg. A clan of vicious wild-folk who prefer the company of their wolves over their own brethren,' said Oscar, with no small amount of disdain. 'Their pack-leader Culann is a brutal, spiteful man who will either agree to help us fight Tarlock or skin us alive for even asking.'

'But doesn't he hate Tarlock too?' said Amy.

'The Wolf-riders live in the long shadow of Mount Arrigal. They might hate him but that doesn't mean they'll turn against him either. They have found safety in silence. In keeping to themselves.'

'Sounds a bit cowardly to me,' muttered Amy.

Oscar nodded. 'We can agree on that, little sionnach.'

Amy looked around. 'So, how do we find Culann anyway?'

'He'll have picked up our scent long before now. He will find *us*.'

Amy could tell by Oscar's tone that he was not

counting on a warm welcome. She drew her cloak tighter. 'So, you're not pen-pals then.' Her eyes darted to the trees looming on either side of them. Every rustle set her teeth on edge. 'How long have you two hated each other?'

'Since we were teenagers.'

Amy looked back at him. 'You've known each other all that time?'

'Longer,' said Oscar stonily. 'We're brothers.'

'Wait. What?' Amy reeled.

Oscar's lips twisted, an old anger hardening his voice. 'Culann was meant to join the Fianna with me. It was our father's legacy. Our destiny. We came up as Greencloaks together, brothers and best friends since the time we could walk. We trained from noon until night in the Elderglen, always pushing each other to be faster, stronger. We fought side by side. Until one day he walked out of the forest and never looked back.'

Amy gasped. 'You mean he deserted you?'

'He'd fallen in love with a Wolf-rider. He ran away to live with her in the mountains.' Oscar shook his head, his expression wounded. 'He found a new calling. A new life. And I was the last one to know about it,' he said ruefully. 'I should have seen it coming. There was always a wildness about Culann. He couldn't be tamed. It look me a long time to see he didn't *want* to be tamed. Or trained.'

'So what happened then?'

'I followed him here,' said Oscar. 'We shouted at each other. I called him selfish and thoughtless, a stain on our family's legacy. He called me stubborn and possessive, said I cared more about the Fianna than my own family. We were both furious with each other. I hated him for leaving me behind. He hated me for not letting him go. So, we fought.'

'Who won?' asked Amy.

Oscar traced the scar on the back of his neck absent-mindedly. 'Neither of us.'

Amy thought of how she and Liam argued back at home, over silly things like the TV channel or who had to empty the dishwasher. She couldn't imagine ever shutting him out for good.

'After that, we vowed to stay away from each other,' said Oscar. 'He's been in the Fang-lands ever since.'

The hairs on the back of Amy's neck stood up. She tried to ignore the icy prickle of dread as it dripped down her spine. The horses were slowing, as if they could sense the danger lurking in the shadows. Behind them, the Pookas had clustered together.

'Sixty years ago, I broke our truce,' Oscar went on. 'When Tarlock was beginning to craft the Dullahan, and Pookas were popping up all over the country, I rode here alone and asked Culann to help us fight him before it was too late. We were both leaders by then. I thought we would be able to see eye to eye on the fate of our kingdom, if nothing else. But he refused.'

'But why?' said Amy incredulously. The Selkies' reluctance to help was one thing, but the Wolf-riders lived right next to Mount Arrigal.

'Culann didn't want to stir up trouble for his people.' Oscar barked a cold laugh. 'Then again, if he possessed any true measure of bravery, he would have followed in my footsteps and joined the Fianna. Which is exactly what I told him.'

'And let me guess,' said Amy. 'You fought again.'

Oscar shook his head. 'He chased me from his lands, and told me if I ever came back, I was dead meat.'

Amy quailed. 'I wish you'd mentioned that part sooner.'

A rush of wind swept through the Fang-lands, dragging dried leaves and dust with it. The horses stopped in their tracks. Behind them, the Pookas vanished from the trail, bolting into the trees or diving behind nearby boulders. Conan stood up on Jonah's shoulder, sniffing the air. He stamped his foot once, in warning.

'Uh-oh,' said Amy.

Oscar gripped his spear. 'Whatever you do, don't—'

Amy screamed as a grey blur came hurtling down from above and knocked Oscar clean off Arrow's back. He fell to the ground with a thud, and the horse reared up in panic. Amy was thrown off, landing hard on the ground. The air whooshed out of her in a ragged wheeze. She blinked at the faraway sky, trying to orientate herself while a chorus of growls filled the air.

They were surrounded by wolves! Amy sat up just in time to see a pack come charging down from the trees, carrying fully grown riders on their backs. They howled as they descended on the Fianna, and in the chaos of clashing spears and snapping teeth, she lost sight of Oscar entirely.

She spun around, searching for Jonah, only to meet with the blunt end of a wooden club. It smashed into the side of her head, the world exploding in a sunburst of colour as she slumped sideways. She blinked once, glimpsing a pair of icy blue eyes and a mouth full of fangs, before the blackness swept in and claimed her.

Chapter Twenty

THE SWORD OF TRUTH

BANG!
Liam sat bolt upright in the dark, blinking away the dregs of a nightmare.

Footsteps echoed along the stone floor and he remembered where he was. What he was.

A *prisoner.*

'Get up,' came a voice from the dark.

There was a soldier standing outside his cell. The door swung open, and Liam was dragged to his feet. He was marched out of the dungeon and up the stairs. *All the way up the stairs.* Until they came to a familiar oak door at the top.

'No, don't.' Liam tried to back up. 'Anywhere but here.'

But the guard blocked his way.

The door creaked open with a low groan, and Liam was shoved through it.

He stumbled blindly into Tarlock's tower room and the door slammed behind him. Liam turned back and jiggled the handle, but it was no use. He groaned as he pressed his head against the wood, willing it to open. 'Please. Please. *Please.*'

'Have you always been a quivering coward?' came a voice from behind him, followed by a deep, rippling laugh. 'Or does my reputation precede me?'

Fear flooded Liam's body, turning his blood to ice. He turned round slowly.

The mage was sitting at his desk, his face hidden beneath the folds of a bright silver cloak.

Tarlock.

Liam pressed himself up against the door. 'P-p-please d-don't hurt m-me,' he stammered.

The mage removed his hood as he stood up, revealing a pale, slender face and a long grey beard. His skin was paper-thin and as wrinkled as a prune. Liam hadn't met very many people since he had arrived in Tír na nÓg, but he was certain this man must be the oldest in all of the land. In *any* land. His nose was long and sharp, and his hooded eyes were ringed in silver.

Tarlock crooked his finger at Liam. 'Let me look at you.'

Liam stuck to the door like a starfish.

Tarlock peeled back his lips, revealing the yellow glint of his teeth. 'Very well. I will come to you,' he said, gliding right through his desk, as though it were made of nothing but air.

Liam screamed, but there was nowhere to run. The door was locked, and the window was too narrow – not to mention too high – to leap through. Tarlock paused at a bookcase halfway across the room, slipping his hand under the topmost shelf and sliding the wooden panel away to reveal a secret compartment.

Liam's eyes widened as he removed a long golden sword from it. It was almost half his size, and the hilt was encrusted with emeralds.

Tarlock swept towards Liam, and angled the blade at the tip of his chin.

Liam stiffened as a terrified whimper seeped out of him.

'This is *Fragarach* – the Answerer,' said Tarlock, like he was introducing Liam to an old friend. 'It belonged to my mother Danú, many, many centuries ago. She used it to cut a hole in your world, and carve out another one for us. A better one.'

The sword began to glow at Liam's throat, illuminating the mage in all his towering terror. He looked like a corpse brought back to life.

Liam scrunched his eyes shut. 'If you're g-g-going t-t-to k-k-kill m-me, j-j-just g-g-get it over with.'

The mage chuckled darkly. 'Now, where's the sense in that? The Answerer is the most powerful blade in Tír na nÓg. It is spelled to cut through any obstacle – human or object – just as assuredly as it can cut through lies.' He used the blade to tilt Liam's chin up, forcing him to meet his silvery gaze. 'And I want the truth, boy.'

Liam felt his tongue loosen in his mouth.

'How many of you came through the waterfall to Tír na nÓg?' asked the mage.

An alarm bell was ringing somewhere inside Liam.

Don't do it. Don't tell him about Amy.

'Speak,' said Tarlock.

Liam ground his teeth together.

'Don't fight it, boy. You'll only hurt yourself.'

And oh, it *did* hurt. A pool of blood was gathering at the base of Liam's throat and suddenly he felt if he didn't open his mouth and say what he knew, all the words would fill him up and drown him from the inside out. The sword flashed, bright and blinding, and Liam's resolve crumbled. To his horror, he opened his mouth and cried out, 'There were two of us. I came here with my sister Amy!'

He slammed his teeth into his bottom lip but it was already too late.

'So, it is as I suspected. The girl belongs to you,' said Tarlock, with no small amount of satisfaction. 'How fortunate for me that interlopers always seem to travel in pairs.'

Liam tipped his head back, trying desperately to fight the sword's magic. 'We weren't travelling, we were adventuring!' he burst out. 'We followed the bird until the headless horsemen found us. Amy hid before they found her!'

'Tell me what you know of the Fianna warriors,' said the mage.

Liam stared up at him blankly, relieved to have nothing to offer but his confusion. 'I don't know who you're talking about.'

The mage's frown was gruesome. 'Useless, quivering child,' he muttered. 'I know your sister rides with Oscar of the Fianna. My wardens have seen her. My hawk has tracked her. My horsemen have scented her. I want to know *why* she is with them, and I want to know *where* they intend to go.'

'I don't know anything about them,' said Liam, the sword flaring in the presence of another truth. He read the frustration on the mage's face and felt himself smile. 'But I'm not surprised you can't find her,' he said, without meaning to. 'She's much too clever for you.'

The mage narrowed his eyes. 'There is nothing lost in this kingdom that cannot be found, boy. Your sister might have disappeared from my sight but she cannot hide from me forever.'

Liam's heart thundered in his chest, hope and fear and worry all jumbling together until he felt like he might explode. Amy was safe and, by the sounds of it, she had fallen in with people who could protect her. *Warriors.* 'Maybe she's coming to rescue me,' he whispered, the words spilling from him before he could stop them.

Tarlock's eyes gleamed, and Liam knew he had made another misstep. 'I was hoping you'd say that.'

'What do you want with Amy?' said Liam anxiously. 'You already have me.'

'Ah, but *you* are not quite enough.'

Liam remembered then what he had read in Tarlock's tower – the final ingredients for his sun ritual. '*Two interlopers, still squirming,*' he muttered, before he could stop himself.

Tarlock loomed over him. 'Someone has been sticking their nose where it doesn't belong.'

'You'll never get your wrinkly old hands on my sister,' said Liam, accidentally. The sword was making him brave as well as truthful, and even though he knew he should be careful, he was swept up in the sudden rush of magic. 'I hope those warriors tear you limb from limb!'

Oh no. Oh no, oh no, oh no.

The mage clucked his tongue. 'What a shame you interlopers can never find your courage on your own.' He moved the sword until the point pressed against Liam's chest. 'You should know I only need your bones for my spell,' he snarled. 'Not your tongue.'

Liam clamped his lips shut, but another insult was already brewing inside him, this one even worse than the last. Before he could spit it out and get himself in even more trouble, there was a knock at the door. Liam stepped to one side, relieved to be out of reach of the glowing sword. The door opened to reveal a warden, her grey hood falling backwards as she poked her head in. 'Pardon me, Your Grace. I don't mean to interrupt.'

'You *are* interrupting,' said Tarlock crisply. 'Speak quickly.'

'The girl's been found. She's not far from Mount Arrigal.'

'*Ah.*' Tarlock's lips curled into a triumphant smile. 'Where?'

'She's in the Fang-lands, Your Grace. Culann has sent word.'

The mage stowed the Answerer in his robe. 'What are you waiting for, you imbecile? Go and get her.'

The warden scuttled away like a frightened mouse. Tarlock shoved Liam out after her, where he crashed into the same soldier as before, stubbing his nose against his shiny armour. 'Oof.'

'I'll come for you,' said Tarlock darkly. '*Soon.*'

Liam was marched back down the stairwell, the mage's threat trickling down his spine like ice.

Chapter Twenty-One

CULANN'S CAVE

Amy woke up in the dark with no idea where she was. The air was stagnant, the silence broken by the nearby patter of water. She groaned as she turned over, but the ground was scratchy against her cheek. It was cold too, and without a blanket to cover her, she was shivering. She sat up, blinking furiously until the ceiling shifted into focus. It was high and rocky, and hung with frozen icicles that glittered in the dimness.

As her memory came flooding back, Amy realised two things in quick succession. The first was that she had been kidnapped. The second was that she was in a cave. She whipped her head around, but there was no sign of Oscar or Jonah, or the rest of the Fianna. There were stray animal pelts spread along the ground and candles burning in faraway alcoves. She let the flickering lights guide her towards the sound of water. With any luck, she would find a river that would lead her out of here.

'I was wondering when you'd wake up,' came a voice from the shadows. A girl stepped out from a crevice in the rock. She was older than Amy, and had silver-blonde hair pulled away from her face in a long fishtail braid, pale skin and icy blue eyes. She was dressed like a warrior, clad in dark fur and leathers, and when she smiled, she revealed two rows of sharp white teeth. 'I thought you might be thirsty so I brought you some milk.' She held out a small cup. 'Sorry about bonking you on the head.'

Amy ignored the cup of milk. She eyed the knife sticking out of the girl's belt instead. 'Who are you?'

'My name is Torrin.' The girl grinned, too widely. 'I've never met an interloper before.'

'And now you've kidnapped one,' said Amy angrily. 'It seems to be a running theme here in Tír na nÓg.' She glanced around them. It appeared that the cave was connected to a series of other caverns by narrow tunnels cut into the rock. She'd have to pick one and hope for the best. 'If you'll excuse me, I really have somewhere else to be.'

The girl supped from the cup of milk. 'I wouldn't try to leave if I were you,' she said mildly. 'It won't end well.'

Amy lunged, snatching the knife from her belt. She held it out in front of her. 'Just let me pass. I don't want to hurt you.'

Torrin snorted as she took another sip. Even without her knife, she didn't appear to be one bit afraid of Amy. In fact, she looked amused.

Out of the corner of her eye, Amy spied a tunnel in the rock and ran for it. There came a low growl, and then a flash of grey as a huge wolf leaped out of the darkness, blocking her path.

Amy yelled as she reeled backwards. She dropped the knife in panic as she tried to put as much space between her and the beast as possible.

The wolf growled, revealing a mouthful of pointy teeth. It was at least three times her size, and its eyes were the same piercing blue as Torrin's, who came to stand beside it.

'Well, I did warn you not to run.' She picked up the knife and slid it back into her belt. 'But don't worry, Mac won't eat you unless I tell him to.' She laughed, like she had just made a joke, but they both knew she was deadly serious. 'In the meantime, I'm afraid you're going to have to come with us.'

Amy stared at the wolf's canines as she got up, hoping it wasn't blood she could see matted in the fur around his mouth. She hoped Jonah and the others were all right too.

'Where are we going?' she said warily.

'My father wants to see you.' Torrin's face turned serious and the humour drained from her voice. 'It's best not to keep him waiting. We Wolf-riders are known for our tempers. Especially my dad.'

Amy followed Torrin and Mac down a dark tunnel that led to a huge cavern bustling with activity. There were hundreds of people perched on ledges that wound up and out of sight. There were just as many wolves too, their sharp teeth glistening from the shadows.

Amy's mouth dried up at the sight of them.

Torrin nudged her along until they reached a stony platform in the middle of the cavern. There was a man standing at the very top of it. He was surrounded by twelve fully grown wolves, grey and black and brown and white, and in the flickering candlelight, Amy thought he looked a bit like one himself. He was draped in fur, and brandishing a huge wooden club. His hair was long and silver-white, pulled back from his pale face and bundled on top of his head with twine.

His teeth were big and sharp, but his eyes were the same as Oscar's; dark and hooded, with a ring of gold around each pupil.

Culann. He was every bit as wild as Amy had imagined him, and judging by his expression, just as unfriendly. She wished more than anything that she didn't have to face him by herself.

Culann's shoulders tensed as Amy approached. When he spoke, his voice was low and threatening, like a growl.

'Tell me, interloper. How has my brother come to be in possession of you?'

Amy tried to swallow the dryness in her throat.

'Actually, it's *Amy*,' she croaked. 'And I'm not Oscar's possession. I don't belong to anyone.'

Culann prowled down the platform towards her, two jet-black wolves lumbering alongside him. 'You do when you're on my land.'

Amy cursed her trembling limbs. 'I mean no harm to anyone here. I'm just passing through on my way to Mount Arrigal. I've got to rescue my brother from Silverstone Castle.'

Culann loomed over her. 'Something tells me you'll be reunited soon enough.'

The scent of wet fur mingled with old blood in the air between them.

Amy tried not to gag. 'What's that supposed to mean?'

Culann curled his lip, revealing a glistening fang. 'It means you won't be staying here much longer. My pack has no business with interlopers. We have no interest in the veil, or what lies behind it. Your people are a poison to this land.'

Amy thought of the sixpence in her pocket. To use it on Culann would buy her seconds at most, but she was certain his wolves would devour her the instant she flung the poisonous coin at their leader.

She folded her arms. 'If you don't care about interlopers, then why did you go out of your way to kidnap me?'

'We have a deal with Tarlock,' said Culann. 'We watch the Fang-lands for him, and in return he leaves us alone.'

She gaped at him. 'So, you don't care what he does to this kingdom as long as he doesn't do anything to *you*?' she said, in disbelief. 'Don't you think that's selfish?'

Culann only shrugged. 'Call it what you want.'

'No wonder you never made it into the Fianna,' Amy muttered.

Culann's eyes flashed. 'What did you just say?'

She swallowed thickly. 'You might be safe for now, but that's only because the mage is using you. You're no better than a warden.' Amy stared up at the wolf chieftain, trying to fathom how someone so closely related to the leader of the mighty Fianna warriors could possibly be so foolish. 'Are you really going to trust the same person who has cursed your sun and destroyed the land, all so that he never has to die?'

A muscle moved in Culann's jaw. 'I will do what I must to keep *my* people safe.'

'Wolves are supposed to be loyal,' said Amy.

Culann narrowed his gaze. 'So are the Fianna warriors. But my brother fled at the first sign of ambush and left *you* behind.'

Amy felt like she'd been slapped. Her eyes stung and her bottom lip began to wobble. It was true that in this cavern full of wolf-folk, she was desperately alone. Was she not worth the trouble of rescuing?

She looked at her shoes and did her best not to cry, but the tears slipped out anyway as Torrin and Mac came to stand at her side.

'I don't see why we can't let her go?' said Torrin quietly. 'She hasn't done anything wrong.'

Amy glanced sidelong at the girl and offered her a small, grateful smile.

Culann shook his head. 'Tarlock already knows she's here. If we let her go, we'll pay for it with our heads.'

Torrin scowled at her father. 'But she's frightened.'

'Torrin,' said Culann sternly. 'We're *all* frightened.'

'THEN SEIZE YOUR COURAGE, BROTHER, AND FIGHT FOR OUR KINGDOM,' came a familiar, booming voice.

Amy's heart leaped. She looked all around. Where was he?

Hundreds of hostile faces stared down at her. The wolves were growling, like they could sense the warrior skulking somewhere in the shadows.

Culann raised his club. 'Show yourself, Oscar of the Fianna, before I set my wolves on you!'

The Fianna emerged all at once from several different tunnels. The wolves snapped at them as they poured into the cavern, but no one moved to attack.

Yet.

Oscar strode out from the tunnel behind Amy, wielding Lug's Spear. It blazed brightly in the dimness, casting shadows along the rocky cavern. The wolves backed away in fear.

'You came back!' cried Amy.

Oscar offered her a brisk smile. 'Don't forget I owe you a debt, little sionnach.' He grabbed her cloak and tugged her backwards. 'Now, get behind me.'

Culann lunged at Oscar without warning, bringing his club crashing down. It met Lug's Spear with a thundering clash, both brothers straining as they pushed against each other.

'How dare you take the girl from us?' said Oscar, through gritted teeth.

'How dare you pass through my lands without permission?' Culann slammed his foot into Oscar's shin, knocking him off kilter. 'Your arrogance never ceases to surprise me.'

'Nor does your selfishness.' Oscar ducked a second blow, and brought his spear around, catching the chieftain behind his knees. Culann stumbled forward and Oscar headbutted him. Amy flinched at the sound of thudding bone. 'You'd turn against your own kingdom for a mage who will tear you limb from limb when he no longer has need of you,' snarled Oscar. 'You would turn against your own *family*.'

Culann bared his teeth. 'It was *you* who turned against me first, brother. Merely because I had the courage to choose a different path. A different life. You couldn't stomach it.'

'You deserted me,' said Oscar. 'You left your fellow Greencloaks behind! You have no honour, Culann. No loyalty.'

Culann threw his arms up, gesturing to his people. His wolves. 'I have an army of my own now, Oscar. And more loyalty than you could ever dream of.'

Oscar rolled his eyes. 'After all these years, you still sound like a petulant brat.'

'You can't stand not being able to order me around any more,' sneered Culann. 'You never could.'

'I don't waste orders on cowards,' said Oscar viciously. 'And a coward is all you've ever been.'

Culann roared with anger. Behind him, two white wolves leaped off the platform and came at Oscar. Niall surged out of the shadows, spinning a sword in each hand as he beat them back. Oscar caught his brother by the scruff of his neck and slammed his fist into his jaw. 'Prove me wrong!' he hissed. 'Do your own fighting!'

Culann shoved him off and spat out a mouthful of blood. 'None of you are going to leave this cave alive.'

Osar spun his spear and then angled it at Culann's chest. 'Then we will die together, brother.'

Culann raised his club over his head, red rising in his cheeks as a wild anger overtook him. 'I mean it, Oscar. I will crack your skull.'

'I will snap your spine in two!' seethed Oscar.

'THAT'S ENOUGH!' Amy burst out, startling the men *and* herself.

She marched into the space between them and knocked their weapons out of the way. She stood her ground, and turned on Culann.

'If I'm your bargaining chip, then you won't dare kill me,' she said, hoping it was true. 'So just listen to what I have to say before you two bull-headed oafs end up doing something monumentally stupid.' She heaved a breath, the silence suddenly so loud she could hear water dripping down the walls. 'You're brothers! You grew up together. You trained together. And now you want to use that training on each other? You'd rather Tarlock destroyed this kingdom and *all of you* rather than see it get well again! Don't you see? This is exactly what *he* wants. You've each made an enemy of the wrong person'

High on a rocky ledge, a wolf howled.

Oscar palmed his spear. 'Culann is the one who sided with Tarlock.'

Culann raised his club again. 'You gave me no choice. You told me the protection of the Fianna no longer extended to the Wolf-riders. That we'd be better off dead.'

Amy turned to Oscar in alarm. 'Is that true?'

'They can't be trusted,' said Oscar tightly.

'You're still angry at me for leaving you behind,' growled Culann.

Oscar scoffed. 'No. I'm angry because I came here a long time ago and asked you to fight with me against Tarlock and you said no.'

'You didn't *ask* me to do anything.' Culann raised an accusing finger. 'You ordered me, Oscar. *Threatened* me.'

'That's not how I remember it,' said Oscar stiffly.

'Your big brother complex clouds your memory,' jeered Culann. 'Just as it clouds your judgement.'

'Wait a second.' Torrin came to stand between the men, her shoulder brushing Amy's as they stood side by side. Together, they made a shield between the brothers. Or, perhaps, a bridge. 'Did you ever think that maybe you're *both* in the wrong?'

Amy smiled. 'You can be loyal to someone even if you don't like them very much,' she offered into the stony silence. 'Even if you're still angry with them …'

Oscar's nostrils flared.

Culann sucked his teeth.

Amy went on. 'I've been tricked and kidnapped more times than I can count since I set foot in this land.' She pointed at Oscar. 'He and I have spent more time bickering than talking, and I can't remember the last time I ate anything that didn't taste like burnt dirt. But none of that stuff matters to me right now because what I truly *care* about is rescuing my brother from Silverstone Castle. And more than that, I *care* about freeing this land from Tarlock's evil grasp once and for all. Now that we know he's dying, there's no better time to strike.'

She turned on Culann. 'I haven't been in Tír na nÓg very long, but I've seen enough beauty and bravery here to know that it's special, even under a curse. If an interloper from beyond the veil can set foot in this kingdom and see how badly it needs saving, then why can't *you*?'

Culann's stare was so withering, Amy had to look away from it. 'If you know so much about the world, then tell me this, interloper. Why should we join a fight alongside an army that doesn't respect us?' He glanced pointedly at Oscar. 'A warrior that doesn't even *trust* us.'

Amy was about to respond when Torrin spoke up. 'To lay old grudges to rest. We can't change the past, Dad, but we can change the future.'

'Better still,' said Amy. 'You can free your sun and make a future possible. That's what you all want, isn't it?'

The Fianna grunted their agreement.

Some of the wolf-folk began to nod.

Amy gave Oscar a pointed look.

The leader of the Fianna slowly lowered his spear. 'I propose a truce, Culann. Let bygones be bygones. Will you come with us to Mount Arrigal and help us save this kingdom, so there may be peace, once and for all?'

Culann stewed in silence.

Torrin turned to her father, her blue eyes pleading. 'Tell the truth, Dad. You're sick of it. We all are. We hate living under this cursed sun, cowering inside our caves and always looking over our shoulders for the day the Dullahan will turn on us. We miss the moon. We long for those nights when we ran free across the Fang-lands, with our gods bright and twinkling as they watched over us.'

Culann's jaw was clenched so hard he looked like he was in physical pain. 'It's not that simple, Torrin. If we march against Tarlock, we'll destroy our truce. We're risking our lives.'

'What lives?' said Torrin softly. 'Is this really living, Dad?'

The silence in the cavern was answer enough. Even the wolves were quiet.

Culann's shoulders slackened. He was thinking ... wavering. He turned to his brother. 'We'll be out-numbered.'

'I never said it would be easy,' said Oscar evenly.

'The Selkies are coming to help us,' Amy interjected. 'They're going to meet us at Mount Arrigal. Tristan pledged to join us.'

Oscar and Culann exchanged a glance, and for the first time in over sixty years, the brothers shared a barking laugh.

'If we're relying on Tristan, then this kingdom truly is doomed,' snorted Culann.

Oscar chuckled in agreement. 'Perhaps we should rely on each other instead,' he said, the amusement draining from his voice. 'What do you say, brother?'

Culann was silent for a long moment. It felt like everyone in the cavern was holding their breath. Waiting.

He looked up, at his people and his wolves, before returning his gaze to his daughter, Torrin.

'Come on,' she said, flashing her canines. 'Let the wolves out.'

Culann's eyes sparked, the gold inside them shining.

He held out his hand to the leader of the Fianna. 'To the future, Oscar. Let's give it a fighting chance.'

Oscar took his brother's hand and shook it.

When he smiled, Amy barely recognised him, but she found she was smiling too.

* * *

Outside the cave, in the dried-up basin of the Fang-lands, Jonah and the Pookas were waiting for the Fianna to return. When he spotted Amy, he bounded towards her and pulled her into a great bear hug. 'Thank the gods! I was sure you'd be half eaten by now!'

Amy pulled back with a grin. 'Actually, I think it all went rather well.'

Jonah's gaze slid over her shoulder, where the Wolf-riders were emerging from Culann's cave, weapon-clad and ready for battle. His eyes went wide. 'They're coming with us? How did you do that?'

'With my incredible charm.'

'How really?' said Jonah.

Just then, Torrin and Mac joined them. Conan shrieked before diving inside Jonah's cloak, where he quivered in fear of the wolf.

Torrin stuck her hand out. 'I'm Torrin. You must be a Greencloak.'

Jonah folded his arms. 'Your wolves are not allowed to eat any of our Pookas,' he warned. 'I'm afraid that's non-negotiable.'

Torrin flashed her teeth. 'Don't worry. We're saving our appetites for Tarlock.'

Conan poked his head out and squeaked gratefully.

Jonah extended his hand to the girl. 'In that case, let's be friends.'

There was no more time for pleasantries. Soon, they were back on the horses and riding out of the Fang-lands. Oscar travelled at the front of the Fianna, while Culann rode a humongous black-and-silver wolf at the head of his pack, both brothers leading side by side, as they forged a pathway north, to Mount Arrigal.

Every time Amy looked over her shoulder, she spied more Pookas pouring out of the trees to join them.

'You know, together with the Pookas *and* the Wolf-riders *and* the Selkies, I really think we can do it, Oscar,' she said giddily.

Oscar kept his eyes fixed on the horizon. 'Keep hold

of that hope, little sionnach. You will need it for what comes next.'

Amy turned back around. In the distance, the silvery peak of Mount Arrigal speared the horizon like an arrowhead. Soon she could see the dark mist that swirled around the bottom of it, marking the shadowy spectre of the Dullahan, a thousand-strong army that now stood between them and the mage.

Above it all, a fork of silver lightning cut a jagged line in the sky, heralding a new storm.

Chapter Twenty-Two

THE DUNGEON PLEA

Liam was running out of time. He had to get out of Silverstone Castle and find his sister before Tarlock kidnapped her and killed them both. But he was trapped down in the dungeon with only the patrolling Banshee for company. He paced his own cell, trying to figure out a plan. When another storm rolled in, the sky thrashing and roaring with the king's anger, it gave Liam an idea.

He began to sing. At first nothing happened, the notes of Gran's favourite song lost in the howling wind. But he refused to give up. Liam sang louder, bellowing out the same verses until they echoed back at him. Still the storm raged. When the Banshee came skulking past his cell, he reached through the bars and beckoned her over.

She opened her mouth to scream.

'Wait!' he said, and to his surprise, she did. Curiosity glimmered in her milky eyes. 'I know you can scream,' he said. 'But can you sing? Because I need your help.'

The Banshee stared at him, quieter now than Liam had ever known her to be.

'I know you're unhappy,' he went on. 'Everyone here is unhappy, and I want to do something about it. If you want to help me, all you have to do is sing with me.'

The Banshee licked her rotting teeth.

Liam swallowed a quiver of fear and began the song again, slipping seamlessly from one verse to the next until, remarkably – almost impossibly – the creature joined in.

The Banshee's singing voice was not silky or sweet – it was a harsh, high-pitched warble – but as Liam sang himself round and round in circles, she found the tune and carried it well enough. And so they sang together, the Banshee and the boy, until the thud and rattle of thunder ceased, and the door to the dungeon flew open.

Gilda came marching down the stairwell, Kit two steps behind. The Banshee took one look at them and skittered back into the darkness.

Liam stopped singing. 'Oh good, you're here.'

Gilda stared at Liam, like she was trying to figure out

who he was. Her eyes were glazed and silver. 'What's the meaning of all this racket?'

'I know you like this song,' said Liam. 'I thought if I sang it enough times, you'd come and find me.'

'Which is absolutely against the rules,' Kit piped up. 'If Tarlock finds out about this, he'll—'

'Grind me into bone dust?' said Liam impatiently. 'What's new?'

Gilda folded her arms. 'So, you lured me here on purpose.'

'I need to talk to you. And it can't wait.' Liam stuck his arm through the bars, reaching for her hand, but she curled it into her chest and stepped away from him. Her frown deepened, and in it, Liam saw no hint of recognition. Without his touch, she was still trapped under the mage's spell – doomed to forget who she really was.

'Whatever this is about, make it quick,' hissed Kit, with one eye on the door.

Liam pressed his face between the bars and spoke to Gilda. 'Please,' he said desperately. 'I need you to help me.'

'Help you?' she said in bewilderment. 'What makes you think I *can* help you? Or indeed that I'd even *want* to.'

'Because we come from the same place, you and I,' said Liam, praying the king would believe him. 'You grew up in a yellow house that sits on the other side of the waterfall. And all around it, there are mountains and wild-flowers and fields full of brambles and briars and nosy sheep, and in the summer, there are butterflies and big droning bumblebees, and if you walk west for long enough you'll find the ocean bubbling up along the coast, and the water there is freezing and full of seaweed but it tastes like adventure and it smells just like home.'

The words spilled out in a panicked rush, and although Gilda was staring at him like he had suddenly sprouted horns, she didn't move away. It was enough – just enough – to keep going. 'That place is called Connemara.'

The girl king blinked. 'Connemara,' she whispered, and in the silence between them, the word felt like magic.

'You used to live there, Gilda,' Liam went on. 'But then you walked through an enchanted waterfall and ended up here. Tarlock stole you away from your family and your home. He bound you to this land with an awful curse and made you forget who you are.'

Gilda's frown deepened, and Liam could tell she was trying very hard to remember the rest.

'I think you have a sister. She's an old woman now, but she misses you very much.' Liam swallowed thickly. 'Her name is Dorothy.'

Gilda's eyes narrowed in concentration. '*Dorothy*,' she said, sounding out the name.

It still wasn't enough.

Liam held his hand out to her. 'Please. Let me show you.'

She stared at his hand, and this time, she took it. She squeezed her eyes shut.

'And your name …' Liam went on. 'I think your name is Peggy.'

The girl's eyes snapped open. They were suddenly a bright, brilliant blue again. 'Peggy,' she said, the name bringing a smile to her face. '*Oh.*'

'My word,' muttered Kit, and when Liam glanced at her, she was shaking her head in disbelief. 'She remembers.'

Liam squeezed her hand. 'You don't belong here. You belong to *us.*'

'I do?' she whispered, with all the fragile hope of a little girl.

He nodded. 'And I think I know a way we can finally go home.'

'What on earth are you doing?' Kit was staring at Liam in alarm.

'You were right, Kit. Gilda and I do have something in common after all. Some*one*,' said Liam. 'So, I'm doing the only thing I can do. I'm making a deal with the King of Tír na nÓg. And if you're the fair and good person I think you are, you won't stop me.'

'As a soldier of Silverstone Castle, I *should* stop you,' said Kit. Then she hesitated. 'But maybe I can't quite hear what you're saying ...' She spoke slowly, taking a step backwards. 'Maybe I'm not even here right now ...'

Liam turned back to the girl, hope swelling like a balloon in his chest. 'I don't know how long you're going to remember this conversation for, after I let go. Maybe you'll forget as soon as you leave the dungeon, but try to hold on to your name, Peggy. For as long as you can,' he urged her. 'I need you to bring me the Answerer. It's hidden in a secret compartment under the top shelf in Tarlock's tower. If you can bring me Danú's sword, I think I can use it to set you free. And then we can go home.'

The king shook her head in a bluster, strands of copper hair flying around her face. 'You must be mad!' she cried. 'I can't just steal the Answerer for you!'

'If you don't try, terrible things will happen,' said Liam gravely. 'Once the mage casts his spell, he'll be more powerful than ever. The sun will be chained for good, and you'll forget every last bit of yourself.' He glanced at Kit, who was staring at her boots, pretending not to listen. 'You can't go on living in fear of what he might do next – to you, to your families, to your animals. This kingdom shouldn't have to suffer under him any more. Not while there's still a chance to defeat him.'

The girl king – Peggy – took a step backwards, shaking him off. 'No, no, no, no. It's too much. You're asking too much.'

'You're the only one who can do it,' said Liam, desperately reaching for her hand again. 'I need that sword. If you don't help me, all will be lost.'

But the spark of Peggy's memory was already fading. Her face shuttered as she backed away from the cell. Liam's heart sank. She had forgotten Connemara already. Her eyes were hazy and silver, and her lids were growing heavy, as if the act of standing had suddenly become a great effort.

'I think I might take a nap,' she murmured, to no one in particular. 'All this talk has made me rather tired.'

She turned from his cell, dragging her feet as she crossed the dungeon, like she was in a trance.

'Peggy – Gilda, please!' Liam stretched his arms through the bars, but he couldn't reach the king.

Kit glanced over her shoulder as they left, and in the flickering half-light, Liam could have sworn she looked just as sorry as he did.

He had failed, and there was nothing else he could think of to do. With the slow thud of the dungeon door, the king and her soldier were gone, and Liam was alone once more, his destiny tightening around him like a noose.

Hours crawled by, every shadow on the wall making him jump until his nerves were frayed and his mind was exhausted. Eventually he nodded off, dreams of Connemara quickly bleeding into nightmares of Tarlock bearing down on him like a vicious hawk. His sleep was brief and fitful, and when he woke, Liam found himself curled up in a puddle of light. It was coming from somewhere inside his cell.

He rubbed his eyes and rolled to his feet, gasping at what he saw. The Answerer stood propped up against the wall, just inside the bars of his cell. Liam heard the quiet shuffle of boot on stone and looked up to where a shadowy figure stood in the doorway.

For a terrifying moment, he thought it was Tarlock, but it wasn't him at all.

It was Kit. 'I hope you know what you're doing, boy.'

She slipped away before he could thank her, the door closing with a faint thud.

Relief trickled through Liam.

Peggy might not have remembered what he said earlier but Kit had been listening all along, and now she had risked her life to bring him the Answerer. Even in the cursed underbelly of Silverstone Castle, there was goodness. Bravery. *Hope*.

Liam picked up the sword. It was light in his hands

and he angled it at the cell bars, bringing his arm down in one fluid swipe. There was a brief moment of resistance, the blade connecting with the first bar in a faint *clink* and then, as easily as if it were cutting through butter, the bars cleaved in half and fell clanging to the floor. Liam gaped at the hole in his cell.

And then, without a moment of hesitation, he stepped through it.

Chapter Twenty-Three

THE SLUMBERING SWAMP

The closer Amy got to Mount Arrigal, the more foreboding it looked. Every time she craned her neck to see where the peak ended and the clouds began, a blinding pain flared behind her eyes. The curse was stronger here. It made every step harder than the one before, but they had come too far to turn back now.

Amy rose to her haunches and searched the mist for the Selkies, but there was no sign of Tristan or his army.

Oscar followed her gaze. 'They're not coming, little sionnach.'

'He'll come,' said Amy hopefully. 'He promised.'

'Some promises weigh less than others.'

'And some weigh nothing at all,' grunted Culann, who was riding alongside them.

'It wasn't that long ago that you two were trying to kill each other,' Amy reminded them. 'People can change.'

'People, perhaps,' said Oscar. 'But not Selkies.'

Torrin was just behind her father, riding her grey wolf. 'We don't need the Selkies anyway,' she said, flashing her teeth. 'We've got each other.'

Amy tried to smile back but the stench of death hung heavy on the wind. It reminded her that despite their new allies, they were still hopelessly outnumbered.

After a brief discussion, Oscar and Culann decided they should head east, looping around the mountain to where the pathway up to Silverstone Castle was steepest and so less populated by the Dullahan. That would give the warriors and the Wolf-riders the best chance of breaching the castle gates. It would also provide the perfect cover for Amy to sneak into the castle and rescue her brother.

The plan was not without risk, however. Heading east meant passing through the Slumbering Swamp, where the land was soft and squelching, and eerie creatures darted about beneath the water. Amy spied huge fish with teeth like needles, and mud crabs as big as her head with shiny pincers. She yelped when a giant octopus darted out from the water and tried to catch her ankle with a long, slimy tentacle.

Oscar responded like lightning, slashing the tentacle with his spear and sending the rest of it skulking back into the stagnant water.

All across the swamp, wolves growled and snapped at the churning waters, protecting their riders from the horrors underneath.

'Whatever you do, stay on the horse,' warned Oscar, as they waded deeper. 'If you set foot on the swamp, something will pull you under.'

Amy wound her fingers in Arrow's mane and tried not to look as afraid as she felt.

Behind them, the Pookas moved carefully, the smaller animals hitchhiking on the larger ones to keep from drowning – or worse. For a long time, the only sound was the careful squelch of hoofprints and the gnashing of wolf teeth, until Jonah's voice rang out. 'The swamp is bubbling! Something's coming!'

The warriors drew their swords. The Wolf-riders raised their clubs.

Amy whipped her head around. Beyond the wolves and the horses and the troop of travelling Pookas, new shadows were skulking in the mist. They were coming up from the swamp, rising out of the water on long, sinuous arms and then standing up – tall and hulking – on two legs!

'It's the Selkies!' cried Amy. 'Ha! I told you they'd come!'

Just up ahead, the swamp water began to churn.

Amy cheered as a fist punched through it.

Then the rest of Prince Tristan emerged, leaping out of the marsh like a superhero. His tail morphed in mid-air, and he landed squarely on two feet.

'Easy!' shouted Oscar, as Arrow reared up.

Culann's wolf bared its teeth, growling at the new arrival.

The prince stood uncowed before them, scarred and smiling, and dripping in seaweed. 'You have made it to the mountain, interloper,' he said to Amy. 'It seems I underestimated you.'

'There's been a lot of that going on here lately,' said Amy breathlessly. 'But I'm glad you kept your promise!'

The prince cocked his head, the spires of his crown glimmering in the mist. 'Did you have cause to doubt me?'

Amy pointed accusingly at Oscar and Culann. 'No, but they did. They said I was foolish to believe you'd come!'

Oscar cleared his throat awkwardly. 'Perhaps I was too hasty in my judgement.'

Culann lowered his club, looking a little sheepish. 'On this occasion, I am pleased to be wrong.'

'Then I suggest you call off your dogs,' said Prince Tristan haughtily. 'Unless you intend to eat your reinforcements.'

Hundreds more Selkies were emerging from the Slumbering Swamp now, brandishing sharpened spears and rusted harpoons. The wolves growled and snapped at them as they shed their seal tails for human legs.

Culann threw his head back and barked a command. It didn't sound like any word Amy knew, but the wolves understood it at once. They drew back, chastened.

They journeyed on – the warriors and the Wolf-riders, the Pookas and the Selkies – through the Slumbering Swamp and up the jagged mountain. It was so large, it hid the sun from them, but there was no comfort in its long, dark shadow. Amy felt like her bones were made of lead.

Eventually the land grew too steep, and the horses could go no further. High above them, the towers of Silverstone Castle skewered the low-hanging clouds. There was at least half a mile yet to go.

'It's time to split up,' Oscar announced. He withdrew the castle map from inside his cloak and unfolded it. 'The Fianna will round the mountain from here, and launch an attack on the Dullahan to the west,' he said, tracing his finger along the parchment. 'That should draw most of them away from the black gates in the south.'

'The Selkies will go with you,' said Tristan. 'We'll herd as many as we can, down to the swamp. The creatures there will help us drown them.'

'The Wolf-riders will then breach the black gates and search for Tarlock,' said Culann, who was palming his club in anticipation. He nodded in Amy's direction. 'That will give the interloper enough cover to sneak around the back of the castle, enter from the east and make for the dungeons.'

'I'll take you,' said Torrin. 'We'll be quicker on Mac.'

Amy nodded gratefully, relieved she didn't have to trek the rest of the way on foot.

'I'll come too,' said Jonah at once. 'I'm not missing out on a daring rescue mission!' There was an emphatic squeak from the squirrel sheltering inside his cloak. 'And neither is Conan!'

Now that the moment was upon them, unease settled in Amy's stomach. The idea of leaving the Fianna behind was as terrifying as the moment she and Liam had been separated. She had come to rely on Oscar's grumpy steadiness and unerring bravery.

He helped her down off his horse and placed a hand on her shoulder now, as if he could sense what she was thinking. 'Remember, little sionnach, the greatest weapon you wield is your courage. Be quick, be smart and be brave.' He handed her the map. 'You should take this with you – you need it more than I do. Once you get inside, head for the clock-tower. The dungeon is directly underneath it. If your brother's still alive, that's where he'll be.'

Amy took the map, and carefully folded it into her pocket. 'What about Tarlock? We still don't know what he'll do.'

Culann flashed his teeth. 'Ten roasted boars to whichever one of us kills him. They'll be good and delicious once the sun is fixed.'

'You're on,' said Oscar, with the confidence of a man who knew he was going to eat well for the next few weeks.

Tristan spun his spear. 'The arrogance of land walkers. Perhaps it's time I put you both in your place.'

With that, the allies split up.

Amy, Jonah, Conan, Torrin and Mac stood side by side and watched the armies go. The Fianna warriors and the Selkies rounded the curve of the mountain as they ventured towards the dark shadow of the Dullahan. The Pookas and the Wolf-riders travelled south, towards the black gates of the castle.

When the last of them had disappeared from sight, Amy and Jonah, with Conan on his shoulder, turned back to Torrin. She scooted forward to make room for them all on Mac's back, and together, the five of them set off to rescue Liam.

Chapter Twenty-Four

THE BROKEN CHAIN

With the Answerer in his hand, and free from the dungeon at last, Liam crouched behind a suit of armour in the upstairs hallway, waiting for the coast to clear.

He was hoping the castle would be quiet, but instead he could hear the shouts of panicked soldiers, and the shrill voices of wardens rattling down the hallways. *What was happening?*

'The Wolf-riders are at the gates!'

'The castle is under attack!'

'Every soldier to the courtyard! *Now!*'

Liam's heart leaped, hope mingling with the swell of his fear. Who were the Wolf-riders, and what were they doing here? And more importantly, whose side were they on? He hoped they were after Tarlock, but he wasn't going to wait around to find out. They'd provided the perfect distraction for his own escape, and he was going to use it.

But first, he was going to free Peggy from her curse. And to do that, he had to break the sun chain. After that, when they were away from here, they would find Amy. And then – *finally* – they would go home. Together.

Once the hallways were deserted, Liam legged it to the rear courtyard. It helped that he was carrying the ancient sword at his side – it made him feel braver, stealthier. Soon, he was standing outside the walls of Silverstone Castle, with the Living Lake glistening over his shoulder. Above him, grey clouds drifted in from the west.

Growling reached Liam on the wind. He heard weapons clashing and people shouting, the black gates creaking as they strained to keep the wolves out, but he couldn't tell who was winning. Only that there was no one around to stop what he was about to do.

Good.

The swans in the Living Lake watched Liam as he crept through the hedges, keeping out of sight of the crescent window that looked out over the water. When he found a sturdy trellis covered in crawling ivy, he anchored the Answerer inside his belt and began to climb. He did his best to ignore the ache burning behind his eyes as the cursed sun beat down on him.

The trellis turned out not to be as sturdy as he'd have liked, and the climb was made harder by the sword knocking against his leg every time he raised his foot. Sweat beaded on the back of his neck and pooled under his arms, but he persevered until the world below him had become very small and the ghastly sound of the sun chain drowned out the commotion at the gates.

After what felt like a century, Liam flung his arm over the top of the parapet and dragged the rest of his body after it. The sword clattered against the stone roof as he rolled on to his back, catching the last morsel of his breath. He clambered to his feet and looked for the horizon through the mist. The wind was picking up now, casting the first droplets of rain on his cheeks.

The thunderstorm felt like it was in his head too, the clanging so loud up here, Liam could barely think. Across the stone roof, where determined turrets continued towards the sky, the sun chain shimmered like a tear in the universe.

It was a rope of pure light, writhing and twisting like a snake. The physical effect of it being so close made

Liam's stomach heave. He turned to be sick, his eyes streaming as he wiped his mouth.

He was too high up to see what was happening at the gates, but more shouts – different shouts – now reached him from near the foot of the mountain.

What is going on?

Liam peered over the edge of the roof. There were hordes of headless horsemen. And in the midst of them galloped a band of warriors wearing rippling green cloaks and dark armour. Although they were as small as chess pieces, he could hear their rallying cry on the rising wind.

Behind them charged a mass of creatures Liam had never seen before. They looked like they had been dredged up from the seabed, and they were moving more slowly – more deliberately. It was as though they were trying to draw the headless riders towards them.

That's clever, thought Liam. It would drive a wedge between Tarlock's army, splitting it in two. Which would make the fight easier.

Liam drew back, piecing everything together. The entire mountain was under attack, not just the castle gates, but the Dullahan too. And not just by one army either. There were wolves and warriors and sea-creatures. Tír na nÓg had come together to wage war on Tarlock.

Liam closed his eyes for a moment. Because, although he couldn't see her, he knew, with every bone in his body, that his sister had come to rescue him.

After all, Amy Bell would never miss a rebellion.

He snapped his eyes open, seized by a sense of urgency. The armies of Tír na nÓg were marching on Tarlock, but *he* was the key to destroying Tarlock's power. *The sun chain was forged with magic,* echoed Peggy's voice in his head. *Which means it will take magic to destroy it.*

If Liam's gamble paid off, he could turn the tide of battle right here and now, and give them all a fighting chance.

He marched across the roof. The chain was anchored to the top of the glass dome that covered the throne room below. It glowed brighter as he drew nearer, until it felt like he was staring into a slice of the sun itself. Black spots swam in his vision as he unsheathed the Answerer and hoisted it in front of him.

He stepped on to the dome, exhaling in relief when the glass held. Another step, and then one more, and suddenly the chain was right before him.

The curse was unbearable now, cold and cloying as the weight of it threatened to crush him. It squeezed his ribcage until the bones creaked and he had to gasp for breath.

Liam drew the sword back and, with a bursting cry, brought it down.

The blade collided with the chain in an explosion of sparks.

He felt the blow deep in his bones, and looked up to inspect the damage.

But the chain wasn't going to yield as easily as the bars of his cell. Only a thin sliver had snapped away. It lashed out, slicing Liam's shoulder before it turned to dust. He gritted through the pain, holding the sword steady as it severed another bind. And then another.

A crack spiderwebbed across the glass dome, but Liam didn't drop the sword. He could feel the curse wavering, like a great tree about to fall. With every bind that snapped away, the pain in his head lessened.

Between the clouds, the sun hinged off kilter, like an orange tumbling from a shelf.

And then there was only one last luminous thread holding it all together. Liam watched the blade slice through it, severing the chain in two. He dropped the sword, relief bursting from him in a triumphant shout.

Then a hand shot out from behind him, and caught the broken chain by its final thread.

Liam knew that hand – it was paper-white, the skin so wrinkled he could see the blue veins beneath it. Fresh blood dripped through the mage's fist as he looked down on Liam with furious silver eyes.

With his free hand, Tarlock caught Liam by the throat and hoisted him into the air until they were nose to nose.

Liam's feet dangled helplessly as he tried to wrestle free. It was no use. The mage was stronger than he looked. With the chain clenched in his fist, and the power of its curse coursing through him, he looked like a demon sprung from hell. His eyes were bursting with blood vessels and his nose was bleeding.

'Just what do you think you're doing?' he hissed. 'My sun needs an anchor.'

'Then find another one,' heaved Liam. 'Peggy deserves to be free!'

Tarlock smiled, dark blood bubbling through his teeth as he spoke. 'Very well then.'

Chapter Twenty-Five

THE UNEXPECTED PRISONER

'Did you guys see that?' asked Amy, as they crept round the back of the castle. 'I swear the sun just wobbled.'

'How many times do I have to tell you not to stare at that thing?' Jonah shielded his eyes as he looked up. 'It looks the same to me. Big and bright and extremely cursed.'

'Feels the same too,' said Torrin, who was sitting in front of them. 'I've got a blinding headache.'

Conan, who was perched on Jonah's shoulder, was nodding furiously at Amy like he'd seen the sun wobble too.

She pulled out the map, studying it one last time before turning to her friends. 'You two don't have to come inside with me. Liam's my brother, not yours. And it's probably going to be really dangerous.'

'Pah! I *love* danger,' said Jonah, entirely unconvincingly. 'Well, I don't *love* it. But it's part of the job description, isn't it?' He puffed his chest up. 'I want to help you rescue your interloping brother. In fact, I think if it goes well, it will be the thing I'm most proud of so far in my life.'

'And if it doesn't?' said Amy.

Jonah glanced at the squirrel on his shoulder. Something unspoken passed between them. 'Even then, I think I'll still be proud of it.'

'We're coming too,' said Torrin. She leaned forward and scratched the top of her wolf's head. 'And besides, Mac's the best accomplice going. Most people run at the slightest glimpse of his teeth.'

True to the plan, Culann's commotion at the black gates provided the perfect cover for them to leap over the outer wall and the hedges in the courtyard, before creeping into the castle. The east wing was empty, save for the suits of armour that craned their necks to watch them go. Mac padded past fancy oil paintings and glittering chandeliers, the ceiling so high, Amy had to tip her head all the way back to see where it ended.

With the map to guide them, Torrin nudged Mac towards the clock-tower, but when they turned on to the hallway that led to it, a pair of wardens came around the corner.

'Hide!' whispered Amy.

They doubled back the way they had come, only to find two more wardens closing in on them.

'Hop off! Quickly!' Torrin rose to her haunches on Mac's back, and held her wooden club aloft. 'I'll create a distraction while you two get into the tower.'

'But they'll take you away!' said Amy.

'They might spot me, but they won't catch me,' said Torrin confidently. 'You've never seen a wolf *truly* run.'

Before they could argue, Mac reared up on his hind legs, dumping Jonah and Amy on to the floor. Torrin threw her head back and howled as they took off down the hallway. She swung her club as they went, toppling suits of armour in a symphony of clanging that echoed throughout the entire wing.

Jonah grabbed Amy's hand. 'Come on!'

While Torrin led the wardens on a wild castle chase, Amy and Jonah vaulted across the hallway and ducked into the clock-tower, following the stairwell into the deepest part of the castle. At the bottom, they squinted into the dimness. At one end of the damp corridor, a Banshee watched them from the shadows.

Amy stuck her hand in her pocket and held the coin

out in warning. The creature came no further.

They tiptoed along the passageway, peering into empty cells until they reached the last one. It was locked. In the very back corner, a quivering figure sat hunched in a ball.

Amy's heart cartwheeled in her chest as she pressed her face between the bars. 'Liam!' she hissed. 'It's me! Amy!'

The figure stirred.

'Are you injured?' she whispered. 'Don't worry, Liam. We'll get you out of this awful place. I promise.'

'Allow Conan.' Jonah removed a small silver pin from his cloak and handed it to the squirrel. 'He's never met a lock he couldn't pick.'

'Even as a squirrel?'

Jonah tapped the side of his nose. '*Especially* as a squirrel.'

After a minute of intense poking and twisting, Conan eased open the lock with a click, and Amy stepped inside.

'Liam. P*lease* get up.'

The figure groaned.

Amy froze.

Jonah curled his fingers in the back of her cloak. 'I don't think that's your brother.'

As Amy's eyes adjusted, she saw what she had missed before – the long sweep of coppery hair and the lace edges of a frilly purple dress. It wasn't Liam – it was a little girl! She was trembling badly, with her knees pulled into her chest and her head tucked tightly between her elbows.

Amy nudged her gently with the tip of her shoe. 'Hello?'

The girl raised her head, revealing a pale face, small round ears and big blue eyes.

'Holy sneezeweed!' muttered Jonah.

'Who are you?' said Amy.

'I'm the king,' sniffed the girl. 'Or at least, I *was* the king. Before I was thrown in here.'

Amy blinked. Then frowned. 'Hang on. *You're* the King of Tír na nÓg?'

'What are you doing down here in the dungeon?' said Jonah, who wasn't remotely surprised by the king's appearance. 'Did something happen?'

The girl nodded. 'The sun chain snapped. I'm not cursed any more.'

'But that's a good thing ... isn't it?' said Jonah uncertainly.

'Tarlock says I'm useless to him now,' said the girl. 'I'm not strong enough to bind the curse again, so he threw me down here while he figures out what to do with me. I expect I'll be a newt soon enough.'

'We won't let that happen,' said Amy firmly. 'But how

did you end up being king in the first place? Sorry if it sounds rude, but adults don't tend to let children do that kind of thing where I come from.'

Jonah stroked his chin. 'I thought you'd be more surprised by the other thing.'

'What other thing?' said Amy.

He gave her a sidelong glance. 'Well, the fact that she looks exactly like you.'

Amy looked closer.

The girl stared right back, the same frown pinching her brows together. Now that Jonah mentioned it, there *was* a certain resemblance.

There was a strange feeling prickling along the back of Amy's neck. A stray memory crept out of the corner of her mind. It was of Gran sitting at the kitchen table, with a silver coin in her hand, talking about a little girl called Peggy.

Was it possible, or was Silverstone Castle playing tricks on her?

Her thoughts were interrupted by Conan, who was jumping up and down on Jonah's shoulder, squeaking himself hoarse.

The girl reached out to touch him. 'I remember you.'

'Conan was there,' Jonah translated. 'The day she was kidnapped and taken to Silverstone Castle was the day he got turned into a Pooka by Tarlock.'

'You're the interloper,' said Amy, in dawning wonder. 'The living sacrifice.'

The girl king nodded.

'And the other interloper. The one Conan helped escape …' Amy's breath swelled inside her. The more she looked at the girl, the more of Gran she saw in her wide blue eyes. Suddenly Dorothy's life-long obsession with Tír na nÓg made perfect sense. She had been here too, long, long ago. Only she had managed to escape.

It occurred to Amy that she should introduce herself. She stuck out her hand. 'My name is Amy. And I come from Connemara.'

The girl took her hand. 'I'm …' She paused, her face straining as she dredged the name up from the depths of her memory. 'Peggy,' she said, with a breath of relief. 'My name was – is – Peggy.'

And just like that, the final sliver of Amy's doubt melted away.

'You're really her,' she said, in quiet disbelief. 'And you're here. After all this time.'

She helped the girl to her feet, squeezing her hands to make sure she was real. Amy had found a miracle tucked away in the dungeon of Silverstone Castle, and she intended to do everything she could to preserve it. 'Stick with me, Peggy. I'm going to get you home, but first we have to find my brother, Liam.'

'*Liam.*' Peggy stiffened, a sudden look of worry crossing her face. 'Quickly! We don't have much time.' She scurried out of the cell and up the stairwell, taking the steps two at a time.

The hallways were deserted, now Torrin was leading the wardens on a meandering wolf chase. Peggy tugged them into a cloakroom halfway along it, which was full of freshly washed grey robes.

'Put these on,' she said, as she shrugged one over her head. It was much too large for her, pooling around her feet like a dark grey puddle, but it hid her perfectly from view. Amy and Jonah did the same. Conan ducked inside Jonah's disguise, his little head peeking out from beneath the collar.

'Stand on your tiptoes and tilt your chins to look taller,' said Amy, as they set off again.

She and Jonah followed Peggy's lead, the three of them sweeping down one hallway after another as they made their way towards the heart of the castle. Soon other members of Tarlock's court fell into step with them. Despite the fighting outside, the wardens were all hurrying in the same direction, and were too distracted to take much notice of the unusually short wardens in their midst. Eventually they shuffled through a pair of doors that opened into a marble throne room with a magnificent glass-domed ceiling. There were hundreds of wardens already inside, assembled around a dais that looked out on to a lake through a huge crescent window.

There was a man standing on top of the dais. He was dressed in a shimmering silver robe and his face was uncovered. His skin was impossibly wrinkled, and a deathly purplish hue lingered underneath his eyes.

It was the first time Amy had seen Tarlock in real life.

She could feel the creeping tentacles of his power from all the way across the room, and noted the way his wardens faced him, with their heads lowered in reverence. The mage was looking back at them, his arms resting on top of the gilded throne in front of him.

Upon it sat a new king.

Amy almost didn't recognise her brother. Gone were his hoody and tracksuit bottoms, his favourite trainers and the messy sweep of mousy brown hair. He was dressed in a blue velvet doublet and dark trousers, and was wearing pointed black shoes. On his head, a glittering golden crown covered his ears and sat heavy on his brow. Beneath it, his face was pale and sombre. His eyes were bright silver.

'Oh no,' whispered Peggy. 'We're too late.'

Chapter Twenty-Six

THE SPOILT RITUAL

Amy wanted to burst out of the crowd and run to her brother, but Jonah caught her and pulled her back.

'What are you doing?' he hissed.

Amy turned on Peggy. 'What's he done to my brother? Why are his eyes like that?'

'He's cursed,' said Peggy. 'Liam's tied to the sun now. He's tied to the kingdom.'

'What are you talking about?' said Amy, panic making her voice louder. Some of the wardens turned to stare at her in annoyance.

'He's the new anchor for the sun chain,' Peggy explained. 'Tarlock must have made the transfer when

Liam cut the chain and freed me. It's made of his essence now, just like it was once made of mine.'

'He's found himself another living sacrifice,' muttered Jonah. 'That's not good.'

Amy hardened her jaw. She was not giving up. 'How do we *uncurse* Liam?'

But the answer was suddenly obvious. It was standing behind Liam, as tall and withered as an ancient tree. Tarlock.

At that exact moment his voice rang out. 'Kneel.'

His wardens flung themselves to the floor, their foreheads kissing the marble until it was just the three of them left standing in a sea of grey robes. Peggy dropped to the floor, pulling Jonah with her. By the time Amy realised what she was supposed to do, it was too late.

The mage's laugh was low and rippling. 'I was wondering when you'd get here,' he said, and although there were hundreds of people in the throne room, Amy knew he was talking to her. 'In fact, you are just in time.'

Before Jonah could stop her, Amy threw off her robe and stalked across the room. 'Let my brother go!'

Tarlock cocked his head, pretending to think about it. 'No.'

'Liam!' Amy called out desperately.

Liam stared past her, his eyes glazed as if he were in a trance.

'Your brother doesn't belong to you any more,' said the mage. 'He belongs to Tír na nÓg. This time, my curse will hold for far longer than sixty measly years. Do you know why?'

'Tell me.'

'Because I will use *your* bones to strengthen it.' His lips curled as he rounded the throne. 'At last, I have my pair of interlopers. One to bind the curse, and one to die for it.'

The mage clicked his fingers, and two special wardens, dressed in dark blue robes, drifted from behind the dais and grabbed Amy's elbows. She struggled and shouted but it was no use. A familiar red blur darted in her periphery but when she snapped her head around, Conan had disappeared.

The rest of the wardens stood up and craned their necks as she was dragged towards the dais. Tarlock came down the steps towards her. He stuck his hand out, and just when Amy thought he was going to grab her by the throat, a fire sprang up between them. The flames were pitch black, but instead of heat, they gave off a terrible coldness.

She screamed at the top of her lungs, trying desperately to rear back from them. 'NO! PLEASE!'

The wardens shoved her closer, until the fire licked the tip of her shoe.

'Liam!' she yelled. 'Liam, wake up! Help me!'

But the boy king glanced at the fire disinterestedly, his silver gaze sweeping over Amy as if he didn't know her. Tarlock snapped his fingers again, and a blue-robed warden scurried over with an ornate chest. He opened it to reveal several small glass vials.

Tarlock removed one that was filled with bronze powder. 'Now that my final ingredient has arrived, we may begin.'

A hush fell upon the throne room.

'*The crushed beak of an Elderglen robin, killed mid-song.*' He tipped the powder into the fire, the flames twisting as they grew. His mocking face flickered between them. 'Once we give you to the fire, there will be nothing left but the dust of your bones. You may die knowing your sacrifice will sustain your brother on this throne for centuries to come and grant me power the likes of which I have only dreamed of.'

'Stop it!' cried Amy. 'Please! You don't need to do this! Just let us go!'

Tarlock reached for a bigger vial, this time tipping several tufty coils into the flames. '*The beard of a Blackthorn druid.*' The fire hissed as it devoured it. He reached for another. '*One thimble of Selkie blood,*' he announced, as he tipped the vial in. The flames thrashed about like they were in pain.

'Stop!' Amy tried to wrest herself free, but the wardens held her firmly in place.

Tarlock removed a narrow vial containing a long white tooth, and tossed it in. *'One bloodied wolf fang.'*

The flames howled.

The wardens laughed.

The mage unstoppered the final glass vial and tipped it over the fire with deliberate slowness. *'Seven tears from the Wailing Wastes.'*

The flames shuddered as they devoured each one. Then they began to spread.

'And last, but not least, my interloper.' Tarlock peeled his lips back, revealing his rotting yellow teeth. *'Still squirming.'*

The flames made a flickering black circle around the dais, cutting Amy off from Liam. The fire was less than six inches from her nose now, and so cold her tongue froze in her mouth. She tried to scream, but a puff of white cloud burst out instead.

The mage recited his spell.

'Foreign bones, freshly ground,
A young king newly crowned,

Will *bind the chain and freeze the hour,*
For the sun's curse to yield new power.'

The wardens released Amy as the flames curled around her wrists, like handcuffs. They tugged her forward, into the flickering abyss. The rest of the room fell away as blackness surrounded her. It slipped down her gullet, trilling along the rings in her throat. It invaded her chest, wrapping itself around her ribcage. Her legs turned heavy as lead, her arms so cold she couldn't feel them any more.

She couldn't feel anything.

Tarlock repeated his spell, looping the words together again and again, until it became a chant.

Amy's eyes grew heavy as the words wormed into her mind, whispering her to sleep.

She swayed on her feet, about to give herself over to the flames.

Her heartbeat stuttered to a slow thud.

Then an almighty crash rang out. The room trembled as glass rained down from above. Shards nicked her cheeks and arms, shocking her back into her body. Another explosion followed, the crescent window behind the dais buckling under the force of two hundred stampeding woodland creatures.

Tarlock broke off his chant with a startled shout.

The flames faltered.

Amy blinked. Then she remembered where she was.

The throne room was in utter chaos. A hundred angry swans had crashed in through the ceiling and were flying in circles, swooping and attacking the wardens as they fled. Conan rode on the largest swan, directing it towards Tarlock, who was fuming over on the dais. The other Pookas, meanwhile, had smashed in through the crescent window, Torrin's triumphant howl ringing out like a war cry as she and Mac chased the mage's followers away.

Amy snapped her eyes up to Liam on the throne. He was the only one in the room who hadn't noticed – or cared – about the ambush. Just as she was about to leap through the flames to get to him, Jonah appeared beside her and pulled her away from the fire.

'Good thing Conan rounded up those swans,' he huffed, 'or you'd be a pile of bone dust right now.'

'We have to run,' said Peggy, who was two steps behind him. 'We won't have the upper hand for long!'

Tarlock's soldiers were already pouring into the room, trying to catch the Pookas. Swans were being ripped out of the air by their feet, deer were being tackled three at a time, while foxes and squirrels met with the sharp end of the guards' swords. Up on the dais, Tarlock had regained his composure. He swept his hand in a wide arc and sent the black flames skittering across the floor like scorpions. He himself walked through it unharmed, guiding the fire as it bled out like a slick of oil, devouring everything in its wake.

Amy turned to Jonah. 'Take Peggy and make for the door before Tarlock catches you,' she said urgently. 'I'm going to get Liam. We'll be right behind you.'

Jonah gestured to the icy black flames that separated them from the dais. 'Do you have wings I don't know about?'

'No, but she has me!' Torrin was bounding towards them on Mac's back. She grinned wildly, her silver-bright hair sweeping out behind her. 'Jump on!'

Amy held on to Torrin for dear life as they leaped over the flames. On the dais, they took the steps two at a time until they reached the throne. Liam turned to stare at them – and where once he might have screamed in the face of a terrifying wolf, now he barely frowned.

'Liam! Look at me!' Amy grabbed her brother by the shoulders and tried to shake some life back into him. The moment she touched him, his gaze cleared and he cried out, 'Amy, you're here! I need your help! Tarlock—'

'I know.' Amy yanked the crown off her brother's head and fired it into the flames. 'Stick with me. We're getting out of here.'

Torrin made room for Liam on Mac's back. The floor was almost completely covered in flames now. There was no pathway left, not even with the wolf to carry them.

'Well, never mind,' said Torrin, coming to the same conclusion. 'Doorways are overrated anyway.' She turned Mac towards the shattered crescent window. 'Keep your arms and legs tucked in and close your eyes if you want to!'

The wolf gave a great, bounding leap, bigger than any that had gone before. The wind howled in their ears as they sailed through the broken window. They landed in the courtyard with a jolting thud.

Before them, the stagnant lake was empty and the courtyard was completely deserted. Amy held on to her brother as they rode away down the rocky slope of Mount Arrigal, where the clash and clamour of battle rose to meet them.

Chapter Twenty-Seven

THE GETAWAY

Culann and the Wolf-riders were not faring well. They had been driven back from the black gates and were down on the slopes of Mount Arrigal, fighting alongside the Fianna. The Dullahan swarmed them, horses rearing and weapons swinging, as they fought ceaselessly and without mercy. It was hard to tell who was winning and who was losing. All Amy knew for certain was that they had to get Liam away from the castle, as fast and far as possible, before Tarlock came looking for his brand-new king.

Mac carried them down the steepest side of the mountain, where the land was rocky and unforgiving. It was there that Oscar met them. His face was streaked with blood and a nasty bruise was blooming on his cheek.

'You look awful,' said Amy in alarm.

'Better a wounded warrior than a pretty corpse,' he huffed, by way of greeting. 'Glad to see you've found the boy. We're losing ground fast.'

'Where are the Selkies?' said Amy, craning her neck to try and catch a glimpse of the prince.

'They returned to the swamp when the fight turned against us. Tristan values his life more than our freedom.' Oscar bit off a curse. 'I told you before. Selkies can't change. They don't want to.'

'If that were true, he would never have shown up in the first place,' said Amy. 'He must have had a reason.'

'Forget about the Selkies,' said Oscar urgently. 'We need to get you and your brother out of here before the horses catch your scent.'

Torrin glanced uncertainly at her wolf. He was panting heavily and his hind legs were starting to buckle. 'I'm not sure how long we'll be able to outrun them. Mac's not used to carrying so many riders at once.'

Oscar set his jaw. 'Then I'll take you to the Elderglen myself. Arrow is the fastest horse in all of Tír na nÓg. And we're not hiding any more. We can cut straight through the middle of the kingdom.'

The change from wolf to horse was quickly made.

'Whatever happens, don't let go of me. Otherwise, I'll start to forget who I am,' Liam told Amy, as she settled behind him on the horse.

'Don't worry,' she said, as she flung her arms around him. 'You're stuck with me.'

Liam twisted to look down at Torrin. 'We need to find Peggy. I promised her I would bring her home too. I can't just leave her.'

'I'll find her,' said Torrin. 'We'll follow you as soon as we can.'

Oscar took off promptly, Arrow galloping down the mountain so fast it felt for a moment like they were about to take flight. They launched into the Slumbering Swamp, where Amy searched for a sign of the Selkies. There was nothing but a few strips of seaweed left behind during their retreat.

'There's no way they just *left* us,' muttered Amy, but doubt was starting to creep in.

The sun chain roiled and thrashed above them, and a moan seeped out of Liam. Amy tightened her arms around him. 'It's all right, Liam. I've got you.'

It wasn't long before the Dullahan came after them. The Wolf-riders and the Fianna did their best to hold them back, but a hundred headless riders broke through their resistance.

Oscar tightened his grip on the reins, urging Arrow to go faster as they set a course for the Fang-lands. Hours passed, the world whipping by in streaks of green and blue as they picked their way down into the barren valley. It was deserted of wolves now, and the wind had fallen silent. Amy could hear her breath punching out of her.

Behind them, the thunder of Dullahan hoofs echoed throughout the Fang-lands. Amy could sense them getting louder, *closer*, but she was too frightened to look over her shoulder and check.

In front of her, Liam slumped in his seat, his hands coming to his head. 'The curse,' he moaned. 'It hurts.' A sob burst out of him, and his shoulders began to shake. 'I don't want to be king, Amy. It was an accident. I only wanted to break the chain. I only wanted to help Peggy.'

'You did help her, Liam. You freed her.' Amy held on to her brother for all she was worth. 'But we're going home now. We're going back to Connemara. And the only thing you can be king of there is the top bunk. How about that?'

Liam sniffed. 'I don't think Tarlock will let me go.'

'He doesn't have a choice.' A familiar anger erupted inside Amy. 'From here on out, anyone who gets between me and my brother is going to regret it.'

Liam looked at her over his shoulder, his eyes swimming with tears. 'I'm scared, Amy.'

'I know,' she said gently.

They passed through the Fang-lands and made for higher ground. In the distance, a smattering of trees gave way to vast fields of corn and wheat, farmland rolling east and west as far as they could see. They were still miles from the Elderglen, but Arrow never slowed, and Oscar never looked back to see what they were up against – he already knew.

Soon Amy's legs began to ache, and her lids grew heavy with exhaustion. When she spied a familiar circle of stone tombs atop a humpbacked hill, she sat bolt upright in her seat. They had reached the Graveyard of the Gods! Oscar bowed his head as they weaved their way between the mighty cairns. Amy risked a look behind and saw the Dullahan were still in pursuit. They were already charging up the hill, their terrifying bone whips cracking in the air.

Oscar urged Arrow on, animal bones crunching underfoot as they made it out the other side of the grave-yard. Suddenly a screeching chorus filled the air. This time, Amy looked up, to where the swans of Silverstone Castle were circling the tombs. There were hundreds of them – their mighty wings spread out in an endless canopy of white. And there, perched upon the swan that led the flock, was a small red squirrel.

More Pookas emerged from the hinterland and

stampeded across the graveyard, squirrels and stags and foxes darting between the huge black horses until they reared back in alarm. The swans dived from the sky like an arrowhead and attacked the Dullahan, buying Amy and Liam precious moments to get away.

By the time Tarlock's army had fought their way through the angry squall, Liam and Amy were long gone. They rode on, and on, and on. Amy was so tired by now that she would have fallen asleep had it not been for the black shadow still inching ever closer to them.

Long after night should have come and gone, with the sun still blisteringly bright above them, Arrow began to slow, the burden of three riders finally becoming too much for her. The Dullahan had shirked the last of the Pookas and were gaining ground again. Now Amy could feel the vibrations of their whips cracking against the earth.

The Well of Wishes shimmered up ahead, and just beyond it, the winding Dabberlock River. Amy gulped as she looked over her shoulder. The Dullahan were a spear-throw behind them now, but with any luck, the current would slow them down. Arrow plunged into the Dabberlock, the water coming up to their hips as they waded across. They moved in maddening slow-motion, the horse panting and straining with every stride.

Liam used his arms as paddles to try to propel them faster, but it was no use. Behind them, the Dullahan entered the river in a whisper and floated through the current like sharks. Much to Amy's dismay, they were almost as fast in the water as they were on land. She yelped as a whip cracked in the air behind her.

'It's no use,' she cried. 'We're too slow!'

The Dullahan were powered by a magic so dark it never slept. The headless riders had no need of food or rest, and neither did their horses. They would run them to the ends of the earth without breaking a sweat or taking a breath, and no matter how hard they ran or fought, it would never be enough.

They couldn't outrun their fate. It was only a matter of time – perhaps even seconds – before it caught up with them.

'I'm sorry,' she said, as she squeezed her brother tightly. 'I should have never dragged you through that waterfall in the first place!'

Liam hugged her arms against his chest and scrunched his eyes shut, trying his best to be brave. 'It's all right, Amy. I forgive you.'

'Hold your nerve,' said Oscar, as steely as ever. 'It's not over yet.'

They pitched backwards as Arrow clambered out of

the water. The moment they were back on solid ground, Oscar turned round and pressed the reins into Liam's hands.

'Hold on to these, and keep your eyes on the horizon. Arrow will do the rest.'

Without another word, he palmed his spear and leaped off the horse. Liam yelped as Arrow took off again at lightning speed, having perfectly understood her master's instruction. Amy whipped her head round.

The leader of the Fianna cut a lonely figure, standing on the edge of the riverbank with only his spear, as the full might of the Dullahan bore down on him.

'Oscar!' screamed Amy.

But Arrow kept galloping. The Dullahan pulled Oscar down into the river and converged on him like a murder of crows. Between rippling black shadows, Amy watched him struggle. He got to his feet, only to be knocked down again, the currents coming stronger and quicker than before.

And then she heard it – a noise like a great wave breaking against the cliffs.

The river heaved in a mighty swell.

A rallying war cry bubbled up from the deep.

And the Selkies appeared in a hail of froth and seaweed.

'Tristan!' cried Amy.

She was right. Prince Tristan emerged from the water with a ragged shout, and launched himself at the nearest rider, dragging him down into the gushing river. The rest of the Selkies leaped and brawled in a mass of pallid skin and gnashing teeth, roaring as they descended on the Dullahan.

In the middle of it all, Oscar sloshed through the water, soaked from head to toe and still fighting. Tristan stood at his back, both leaders putting themselves between the Dabberlock and the fleeing children.

Their cries chased after them on the wind, but Amy couldn't tell if they were born of triumph or defeat, only that she and Liam were alone now, and their freedom was waiting for them just beyond the horizon.

Chapter Twenty-Eight

THE GROANING FOREST

A my fixed her gaze on the horizon as they rode on and on, through endless farmland and villages, the thud of Arrow's hoofbeats keeping time with her pulse. She pictured the Elderglen in her mind, willing herself to stay awake until they reached it.

Hours passed in strained silence, Liam gripping the reins so tightly his knuckles turned white. When the leafy canopies of the Elderglen finally appeared in the distance, he thought he was imagining it.

'Amy, look!' he cried. 'Do you see the trees?'

Amy stiffened. 'I see them, Liam! We're going to make it!'

As the forest loomed ever closer, so too did the rattle

of hoofprints behind them. Amy's heart sank as she realised that ten or so Dullahan were still chasing after them.

Surely they'll never catch us now? she thought. Once Arrow crossed the treeline, the Elderglen would protect them.

But as Amy and Liam entered the forest, the trees of the Elderglen huddled together, as though to block their way. The trail, half swallowed now by dried mud and fallen leaves, was twisting and narrow, and the birds had fallen unusually quiet.

'Do you feel that?' Amy whispered into the eerie silence. 'It's like the forest doesn't want us here.'

In front of her, Liam said nothing. He simply ducked his head and tucked in his arms as if he was trying to make himself disappear.

'Listen for the sound of water,' said Amy, straining to see through the branches. 'We can't be far from the waterfall.'

They wound their way deeper into the Elderglen, but nothing looked familiar to Amy. Soon, a rotting stench filled the air. The trees groaned like they were in pain, twigs dropping to the ground and slithering away from them.

Amy whipped her head around, searching the gloom. Leaves fluttered down from the boughs and decayed before they hit the ground. Maggots crawled out of the mud and devoured them. A mighty thud shook the forest.

She glanced over her shoulder, just in time to see another tree fall. From its charred and rotting bark, a horde of spiders scuttled free.

'Liam,' she hissed. 'There's something wrong.'

Liam released the reins and turned to look at his sister. His face was blotchy and his bottom lip was trembling.

'It's not the Dullahan,' he whispered. 'It's *me*.'

'But you're not doing anything,' she said.

Liam clutched at his chest, a look of intense agony crossing his face. 'The forest knows I'm cursed. I'm making it sick just by being here.'

'No, you're not,' said Amy quickly. 'You're all right now, Liam. You're going to be fine.'

'I don't think so.' Liam removed her hands from around his waist and scooted forward on the horse.

The silver mist returned to his eyes.

Amy grabbed his hand. 'What are you doing? You're not supposed to let go!'

'I'm trying to show you that it's still here,' said Liam, with rising desperation. 'It's still inside me.'

Amy waved his words away. In her mind, the simplest thing to do now was to get her brother back to the waterfall and into Connemara, where the curse – not to mention Tarlock – would have no power over him.

She looked up at the trees. 'I know you don't want us here, but I promise we don't mean you any harm,' she called out. 'If you help us find our way to the waterfall, then my brother and I will leave you alone forever.' The silence lingered, but Amy could tell the trees were listening. '*Please*,' she begged. 'We're not your enemies. We just need your help to go home.'

'They don't trust me,' said Liam nervously.

'They're thinking,' said Amy. 'Give them a minute.'

There came a gentle rustling of leaves. The trees creaked as they parted, revealing a pathway through the forest. A ruby-chested robin soared down from a nearby branch and flitted in front of them, ruffling its feathers in a way that left no doubt that they were to follow it.

Amy sensed the trees holding their breath as they passed. The rotting stench clung to them as they went, the delicate flowers that lined the trail dying under their strides.

'I'm sorry,' whispered Liam, over and over – he could sense the forest's discomfort and he knew he was slowly killing it.

When the sound of rushing water reached them, Amy sagged in relief. Arrow cantered towards it, stopping at the edge of a familiar clearing. The water was crystal blue, the mighty waterfall tumbling down to meet it in a rush of white froth. Amy slid off the horse and helped her brother down after her. He stumbled when his feet hit the ground, but she caught him before he fell.

Liam was even paler now, and shivering.

'It's all right,' she said, squeezing his hand tightly. 'We've made it, Liam. We're here.'

Liam's teeth chattered. His eyes were still blue, but there was a shadow moving in them, like the curse was trying to peer out. Amy pressed her free hand to Arrow's head in thanks and hoped that she would find Oscar again, that he and Jonah and Torrin would all make it out alive and finish what they had ridden to Silverstone Castle to do. At least with Amy and Liam back in Connemara, Tarlock would have no interlopers to help continue his wicked spell.

At the edge of the water, Liam hesitated.

'Come on, Liam. The best thing we can do for Tír na nÓg is to leave. Now.'

But Liam was straining at his reflection in the pool, as if he hardly recognised himself.

'We have to go before the Dullahan find us.' She squeezed his hand again. 'Are you ready?'

Liam didn't say anything as he waded into the water, but with every step he got slower. The strain on his face was obvious now. Sweat was beading on his brow and his eyes were bloodshot.

'Amy,' he said, through his teeth. 'I c-c-can't go any further.'

'We're almost there, Liam.' Amy tugged her brother after her. 'You can't give up now.'

Liam clutched at his throat, his breath coming in a laboured wheeze. 'But it *hurts*.'

Another step. His cheeks turned purple. And then another. His eyes began to stream.

Amy stared at her brother with dawning alarm. They were less than ten feet from the waterfall now, so close she could feel its icy spray kissing her cheeks, but every step was killing him. He took one more and fell to his knees, the water coming up to his chest.

Amy stood over him, hot tears spilling down her cheeks. 'I don't understand,' she said, even though she was beginning to. 'Why can't we go home?'

She was answered by a deep, rippling laugh. It echoed through the little clearing, raising the hairs on the back of her neck.

'Because he is bound to Tír na nÓg now.'

Across the clearing, Tarlock emerged from the trees, his silver eyes glittering with triumph. 'Isn't it obvious? If your brother passes through that veil, he'll die.'

Chapter Twenty-Nine

THE SNEAKY SIXPENCE

'Perhaps you thought you had saved him,' Tarlock went on, in a mocking voice. 'That your little escapade across Tír na nÓg would amount to something. But the minute that boy cut my sun chain, he doomed himself. There is nothing you can do for him now.'

Amy's eyes darted, scanning the shadows between the trees. The Dullahan were lurking in the forest, waiting for their master to summon them. The children were completely surrounded.

Liam feebly pushed her towards the waterfall. 'Go,' he rasped. 'It's too late for me.'

Amy stepped in front of her brother, positioning herself like a shield. She levelled the mage with her meanest look. 'You're *not* taking him.'

Tarlock withdrew a glittering golden sword from the folds of his cloak. He angled it towards her. 'If you don't release *my* king, I'll take him by force and I'll take *you* in pieces.' Summoned by some unspoken command, the Dullahan stepped out of the forest, forming a ring of darkness around the pond. There was no escape. The only path left was through the waterfall – without Liam.

Tarlock stepped into the water. 'You wouldn't be the first interloper to abandon their sibling,' he told Amy. 'To flee at the first sign of danger. To save yourself in place of the person you love most in the world. In fact, I would say it runs in your family, doesn't it?'

A blinding rage took hold of Amy. She felt like she'd swallowed a bolt of lightning, and she wanted to spit it at Tarlock. But she had no one to back her up and nothing to fight with, except for the laces in her shoes and the coin in her pocket. Amy froze.

Could she … ?

She stuck her hand into her pocket and curled the sixpence in her fist.

'Go,' pleaded Liam. He was too weak to raise his head now, the water lapping at his chin. Whatever Tarlock was doing was making his suffering worse.

Amy set her jaw. 'Not without you.'

'The curse already has its claws in him. He is tied to the sun. Tied to *me*.' Tarlock trailed his sword through the water, setting it aglow as he came towards her. 'Every time your brother moves, I feel it. Every time he *breathes*, I hear it. The time for fighting has long past. You may try and flee if you're brave enough.'

He nodded towards the waterfall, but Amy could tell by the gleam in his eye that if she ran, he would cut her down just as quickly. After all, she was as valuable as Liam, and he hadn't brought that big fancy sword to use on her brother. In that moment, she knew she would never see the soil of Connemara again.

She'd never go back to school and win a race against Melissa Talbot, never see her best friends, Lily and Gita. Mum would come home from her holiday and never know what happened to her children, and Gran would spend the rest of her days in that little yellow house, grieving for all the people she had lost to the enchanted waterfall.

'Stop fighting your fate,' said Tarlock, like he could read her thoughts. 'To run from it will only make it worse.'

Four Dullahan riders slipped off their horses and waded into the water. They sloshed towards Liam. Amy spun around, in a panic. The coin burned white-hot in her palm but she didn't know what to do with it. She was hopelessly outnumbered.

Tarlock raised his sword, beads dripping from it like luminescent pearls. While the Dullahan converged on Liam, the mage stalked through the water towards Amy.

She cried out just as a chorus of screams filled the air. For a heartbeat, she thought the trees were screaming too.

And then she spotted a flash of green moving in the trees. From the dark mouth of the forest came a gaggle of hollering young boys clad in green cloaks. Cade, the sour-faced one, led the charge, firing an arrow at one of the Dullahan and skewering him in the side. The rest of the Greencloaks charged for the other riders, wielding their wooden weapons with the strength and speed of long-seasoned warriors.

Tarlock's attention wavered, and in that split second, a faint whizzing filled the air. A flash of amber came shooting over the trees and hurtled into the clearing, like a meteor. It landed in the water just in front of Amy and sent out a single, silent ripple. Her eyes widened.

Oscar's spear.

His words rang in her head. *The Spear of Lug will always find its mark.*

Oscar must have thrown it from somewhere far beyond the forest, and it had come to her when she needed it most. She pulled it from the water and hurled it at the mage with all the strength she had.

The spear whipped across the pond, flying straight and true, and sank deep into his right shoulder.

Tarlock froze, and a sucking gasp escaped his lips.

Then, just when Amy thought he would collapse, or at the very least *bleed*, he released a low chuckle.

He lumbered towards her, the weight of the spear tipping him to one side. His sword trailed in the water. 'You *pathetic* child. I am immortal. No weapon in this world can kill me.'

'Not even that?' Amy gestured at the sword in his hand. Tarlock turned to glance at it, and she seized his distraction. She let go of Liam, and lunged at the mage, sending him crashing backwards into the water. She kept one hand on the spear lodged in his shoulder to stop him from springing back up.

The mage's eyes flashed in warning, but he did not yet look afraid. In fact, to Amy's annoyance, he almost looked amused. 'If you think you can kill me with the Answerer, you are sorely mistaken,' he snarled. 'My mother's sword would never turn against me.'

Amy stuck out her tongue. 'Keep your stupid sword. This is from Peggy.'

Confusion flashed across the mage's face. He opened his mouth to shout – and Amy seized her moment.

She jammed the silver sixpence between his lips, then

clamped her free hand over them to make him swallow it.

The mage choked as it lodged in his throat. His eyes went wide, horror spreading across his face as he realised what it was – not just a coin, but a poisonous coin.

The only weapon that could kill him was stuck halfway down his gullet.

Now it was Amy's turn to smile.

A shadow rider ripped her off the mage, but the damage was done. Tarlock grasped feebly at his throat as his fingers turned to dust, the bones scattering in the wind. He opened his mouth to scream, but his skin crumbled away, revealing rotting yellow teeth. His eyes turned white as they rolled backwards, and then disappeared into nothing as the rest of his body turned to ash.

For a heartbeat, his cloak stood suspended over the water, like a ghost. Then it collapsed in a heap, floating on top of the pond like a silver lily-pad.

A cool breeze swept through the clearing. The Dullahan halted their battle with the Greencloaks, grasping helplessly at the shadows above their necks.

Liam wrenched himself free.

All around them, the Dullahan fell, one by one by one, leaving only their black cloaks behind.

The Greencloaks erupted in cheers at Tarlock's demise, but Amy sloshed towards her brother and seized him by his shoulders, terrified he was going to collapse too. 'How do you feel? Are you all right?'

Liam was very pale.

His whole body shuddered as he began to retch. He pitched forward in the water, but Amy held him up, as a dark, slimy shadow poured out of him.

It seemed to take an age before the darkness stopped coming, yet at last he stood up on shaking legs. Then he looked at his sister with crystal-blue eyes and a smile she hadn't seen in forever.

'I'm OK,' he rasped. 'I feel like *me*.'

With relief came the heavy pull of exhaustion. They waded out of the water and collapsed in a heap on the forest floor, where they waited for the world to stop spinning.

* * *

Sometime later, Oscar emerged through a break in the trees, looking battle-worn but very much alive. He spotted the mage's robe floating in the water, and smiled so broadly that for a moment Amy didn't recognise him.

'I believe you have something that belongs to me, little sionnach.'

Amy stood up. 'And I believe *you* owe me ten roasted boars.' She fished Lug's Spear from the water and handed it back to him. 'Thanks for the loan.'

Oscar winked at her. 'I'm always happy to save your life at short notice.'

'I thought you were a goner,' said Amy. 'It's a lucky thing Prince Tristan came back.'

'As it happens, he never really left,' said Oscar, a touch sheepishly. 'Tristan saw the dome shatter back at the castle and knew you'd need help on your getaway. That's why he swam to the Dabberlock.'

Amy beamed. 'I told you so!'

Just then, the sky let out a curious groan.

'*Look*,' said Liam, pointing at the sun chain through a break in the trees.

It clanged as it twisted, the links straining as they stretched and stretched and *stretched*. There was a long, keening creak and then a sudden thundering crack as the chain snapped in two.

They watched in silent wonder as it streaked across the sky like a falling star, and exploded in a shower of silver sparks that fell upon the trees of the Elderglen.

The sun sighed as it floated down to meet the horizon. The sky turned from orange to pink, and then, in a single breath, night fell across Tír na nÓg.

Amy took her brother's hand as the stars came out to gaze upon them. They were brighter than any she'd ever seen before, each one glistening like a diamond.

'The gods are back,' said Oscar, his shoulders slumping in relief. 'The curse is finally broken.'

The Greencloaks pressed their fists to their hearts as they looked up, hope shining in their eyes.

For a long time, no one spoke. As the last whispers of dark magic melted away, and the land of Tír na nÓg shimmered once more under the gaze of its gods, a crimson squirrel came darting out of the forest. By the time he reached the water, he was a boy again. A boy with dark red hair and eyes so big and green, they held the forest inside them.

His smile was toothy and wide.

'CONAN!' yelled the Greencloaks, and before Amy could get a proper look at him, they descended on him in a scrummage. Even Cade joined in.

Jonah wasn't far behind. When he arrived in the clearing, he was accompanied by the rest of Pookas, who, having fought so bravely in the graveyard, were turning back into themselves too. One by one, boys and girls, men and women, old and young, appeared where a deer or a fox or a squirrel or a swan had just been. Many of them were limping and had lost clumps of hair, but they seemed not to mind too much. They were great heroes, returned from war.

Jonah came up to talk to Amy with Conan, the red-haired boy revealing a grin so wide and infectious it made Amy grin right back.

'It'll be a while before I get used to not having a tail,' he said. 'But I don't mind being tall again.' He held out his hand to Amy and she shook it vigorously.

'I suppose this means you won't be throwing acorns at me any more?' she teased.

'I'm afraid those days are behind me,' said Conan regretfully.

'What about your fleas?' asked Jonah.

Conan glared at him. 'I *never* had fleas.'

* * *

The next exciting thing to happen was the arrival of Torrin. But the young Wolf-rider wasn't alone. She slid off Mac's back, revealing the smaller figure of Peggy who had been sitting behind her. She had got away too! Torrin helped her down, both girls running to the edge of the pond, where they stared in disbelief at the mage's floating cloak.

'You really did it,' Peggy cried. 'You freed us!'

'You freed yourselves,' said Amy, hurrying to meet them. 'Where I come from, we call that a group effort.'

Torrin offered her a wolfish smile.

Peggy stepped into the water. She reached into the cloak and plucked the sixpence from inside it. She held it up to the stars.

'Are you ready to go home, Peggy?' asked Liam gently.

She curled the sixpence in her fist. 'More ready than I've ever been.'

Oscar and the Greencloaks gathered by the waterfall to see them off. It was flowing gently now, the thunderous rush replaced by the soft patter of water.

'Will you come back?' Jonah asked Amy, a little anxiously. 'I know we used to operate a strict no-girls-allowed policy, but I've had a chat with the boys and we've decided to officially change the rules. Even Cade says it's OK if you want to join us, and it took him three years to accept *me*!'

Amy chuckled. 'Maybe I'll take you up on that one day.'

Jonah's eyes lit up.

'That reminds me ...' She bent down and retrieved the Answerer from where it was still languishing in the water. She handed it to Jonah. 'I think it's time you gave up your wooden sword for a real one. Don't you?'

Jonah clutched the sword proudly to his chest as she stepped backwards, into the waterfall. She held out her hand to her brother. 'Are you ready?'

Liam took it and squeezed tightly.

Peggy slipped her hand in his other one, and together, the three children of Connemara stepped through the veil between worlds.

Chapter Thirty

THE FOUND GIRL KING

A my held her breath as she ducked under the waterfall. At first there was nothing. Just the gentle pitter-patter of water sliding into her hair and down her face. Then the world shifted. In a whoosh of warm wind, a different one slid into place. Where once there was water at Amy's back, now there was rock.

'Liam?'

Liam squeezed her hand. 'I'm here.'

The rock nudged them onwards, the darkness rippling until Amy spied a glimmer of gold up ahead. The sound of trickling water beckoned them. When they ducked their heads and stepped through it, they emerged into the wildlands of Connemara. The Atlantic wind kissed their cheeks and tugged them out by their sleeves.

Evening had come, and Peggy stepped out of the waterfall as the last rays of sunlight melted along the mountains. Liam squinted up at the darkening sky. 'We *did* it,' he said, with a great breath of relief.

'Here,' said Amy, removing his glasses from her pocket. 'I think you might need these again. Sorry they're a bit cracked.'

Liam grinned as he settled them on the bridge of his nose. 'Much better. Even with the crack.'

Just then, Peggy gasped. Liam and Amy watched in muted wonder as she grew tall before their eyes, her long hair curling up around her ears as it turned to silver. Her face puckered and creased as new crevices deepened the lines around her eyes and mouth. Her lips thinned as she examined her hands, each new wrinkle settling as though it had always been there, just beneath the surface.

'There now. *That* feels right,' she said, in a voice croaky with age. After all this time, Peggy had finally become who she was supposed to be. She peered at her reflection in the stream and met it with quiet satisfaction.

'I swear you look just like Gran,' said Liam.

Amy was having the very same thought.

'Let's go home, Peggy. We'll show you the way.'

The old woman drew a deep breath as she stepped out

of the water. 'I know the way,' she said, with a smile. 'Thank you for reminding me.'

They set off across the fields, skipping towards a familiar yellow house that sat, quiet and unassuming, on the fold between two worlds.

EPILOGUE

Way out west, where the roads run out and the craggy hills of Connemara slope down to meet the Atlantic Ocean, an old woman stood by the window in her yellow house. She was watching the sun melt along the horizon and thinking of her grandchildren, lost somewhere in its shadow.

There was something in the air this evening. Not just the dewy aftertaste of rain, but the promise of magic stirring in the hills. She remembered it from long ago.

There was a shepherd's pie warming in the oven. Amy and Liam had been adventuring for hours now, but Dorothy knew if the setting sun didn't lead her grandchildren home to her, their grumbling stomachs would. She bustled about the kitchen, keeping one eye on the wilderness until not two, but three shadows came strolling over the hill.

The echo of their laughter reached her on the wind, and in its chorus, she heard the voice she had been missing since childhood.

She rushed from the kitchen, apron strings streaming out behind her as she launched herself into the sunset, flinging her arms out wide to gather up her miracle.

When Peggy spotted her sister rushing out from the yellow house, she ran to her with the sprightliness of a little girl, her old sixpence flying from her hand and landing in the long grass behind her. Amy bent down to pick it up, wondering at how something so small could bring about such a powerful change.

Liam was smiling at his sister, like he was thinking exactly the same thing.

Peggy and Dorothy met each other in the stream behind their house, sloshing through the shallows in their shoes and socks. They hugged for a long time, joy hiccuping from them as they pressed their faces into each other's shoulders. To anyone else, they looked like two old women giggling in an ancient river, but when Liam and Amy looked at their sunset shadow on the water, they saw two little girls.

Two lost sisters, each found again.

When Fionn Boyle sets foot on Arranmore Island, it begins to stir beneath his feet. Deep underground, someone has been waiting for Fionn, and soon a new Storm Keeper will rise ...

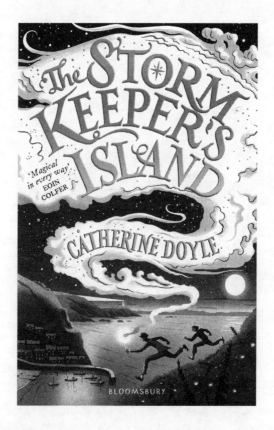

Read on for a gripping extract from the first book in this magical, spellbinding trilogy ...

AVAILABLE NOW

THE WOMAN WHO FOUGHT
THE SEA

Just after midnight, Fionn sat bolt upright in bed with a scream trapped in his throat. He wiped his brow, his gaze travelling the length of the shoebox he and Tara were sharing. Moonlight seeped in through a crack in the curtains, casting strange shadows across the walls.

Tara sighed and turned over in her bed. Fionn knew she hadn't found the enchanted Sea Cave earlier, but whatever she did get up to had kept her away for most of the day.

We're going to try again tomorrow. That's the thing about adventures, Fionny. They take a bit of time.

This time, Fionn hadn't asked if he could go with her.

He knew she would say no. She was still stewing about the doll thing. Plus, the fact remained: he was afraid of the sea. And now everyone knew it.

It needled him that Tara was right. He was not brave. He didn't know how to be brave. Whenever he watched *The Lord of the Rings*, he imagined himself as a lone rider galloping away from a battle while all the other characters were marching into it. When everyone else was in Helm's Deep, he'd be back in the Shire, making a sandwich.

Even so, he couldn't stop thinking of the Sea Cave. If there really was a wish hidden somewhere on the island, would he have enough courage to go and get it? What if he met the same fate as his father? He had fallen asleep imagining himself crawling inside it, through seaweed and seafoam, shouting his wish at the top of his lungs. It was only when the dream turned to visions of a cave swallowing him up like a mouth, that he lurched wide-eyed from his sleep.

He slipped out of bed and into the hallway, trailing his fingers along the shelves of candles as his grandfather's snores echoed through the little cottage.

In the sitting room, Fionn was surprised to find the giant candle still blazing on the mantelpiece. It was a fire hazard, surely, and yet, considering the way the wind was squeezing itself through the cracks in the walls and howling down the chimney like a banshee, the candle was probably the least of this place's problems. He watched the flame for longer than he intended to. The sea settled in the air around him, and Fionn opened his mouth and tasted a storm on his tongue.

His gaze was drawn to a shelf tucked away in the corner of the room, where a small, dark blue candle was peeking out from behind a lopsided wax snowflake. It was round and squat, like a piece of fruit, with a silver thread zigzagging through the centre.

The label glinted at him in the dimness.

Evelyn, it said.

Fionn climbed on to his grandfather's chair and plucked the candle from the shelf. Why would he name a candle after his mother? And why was it hidden away in the furthest corner of the cottage?

He traced the silver streak with the pad of his thumb as he lifted the wick to his nose. There was no smell. He hopped off the chair and found a box of matches at the end of the mantelpiece. He lit the wick and the flame sparked with a faint *whoosh*. The scent enveloped him: hurried strides across damp earth, grass collecting between toes, the bite of an unforgiving wind. And there beneath the rest of it, two different kinds of salt: warm teardrops in a freezing ocean.

What on earth … ?

Fionn held the burning candle in his hand until his curiosity yawned and stretched itself into action. A rogue breeze had slipped underneath the front door and was curling around him.

It pressed itself against his back.

Walk, something inside him said.

He waded out into the night.

This way.

The air shimmered as he pushed through it, the wind shoving harder until he was running so fast his feet were barely touching the ground. The flowers shrank into the earth around him and the grass grew until it brushed his ankles. He didn't notice his bare feet scraping on the rough earth, or the cold seeping through his pyjama bottoms. He followed the moon with the flame in his hand and the wind at his back as the island swept by him.

He stumbled past sleepy houses and little cars, the secondary school and the corner shop and the pub. The island was beautiful dappled in moonlight. It looked like a black and white painting, punctured with amber flecks, where stragglers were still awake, reading or watching television. They winked in and out as Arranmore rose and disappeared above him, and a new one crept up from the ground.

When the wind finally settled, Fionn hovered on the edge of the beach and watched the sea get angry. The waves swelled, spraying the pier with foam as thunder rumbled through storm clouds so dark they ate the stars.

There was a girl standing in the middle of the sea. The fractured moonlight danced on the crown of her head, and dark hair tumbled down her back, tangling and swaying like ropes.

Fionn hopped over the wall and ran on to the beach, panic guttering in his throat.

'Tara!'

The wind took the name from him and gobbled it up.

'Tara!' She was so far in, he didn't know if she could wade back out again. Not with the waves tugging at her elbows. She started flailing her arms, like she was trying to beat up the sea with her fists. The clouds swirled lower, static crackling along their underbellies as the thunder growled like an angry bear.

Fionn raced to the edge of the beach, where it curved into the sea in a peninsula. The candle was still clamped in his fist, the flame fighting the wind the way his sister was fighting the sea. The wax was melting over his knuckles but he didn't feel it.

When he reached the end of the peninsula, the waves dipped and Fionn saw a bump protruding from the girl's stomach.

He looked at her face. More closely, this time.

'Mam?' This time, the storm didn't steal the name. It spluttered out all on its own.

Fionn's mother was screaming at the sea. The sky was roaring back.

'Mam!' Fionn waved the candle in the air, like a flare. 'Mam! Come back!'

A wave crashed against her and she fell backwards, a hand cupping her swollen belly. She scrambled to get back up but another one washed over her head, burying her from view.

Fionn launched himself into the water. The waves spat in his eyes and tangled salt in his hair, pushing him back to shore. The harder he tried to get to his mother, the harder the ocean fought back.

And then from the darkness came a flash of pale skin and long limbs. Fionn's grandfather appeared as if from nowhere, hurtling across the strand like an Olympic athlete and flinging himself into the sea head first.

He resurfaced ten strides later, his bald head shiny with droplets. He seemed so much younger now, so agile and fearless. The wind didn't steal his warnings the way they had taken Fionn's – they tornadoed round and round, as loud and stubborn as a ship's horn.

'Evelyn!' He yelled, his arm looping around her as he tugged her backwards. 'Come out of there before you drown, Evie!'

Fionn tried to wade towards them but the sea danced around him in a prison of salt and brine until he lost his balance. He dropped the candle and the flame went out.

The island inhaled.

Fionn's grandfather disappeared and took his mother with him. The tide sank and the clouds evaporated into a star-laden night. Without the clash and clamour of a troubled sky, Fionn could hear his heartbeat in his ears. He remembered to be afraid, and once he did, the fear climbed down his throat and stole his breath.

He was in the sea! And the sea was going to drown him! He stumbled backwards and tripped on a rock, his body twisting as he fell. He landed face first in the ocean and inhaled a lungful of seawater. A wave rolled over him. And then another.

Come out of there before you drown, Fionn!

It wasn't his grandfather's voice now; it was his own.

Fionn dragged himself from the water, spluttering

and vomiting on to the sand. He crouched there, shaking and panting, until the stars in his vision winked out. Then he rolled on to his back and stared out at the empty sea. It was calmer than he had ever seen it, the sky above a star-speckled obsidian.

He got to his feet. He had only been underneath the water for a few seconds, but the sea had made the most of it. He was sopping wet from head to toe. Crystals of salt were stuck to his eyelashes and streaks of seaweed had woven themselves into his hair.

He trudged home, wincing from the pain in his feet.

Slowly, slowly, the world reset itself.

He did his best not to think about the island as it watched him go by. What it had taken from his family all those years ago. Why his mother had waded into the sea and screamed at it like that.

Where was she now? Was she there, or here?

Where was his grandfather? Swimming underneath the tide like a fish or at home in bed where Fionn had left him?

Where am I?

In the cottage, Fionn peeled off his wet pyjamas and changed into new ones. He dried his hair with a tea towel in the little hallway outside his grandfather's bedroom, listening to the steady rise and fall of his snores. How could he have been in two places at once? Fionn couldn't wrap his tired brain around it.

In the kitchen, he made himself a cup of tea, then took it through to the sitting room where he watched the candle on the mantelpiece with a new sliver of mistrust. Why was it lit? And what was it doing to him? He peered around the dusky room, half expecting a ghost to unfold from the patchwork chair. It was stupid to leave a candle burning at night. Hadn't anyone ever told his grandfather that?

This thing could kill us all.

Fionn set his mug down.

Then he stood in front of the fireplace and blew the candle out.

It exhaled like a sleeping giant and pushed a breeze through the cottage that rattled the windowpanes. Fionn felt it on his ankles as he sank into his grandfather's chair.

There. That's better.

Exhaustion swept over him as the tea settled into his bones. Sleep dragged him to a dark place, where he forgot his name and the island along with it, until –

'HELP ME!'

Fionn jerked awake to the sound of his grandfather

shouting the walls down, his fingers scrabbling to light the candle on the mantelpiece. Spittle was gathering at the sides of his mouth and his breath was stuttering out of him in laboured gasps.

'WHAT HAVE YOU DONE!' he shouted, his fingers slipping and sliding as another match snapped in half.

Fionn sprang to his feet and grabbed the matches from his grandfather's shaking hands. He lit the candle on the first strike. The flame hissed as it climbed towards the ceiling, raging and thrashing as if it was angry with him for blowing it out. The darkness broke apart and flecks of dust floated around Fionn's surprised face.

He shuffled backwards. He was afraid of his grandfather, wild-eyed and unkempt in his mismatched pyjamas. He was so much frailer than the man Fionn had seen in the ocean, dipping and diving like a fish. He towered over him now, the light bleeding back into his eyes as he took Fionn by the shoulders and pulled him close.

'I will tell you this once and once only, lad. As long as you live here in this house, as long as you live on this island, as long as you draw breath and pump blood around your body, you are never, *ever*, to touch that candle again.' He brought his nose right up to Fionn's, two sides of the same coin staring into the same deep blue eyes. 'Do you understand?'

Fionn could feel his pulse in the tips of his ears. 'I understand.'

His grandfather turned and stalked out of the room like a storm cloud, his footsteps thundering back to his bedroom where he slammed the door behind him. Fionn froze in the middle of the sitting room, surrounded by hundreds of candles that peered over him judgementally.

His sister stood across from him in her Hogwarts pyjamas, her arms folded across her chest. 'I told you never to touch that candle, Fionny.'

Fionn wanted to launch himself across the room and shake her and shake her and shake her until all of her meanness fell out.

He swallowed the quiver in his throat. 'No, you didn't.'

'Oh,' she said, shrugging her way back into the darkness. 'Well, I meant to.'

'You didn't tell me anything!' Fionn called after her, but she was already gone.

In the seething silence, Fionn's mind started to whirr. The truth was unavoidable now – he had seen it. He had *lived* it. Arranmore was full of secrets.

The island was full of impossibility.

Be brave.

The island had magic.

This is your adventure.

And he was going to find a way to use it.

Read the whole magical, spellbinding trilogy

AVAILABLE NOW

ABOUT THE AUTHOR

Catherine Doyle grew up beside the Atlantic Ocean in the west of Ireland. Her love of reading began with the great Irish myths and legends, and fostered in her an ambition to write her own one day. She holds a BA in Psychology and an MA in Publishing from the National University of Ireland, Galway. Her bestselling Storm Keeper trilogy was inspired by her real-life ancestral home of Arranmore Island, where her grandparents grew up, and the adventures of her many seafaring ancestors. *The Lost Girl King* is her fourth novel for Bloomsbury. Catherine lives in Galway with her husband, Jack, and their dog, Cali.